Gordon Nimse lives in Ewell, Surrey.

THE INTERPRETER

In war-torn Burma the Japanese jungle warriors are in full retreat. British agents, weapons and silver rupees cascade from the skies to aid the Karen resistance groups. However, the brutal Japanese Kempetai strike back and double-dealings and split loyalties become the order of the day . . . With the war over and martial retribution taking the stage, peacetime journalist Captain 'Robbie' Roberts insists on defending an Anglo-Burman sergeant accused of waging war against the King. The trial becomes a contest that sensationally brings to light a sinister backdrop of intrigue at the highest level.

GORDON NIMSE

THE INTERPRETER

Complete and Unabridged

ULVERSCROFT
Leicester

First published in Great Britain in 2006 by
Robert Hale Limited
London

First Large Print Edition
published 2007
by arrangement with
Robert Hale Limited
London

The moral right of the author has been asserted

British Library CIP Data

Nimse, Gordon
    The interpreter.—Large print ed.—
    Ulverscroft large print series: adventure & suspense
    1. World War, 1939—1945—Campaigns—Burma—Fiction
    2. War crime trials—Fiction 3. Suspense fiction
    4. Large type books
    I. Title
    823.9′14 [F]

    ISBN 978–1–84782–023–5

Published by
F. A. Thorpe (Publishing)
Anstey, Leicestershire

Set by Words & Graphics Ltd.
Anstey, Leicestershire
Printed and bound in Great Britain by
T. J. International Ltd., Padstow, Cornwall

This book is printed on acid-free paper

PART ONE

WAR CRIME

1

The ancient Burmese fort gave Mutaguchi a grandstand view. It was like watching a demonstration of air power at a bombing range at home.

He made a grimace of contempt. The town's defence had been taken by surprise for, at rooftop height, the British planes had swooped in from the south and laid the railway yards in ruin. Out of the blue, the roar of engines and the crash of bombs had torn across Toungoo, had swept across the river and rumbled in the hills. Now from the stricken sidings came the chatter of the guns, the bellowing of cattle and the shriller screams of men, all orchestrated by a crackling as the flames took hold.

Mutaguchi felt remote. The hard, deep blue of the cloudless sky made a backdrop for the flames: a vivid reddish orange topped by a jet-black smoke that seethed and boiled and cast a pall across the town. Mutaguchi was entranced. How wonderfully those contrasting colours combine, he thought. So beautiful. Only war could paint a picture such as this. He drank it in, absorbing every sight and sound. He knew that, later, he would transcribe it into verse. Verses that would join all the other poetry he had written. Poetry that one day would tell his unborn sons that dying for the Emperor was the ultimate boon of life. For a moment an exaltation filled his soul. But enough. Mutaguchi turned his attention to the planes.

The gunfire crescendoed. Belated tracer streaked. It was all too late. Now out of range, the planes had made a climbing turn and were heading eastward to where the green-clad mountains shimmered in the heat. Through his binoculars he watched them go. Watched them growing smaller and dwindle into dots. Then Mutaguchi froze. Almost out of sight, a section of the planes had veered away. Had turned. Now they were flying just above the ground. He steadied the binoculars against the wall. He gasped. Caught by the sun a shower of confetti was being sprinkled in the air. A myriad of coloured spots that drifted briefly before being swallowed by the trees. Parachutes! Reacting swiftly he took a compass-bearing on where the spots had gone.

So there was another purpose to the raid. The British had been out to 'kill two birds . . . ' They had succeeded, there were no two ways on that. Not only had they wrecked the Toungoo marshalling yards, they had resupplied the guerillas too. The two events were linked. That the raid had taken place right now was not by chance. No, for throughout the last ten days stores had been gathered at the railhead: petrol, ammunition, rice, a herd of cattle — rations on the hoof. Tomorrow trucks, mules and bullock carts were to have moved the supplies to the hard-pressed 15th Army, falling back on Mandalay. The British guerillas in the hills had put a stop to that.

Mutaguchi trained his binoculars on the yards. A wreck. No, they were more than just a wreck. Seen through the smoke and flames they were literally a hell on earth. Not a building had escaped. The sleepered rails festooned in whirls. Telegraph posts lay strangled in their wires. Everything in sight was shattered, shot to bits. Craters overlapped and, amongst them, locomotives, carriages and trucks had been tossed about like toys. There was movement too as broken men and animals dragged themselves about.

To Mutaguchi the scene was nothing new. In China, Singapore and Mandalay he had seen much worse and had taken it in his stride. It was the price that war demanded to give the warrior his pride. It was the stake that made it real, for to inflict and suffer

5

death in the service of the Emperor was the highest honour of all.

But enough of that. He had a job to do. A repeat of what he'd done in '43: the expedition that had wiped out the legendary Major Seagrim and his men. However, this time the need was more acute for, following the disaster of Imphal, the armies of Nippon were in retreat. Now, not only were the British agents spying out the land, they were training guerilla fighters too: bandits who would stab the Nippon armies in the back. The planes of the Nippon airforce had been swept aside. Now, British explosives, arms and cash descended from the skies.

Mutaguchi lit a cigarette (British 'Players', loot from captured stocks). Then with his map spread on the bonnet of his jeep he planned what he would do. He would strike at once and hard, for time was running out. In the next few days he would teach the British officers and their men a lesson. It would be a repeat of '43 all right. The British infiltrators would be crushed, the treacherous villagers brought to heel. As before, he would use a combination of the carrot and the stick. A wintry smile. Just a little carrot but quite a lot of stick. He would teach them what it meant to thwart the Kempetai.

Applying the compass-bearing to the map

he judged the distance to where the parachutes had dropped. Around this point he drew a ring of roughly twenty miles. If necessary he would destroy every village in the ring. Getting to them would not be all that easy for there was just one metalled road. The rest were jungle paths and tracks. So they would need to go on foot. That would be no problem. The jungle was home to the battle-hardened warriors of Nippon.

Mutaguchi had no doubts or fears. He would crush the British group in under fourteen days. With luck it would be less. Putting away his map he eyed the scene of devastation down below. It made him clench his fists. He bared his teeth. 'Woe betide everyone responsible for that,' he rasped.

2

The major punched a fist into a palm.
Everything had gone to plan. From the
platform in the trees he had seen the flashes.
Then, as the smoke reached up, he'd heard
the distant thuds. With his face alight he gave
a thumbs-up to the expectant men below. It
raised a cheer. Catlike, he clambered down.
'Raff's bang on time,' he said. The phrase
amused him. Judging from what he'd seen
and heard, 'bang' was pretty apt.

His hands clapped a double pistol shot.
'Right, on your marks. The milkman's on his
way.'

Action. The soldiers scurried to their posts.
Matches scraped and flared and the little
piles of wood that lined the glade began to
smoke. Soon twenty small but billowing
towers were reaching up. To the left, ten red.
Opposite, ten yellow. Jollying, encouraging
and checking, the major seemed to be
everywhere at once.

Captain Washington watched him from his
station by the mules. God, what a ball of fire,
he thought. What energy. It never fails. But
then, he loves it. Loves the excitement and

8

the risks. He even loves the war. He'll be sorry when it ends. And when it does he'll go looking for other wars to fight. Well, he's welcome. For me, it can't end soon enough. Washington thought of the catastrophe that had engulfed this pleasant land. The untold misery and waste. His mind went back to a Burma still at peace — Rangoon and the evenings at the club; the Shwedagon pagoda; the royal lake. He recalled the Irrawaddy, with its river-boats and the sun-drenched villages that nestled on its banks; old Pagan with its myriad pagodas; garish Mandalay; Fort Dufferin's moated walls; Maymyo with its Victorian England charm and blossomed roadside trees. In memory, he went back to the weeks spent in the forests, living rough with his gangs of happily lazy men: men who knew and cared so little about the outside world. The bungalow by the river. Shooting snipe at dawn. The laughing Burmese women in their snow-white lace and multicoloured *longyis*. Yes, and peeping sandalled toes and forest flowers in their jet-black hair. Above all he thought of Ma Ma Gyi and her honey-coloured skin. Ah yes, Ma Ma Gyi: doe eyed, soft and smoothly warm with gentle hands and even gentler ways. Worshipping everything he said and did. Uncomplainingly happy in living for the day (and yes, by God, the night). A wave of melancholy came over him. Ah, where is all that now? Gone, gone, gone. His eyes began to prick.

Then the major was standing by his side, had clapped him on the back . . .

★ ★ ★

Major Willis was a regular, Sandhurst-trained. However, from the way he was garbed right now no one would have guessed. He was a giant of a man, his face and arms mahogonied by the sun. He had let his hair grow long to complement a luxuriant auburn beard. Unlike the captain at his side he was wearing Burmese clothes: a snow-white cotton shirt with rolled-up sleeves, a ruby-coloured *longyi* and a pair of open shoes. Suspended from an army webbing belt was a jungle dah, an army-issue compass and a holstered .38. A cloth bandoleer carried bullets for the .303 Lee-Enfield that was slung across his back. To Washington, he was the image of the English adventurer in Rider Haggard's *She*.

Washington had never been to Sandhurst. Events had seen to that for, as a forestry official, he had been hurriedly commissioned when the Japanese armies struck. In the ensuing débâcle he had struggled back to

10

India on foot, where he had arrived a skeleton, burning with malaria. Burning for revenge as well. After a spell in dock he had volunteered to join the resistance in the Toungoo hills. He received a somewhat sketchy training, then he and a radio team of three Karens were parachuted in. There he joined the buccaneering major. In appearance they couldn't have differed more, for Washington, small and dapper with a Joseph Goebbels face, barely reached the major's shoulder.

Different though they were, they got on well. They had faced a daunting task for, with Major Seagrim's capture, the Japs were in the saddle. However, with radio contact made, the training and supply began. Inspired by the resolute Major Willis the demoralized Karen villagers rallied to his call, determined to rid the country of the hated Japanese.

Events were on their side for, with the British victory at Imphal, the tide had turned. Now it was the 'jungle supermen' who would be ambushed and harried to defeat. The strength of the guerrillas was growing all the time. Arms and ammunition flooded in. Today they would be receiving yet another drop: yet more explosives, arms and cash. And, just as cheering, reinforcements too, for an officer and his signals team would be included in the drop.

11

The major's voice broke in. 'Wake up, Georgie boy. They're here.'

Washington 'woke up' with a start. The planes were there all right! In line astern the Dakotas came hurtling in, breaking through the lines of coloured smoke. With side doors gaping wide they swept across the clearing and the roar of their engines shook the world. As each plane thundered past elongated pods came tumbling out. Parachutes snapped open and the pods gave birth to multicoloured flowers that blossomed briefly before crumpling on the ground.

Roar after roar. Then, as suddenly as they'd come, the planes were gone, were nothing but a drone that faded quickly into quiet.

Dropped from a greater height, four white parachutes drifted down. On each of them a man was tugging at the shrouds to steer towards the smoke. They landed on the run, their canopies collapsing as the harnesses were slipped. Once free, the parachutists froze, took in the surrounding scene. Then, bunching in a loose-knit group they were crouching, facing outwards, their automatic weapons facing outwards too. Then the four made a beeline for the shelter of the trees.

But already the major's men were pouncing

on the stores. Loads were shouldered, parachutes rolled up, the ashes of the signal fires stamped out. In next to no time the dropping-zone was clear and the equipment, stores and men were safely out of sight.

Cock-a-hoop, the major slapped a thigh. Too many of the night-time drops had gone astray. He had overcome the doubters. Now events had proved him right. The 'manna' had been safely gathered in. OK, so a daylight drop so close to a Jap-held town was quite a risk. Well, so what? The bombing of the railway yards had taken care of that. With all that going on, the Japs would take no interest in the distant planes. So now, the next task was to squirrel it all away. But first, the new arrivals must be attended to.

The newly arrived officer was talking to his men. Willis summed him up: tall for a Burman with that over fullness so many Burmese had while usually lithe and muscular underneath. He would be . . . what? Twenty-five or six. Carried himself like a man who'd been around and was confident of going places too! With his overbright green uniform he seemed somewhat of a dandy, albeit in a toughish sort of way.

The major walked across. 'I'm Willis. Gordon Willis. Welcome to the firm.'

It was clear that his appearance had given

the officer a jolt. Willis was amused. It was not surprising for, in contrast to himself, the Burman was smartly uniformed in American jungle green, a long-peaked 'baseball' cap and USA-type boots. All brand new at that. His carbine and automatic Colt were American issue too.

Willis flicked an audit, top to toe. He gave a friendly grin. 'Lease-Lend?' he asked.

A smile. 'No, Major. A full house and a royal flush got me the uniform.' The smile became a grin. 'Four aces got me the carbine and the .45.'

Willis was impressed 'Did it, now,' he said. He turned to Washington. 'Did you hear that, Georgie?' He clicked his tongue and then said drily, 'We'd better count the spoons!' Then, to the Burman: 'Uncle Sam, meet George Washington.'

The Burman was not amused. It showed.

Willis laughed aloud. 'No, that really is his name.'

Mollified, the new arrival touched his cap. The salute was USA issue too. He introduced himself. 'Captain Po Kyin. Attached Burma Rifles.' He then introduced his men, all Anglo-Burmans: 'Sergeant Anderson. Riflemen Hill and Fraser.'

'All radio trained?' asked Washington.

The reply came proudly. 'Combat trained

14

as well. You won't find better.'

'Good.' The major shook each of them by the hand and looked them in the eye. He liked what he saw. These three men were good. That went for Po Kyin too.

'I'm Willis. Major Willis,' he told them. 'Glad to have you here.' He pointed past the line of tethered mules. 'There's some cha back there. Grab some before they swig the lot. Oh, and tell them to bring a couple of mugfuls over here.'

'Sir.' The men moved off.

Willis turned to Washington. 'Georgie, I'm going to brief Po Kyin. Be a good chap. Get yourself some cha. Then check and load the drop. When you're ready . . . let me know the score.'

'Sir.' Washington moved off too.

Willis spread a map. 'You've been told the overall set-up?'

A nod. 'I have.'

'Good. That'll save us time. Now I've marked most of the detail on this map. As you see the area's divided into two. Boundary according to the numbers and location of the villages.' A finger stabbed down twice. 'I'm holed out there. Georgie's here. OK? Good. Now that there are three of us I'm opening up this area.' His hand described the area on the map. 'I'm giving it to Georgie, he knows

15

the district well. Was in the forests there pre-war. You'll take over Georgie's patch. He's got it running well. Bloody well in fact — '

A voice broke in. 'Major.'

'Good, the cha.' The major took two steaming mugs from a uniformed Karen. 'Thanks, Win Maung. Usual bags of sugar? Good.'

Sipping his tea he turned back to the map. 'All three areas will be self-contained. That applies to both stores and personnel. So, if one lot gets the chop we're still in business.'

The finger stabbed again. 'That's our central dump. Carries a reserve of everything we need. The monsoon's coming up. Means we can live off our fat when drops are scrubbed. Covers emergencies as well.'

His fist thumped down. 'Now don't, repeat don't, mark it on your map. For security, it's known only to Georgie and to me. Now to you as well. It's strictly, and I mean strictly, officers only. I don't have to remind you that the Japs play rough. So, if people don't know they can't blab, whatever the pressure. Clear?'

'Clear.'

'Now here are the call signs and radio frequencies. And, most important, the proce-dure if you've a Tojo breathing down your neck.'

Po Kyin raised his eyebrows. 'Meaning?'

'If you're nabbed. Forced to transmit under, to put it delicately, duress. Make sure your chaps know this. All of you, commit everything you can to memory. What you can't, make sure it's quickly disposable. If you're nabbed, burn it, swallow it, stick it up a leprechaun's bum but don't, repeat don't, let the Japs get hold of it. Clear?'

'Clear.'

'Now you don't know this but today's drop included cash.'

'Notes, of course?'

'For the most part, yes. Jap-Burma notes. All forgeries but good ones. From De la Rue, I'm told.'

'You said 'for the most part'?'

'I did. We're winning the war, so Jap-Burma notes are going out of favour. Some of our customers don't like paper money. Particularly the Jap kind.'

'So?'

'This drop should include thirty-bags of silver. Rupees in coin. As I said, it's for people who have lost all faith in what your poker-playing friends would call the 'green stuff'.'

Another nod, a smile.

'The silver, all of it, is going to the dump.'

'And the 'green stuff'?'

'I'm taking it to a courier. A chap in the timber trade. A peacetime friend of Georgie's. He'll take it on a timber-raft and give it to a contact in Rangoon. Slow but sure. The timber-raft, that is. The money's to help shift a certain Burmese gentleman off the fence. All very cloak-and-dagger.'

'Anything else?'

'Yes. That fancy uniform of yours.'

Captain Po Kyin looked miffed. 'Uniform going out of favour too?'

The Burman's disapproving glance made Willis smile. He said: 'Po Kyin, it's no longer *de rigueur* to dress for dinner in the jungle. Mufti's good security. Makes us less conspicuous. However, uniform has its points. If you're nabbed, get nabbed in uniform. Seagrim wasn't. That made him a spy. He was nabbed by the Kempetai. By a Major Mutaguchi and two other mark one bastards, a Sergeant-Major Ekesta and a deserter from 2 Burma Division, a Sergeant Stevens. The locals nicknamed Ekesta 'the Gorilla'. A real nasty bit of work — Mutaguchi's hatchet man, in fact. Stevens, by all accounts, is quite a linguist. He's an Anglo-Burman. Worked in a Japanese firm in peacetime. Speaks their lingo well. English and Burmese too, of course, plus Hindi and most of the local dialects. A right royal trio. Seagrim's chaps

18

knew them as the TUT.'

'Oh?'

'Stood for 'The Unholy Trinity'. They were that all right. They terrorized the villagers, torturing and killing till someone spilled the beans. When they caught Seagrim they stood him against a wall. Shot most of his men as well.' Willis clenched a fist. 'They'd probably have shot him anyhow. They'd lost a lot of faces.' He gave a sigh and shook his head. 'Odd little men, the Japs. Not so much inscrutable as unpredictable. Contrary to rumour, some of 'em do take prisoners. Don't treat 'em all that well but better bled than dead, I'm told. So, Po Kyin, as far as uniform's concerned, it's up to you. Security versus . . . ' Willis drew a hand across his throat.

Po Kyin gave it thought. Then: 'I'll stay in uniform. Pity to waste that poker-game in Cal.'

Suddenly, Washington was back. He raised a thumb. 'Everything OK. One 'chute snagged a tree. One free-dropped.' He chuckled. 'Nearly parted Win Maung's hair. Otherwise everything's spot on.'

'The cash?'

'All accounted for, but that silver weighs a ton.'

'Nothing the mules can't handle?'

19

'No, but it'll mean a couple of extra trips.'

The major shrugged. Then: 'OK, Georgie, thanks. Po Kyin and I will see to that. Now, you've quite a way to go. Cut along now and you'll be there before it's dark.'

'Right.'

'Now this applies to both of you,' the major said. 'Once the silver's in the dump I'm off to fix that Rangoon business. It'll take about a week. I'll be back on Monday. If my memory serves me right, that's the tenth. Georgie, you're in command till then.' He gave a smile. 'Po Kyin, any problems, contact Georgie.'

Washington nodded to Po Kyin. Then, raising a hand to Willis, he said; 'See you on the tenth.' Then, walking briskly, he turned the corner and was gone.

The major drained his mug. 'Right, Po Kyin. Let's see how good you are with mules . . . '

With the major in the lead the mules were plodding up the track. There were six of them, in single file with Po Kyin bringing up the rear. When they had gone about a mile the track veered sharply. As soon as they had cleared the bend the major stopped. The mules stopped too. The lead mule began to nibble at the grass. The other mules nibbled too. The major joined Po Kyin and pointed off the track.

'Po Kyin. Get in there. Keep out of sight. Make sure we're not being followed. I'm pushing on. Give it ten minutes, then catch me up.'

Po Kyin unslung his carbine 'And if we *are* being followed?'

The major pointed to the carbine. 'Use that.'

'You mean kill them. Just like that?' said Po Kyin, uncertainly.

The major nodded. Then he said, coldly. 'Po Kyin, you're not playing poker now.'

He turned on his heel and continued up the track. The lead mule did the same. The others followed suit. Po Kyin was on his own.

Dropping out of sight, he put the safety catch to 'Fire'. Then he fixed his eyes upon the track The day was hot. Nothing moved. There was no sound of any sort. He was astonished at how quiet the jungle was. It was mostly thick bamboo with scrubby clumps of thorn. It gave good cover. His thoughts turned to Major Willis. *Quite a character*, he thought. *He certainly knows his job. That goes for Washington too. Two tough cookies whom I wouldn't like to cross. What would the Japs give to get their hands on them!* But first things first. What if someone did come round the bend? Simple. He would have to kill them. Suddenly he knew a trickle of desire. A need that was almost sexual. The carbine was heavy on his lap. The breech was smoothly oiled. Gently, he worked the slide, ejecting the cartridges one by one. He was conscious of the smoothness of the slide. For a moment he held the bullets in his hand, turned them with his fingers. They were smooth, so smooth, as well. He reloaded, raised the gun and aimed where the track bent round. He knew a surge of power, of lust. Suddenly, everything in him craved for someone to turn the bend. He took first pressure. His imagination raced — took over. Just imagine: a questing face. Lining it in his sight. Two eyes peering down the track. Just the slightest squeeze, a jolt. Then seeing a third eye appear between the other two. Blood and splinters flying. Then another face, and yet another appearing. Again the splinters and the blood. The slide moving smoothly all the time. The bullets ejecting in a stream . . .

But no one came. His arms had tired. The carbine barrel dropped.

At last, sick with want, he laid the carbine down. His head began to ache . . .

Twenty minutes later he caught up with the mules. Without turning, the major raised a hand and waved, then continued on. After a little while he and the lead mule turned about. Like sheep the others followed. They pushed off the track, and milled around, flattening the scrub. Then they returned to the track and, to Po Kyin's astonishment, were plodding back the way they'd come.

They continued for a while. Then the major stopped again. He beckoned Po Kyin and pointed off the track. To the Burman it seemed to be just like any other stretch of track but, followed by the mules, the major pushed a way between the thickets, continued for about thirty yards or so, then stopped. They were in a clearing. All down one side stretched an opensided cave. Canvas flaps hung down.

'The dump,' the major said.

Po Kyin pulled aside a canvas sheet. Peering in, he saw that the cave was sandy-floored, and cool and dry and packed to the roof with stores.

'Right,' said the major, stripping off his shirt, 'off with the fancy jacket and get this lot inside.'

It took seven trips to clear the drop and Po Kyin realized just how well the dump was hidden. It took him several trips before he could find the exit off the track. Each time the procedure was the same. Each time the ambush albeit at a different bend. Each time the false turning off the track. Between each

23

trip Po Kyin's signallers loaded up the mules whilst the officers had a rest.

At last the job was done. Po Kyin's once impeccable jungle green was black with sweat. The major noticed this and grinned. 'Nothing that a dip in a stream won't cure,' he said. Then: 'You'd better push off now. The headman'll be waiting by the twin pagodas just this side of Pindale village. He'll have a meal ready.' Another grin. 'If I know him, other comforts too.' He slapped the Burman on the back and said: 'No need to live like monks, you know.'

Po Kyin looked around. There were now just the five of them and the line of patient mules. 'What about the mules,' he asked.

'They come from way down there.' The major pointed in the direction of Toungoo. 'That lead mule's on the ball. He'll lead the others down.' Suiting action to his words he slapped the lead mule on the rump. The animal tossed its head, then moved off down the hill. In line, the others followed.

'Very useful,' the major said 'Means that the muleteer is not involved. He's an odd bloke. Looks about a hundred and ten years old. Says it's not his war. That he's strictly neutral. He works for the Japs as well. Sort of live and let live.' He shrugged. 'Well, they can't all be heroes.'

The major swung the pack of money on his back. 'I'll see you on the tenth. Anything you can't handle, contact Georgie. Right?'

'Right.'

The major strode away and was swallowed up in the trees.

Po Kyin took a quick look at the map, then he too was on his way.

★ ★ ★

The Kempetai arrived in record time. But despite their efforts they were just an hour too late.

But Mutaguchi took the setback in his stride. There were more ways than one to skin a cat. Someone, somewhere, would be made to talk. His Samurai sword would see to that.

3

Thandaung was now ringed with troops. The men were short, stocky, and grim-faced. They wore rough uniforms with neckflapped caps, and their overlong fixed bayonets glinted in the sun. They were veterans of the Imperial army's wars, the bravest, toughest, cruellest troops on earth.

The villagers rounded up like sheep, were cowering on the ground, trembling, fearful of the wrath to come.

With interpreter Stevens at his side, Mutaguchi was sitting upright at a table, his sword laid out in front of him. Ten paces off, the 'Gorilla' was chivvying the village elders into line.

Mutaguchi eyed the villagers with contempt. Karen peasants who had proved their disloyalty to the Emperor and who would now be taught a lesson. Through Stevens, he took the assembled throng to task.

'As the village adjacent to the drop, you must have known about the British planes. Must know where the British radio teams had gone. Must know where the parachuted stores were hidden.' More in sorrow than in

26

anger, Mutaguchi shook his head. 'But you are keeping all this knowledge to yourselves. This is very foolish, for you are betraying your Nippon friends. Betraying the sacred cause of Asia for the Asians. Above all, you are betraying the hopes of His Imperial Majesty the Emperor.'

Mutaguchi paused to let his words sink in. Then he told them icily: 'For this, your village will be burned and your elders put to death.'

A gasp gushed out. It was followed by a moan. Children began to howl.

Mutaguchi flicked a hand. The noise cut off. He carried on.

'You, the disloyal people of Thandaung, have brought this on yourselves. However, there is hope. His Imperial Majesty is kind as well as just. Therefore if the people of the Toungoo hills will make amends he will spare their lives and houses.'

Stevens translated, trying hard to emulate the officer's tone of voice. Again Mutaguchi paused to let his words sink in. Then he gave an ultimatum.

'You, the people of Thandaung, will spread the word of what has happened here. You will tell every village that unless the British spies are caught they too will have their elders put to death, their possessions taken and their houses burned.'

27

Another gasp. A wail of helplessness and fear rose up.

'However, the Kempetai will honour and reward any friend of Nippon who will lead them to the spies.'

Again a pause. Nervously, Stevens cleared his throat and spat. In the silence this somehow sounded wrong.

Mutaguchi thumped the table with his fist. 'This kindness will not apply to you. You will be punished. Your punishment will prove that the Kempetai does not make idle threats.'

Mutaguchi barked in Japanese. Instantly the soldiers brought their rifles to the ready. There was the sliding-clicking thud of bolts. Bayonets stood stark against the sky. Suddenly the feel of blood hung heavily on the air.

The elders were on their knees, hands tied behind their backs. The 'Gorilla' grasped the headman's wrists and raised them, causing the captive's head to jut forward.

Mutaguchi rose. Slowly he drew his sword from its ornamental sheath. He paused. Then he stalked to the pinioned man. He paused again, then raised the sword towards the sun. Turning on his heel he held the blade aloft. Then, two handed, he brought it slowly down to touch the doomed man's neck. Just as slowly he raised it high above his head. Every

28

eye was on the blade. The wait seemed endless. With bodies rigid, everyone held their breath. No sound of any sort. Then Mutaguchi's mouth gaped wide. SWISH. As the blade slashed down an 'Aagh,' exploded from his lips. it was echoed by his men. A gush of blood spouted. The head bounded and rolled along the ground, then came to rest, face up. There was a gasp of horror from the penned-in crowd.

Mutaguchi stood motionless, his feet apart, the sword point resting in the blood. The 'Gorilla' had bared his teeth. Stevens, the interpreter, vomited.

Mutaguchi straightened, wiped the sword blade clean and returned it to its sheath. He stalked back and resumed his seat behind the table. Once more he was sitting upright in his chair. Immediately in front of him, the flies were busy in the headman's blood.

Now the 'Gorilla' took the stage. The four other victims had been set to kneel in echelon, just a pace apart. A soldier moved behind each man and raised his fettered hands. With his feet apart, the 'Gorilla' balanced on his toes, his sword held high, his eyes on Mutaguchi. Again an eternity of time. At long, long last, a nod.

The sword slashed down. The same explosive 'Aagh'. The 'Gorilla' zigzagged back in three quick steps. Each time the sword slashed down. Each time came the 'Aagh'. Each time the blood spouted and the head bounced and rolled. One. Two. Three. Four. Each time the 'Aagh' was echoed by the watching troops. Within seconds, all four headless trunks were quivering on the ground.

The 'Gorilla' saluted Mutaguchi with his bloodstained sword. Turning, he flung up his arms and screamed a 'Banzai' to his men. As one, with their rifles held on high, they 'Banzai'd' back. Their voices echoed in the hills.

Then the soldiers got to work. Systematically they looted every house. The pigs and chickens were trussed to bamboo poles. The village dogs were shot. The dwellings were set on fire.

The villagers could only watch. Shaking, crazed with grief and fear, they milled helplessly around, wailing and moaning and beating at the ground. Some wandered off in shock. The huddled children screamed.

Mutaguchi watched as well. Impassive, he sat easily in his chair. It was a scene he had witnessed many times before, in Nanking, Manchuria, Shanghai and Singapore, Malaya. And now in the traitorous Burma hills.

Mutaguchi was content. He would now

return to Kempetai HQ and let the medicine do its work.

The punitive force marched out loaded with their loot, singing their martial songs, looking forward to bathing in the river, to getting drunk with complaisant Burmese women. And, if the mail had come, to receiving letters and snapshots from their loved ones back at home. Yes, like Mutaguchi, the soldiers were content.

At the head of his marching men Mutaguchi sat easily in his saddle. Already a poem was forming in his mind. Gradually the words took shape. By the time they had reached Toungoo the poem was complete. He felt a glow. When he had bathed and made his evening obeisance to the Emperor he would ink his brush and enshrine his deed in verse.

4

It was late. Stevens was in the cubby-hole adjacent to the office. He had turned the light out and was lying on his bunk. But, exhausted as he was, he couldn't sleep. He lit another cigarette. The Thandaung episode had left him drained. First the 'speedo' march to get there, the appalling things that followed, and then the long march home. He shuddered. It was all too much.

During the past two years he had been involved in happenings just as bad and, by now, his feelings should have dulled. But no, if anything they were worse. Thandaung had been a case in point. Three nights now and he had hardly slept a wink. Hadn't dared. He couldn't face the dreams. Another shudder. Tears were not far off. He could not go on like this. He simply couldn't. He must do something to end this living hell. But what? Despairingly he knew what the answer was to that — nothing! The Kempetai would never let him go. The only hope of escape was for him and his family to bribe their way across the border. True, the Japanese were there as well but the officials in Siam had itching palms and, for cash, were prepared to take a risk, but only at a price. Again he felt despair. Apart from the awful risk there was the problem of where he would get that sort of money? All he got from the Kempetai was his uniform and a sergeant's pay and rations. Again he was on the treadmill of his thoughts. *What* could he do? What? What? What?

His thoughts were interrupted by voices. Stevens pricked his ears. It was Mutaguchi and someone else. He didn't recognize the other voice. Whoever the stranger was, he was not a Japanese. His accent was proof of that. Suddenly, a light was shining above the map-room door. The glass of the open fanlight, acting as a mirror, reflected the office desk.

Mutaguchi's disembodied voice said: 'Right. Now show me on the map.'

Then the desk lamp came on too and Stevens could clearly see the reflection of the map. He could see Mutaguchi's ornamental cuff and his hand. Then another hand appeared. It was not Mutaguchi's, the forefinger was a stump. Again he could hear the voice. Stevens lay quiet and still, his stomach in a knot. Mutaguchi would not take kindly to anyone listening in.

The stranger's voice said: 'There are now three radio transmitters. One here . . . ' The maimed hand pencilled in a ring. 'One here and the other, here.' Two more rings.

'And the dump?' asked Mutaguchi.

'I do not know as yet,' replied the stranger.

Mutaguchi gave a grunt. Then: 'Find out. Then let me know.'

'Of course,' came the stranger's reply.

Now he could see just the map. Then came a click of glasses and the map was pulled away. Two tumblers and a bottle of what looked like British whisky took its place. Mutaguchi's hand appeared. The bottle was tilted and the whisky was poured. Two very generous measures. The tumblers disappeared, the maimed hand taking one, Mutaguchi's hand the other. Now there was just the bottle on the desk.

Mutaguchi spoke again. 'You've done well. Very well. The general will be pleased.' There was a pause. 'And now, my friend, a toast.' Stevens heard the click of heels. Then: 'To Asia for the Asians.' He heard a clink of glasses being touched. 'And may the British rot in hell.'

The stranger's voice added: 'And to the Imperial Nipponese Army, which will make the dream come true.'

Another click of heels, another clink and then the empty glasses joined the bottle on the desk.

'Have no fears my friend,' said Mutaguchi. 'It will be like it was in forty-three, with Seagrim. At dawn tomorrow the British spies and their radios will be silenced.'

'A rude awakening,' rejoined the stranger. This was followed by a laugh.

'Some will not awake.' Mutaguchi's voice was grim.

Another laugh. The maimed hand reached across. It was gripped by Mutaguchi's. Then both hands disappeared. Shadows appeared on the desk. Then came the sound of someone leaving, the slam of the shutting door. Then Stevens heard the whirr of a telephone being cranked.

Mutaguchi's voice was urgent. 'Watanabe. Three standby sections, ready to move at 0 two hundred hours. 'Speedo' marching order, two days' rations. You and the sergeant-major, orders group, Battalion office 0 one hundred. Oh, and Stevens to be there too.'

The phone banged down. The lights went out. Again came the sound of a slamming door. Mutaguchi's footsteps clopped along the concrete path and faded into quiet.

Stevens groaned. He stubbed out his cigarette and fumbled for his clothes. So Mutaguchi was right again. The 'medicine' had worked. Just as it had in forty-three. He shuddered. Suddenly he was overwhelmed with dread of what the next few days would bring. His stomach heaved and there was a hard metallic taste in his mouth. Then he was retching, retching on nothing but retching just the same.

Gradually, the convulsion eased away to leave his body soaked in sweat and his head splitting. In a frenzy of despair he began to curse the British ineptitude that had led to this. He cursed the savagery of the Japs. But most of all he cursed the living nightmare he was in. With an effort, he pushed the nightmare from his mind. For the sake of his family he must carry on. There was always the Siam border, and the money *might* turn up.

He reported to the Orders Group at 01.00 hours, a well-turned-out sergeant of the Imperial Nipponese Army. Mutaguchi answered his salute. The group got down to work.

★   ★   ★

At precisely 02.00 hours the Kempetai set out. They would go by road as far as trucks could get. Then the three sections would go their separate ways, all travelling by secret jungle paths. All three sections would strike at dawn.

5

Sergeant Ne Win's bladder woke him up. He would have to go downstairs. Not surprising, he'd had a lot to drink the night before. He could just make out the dial of his watch — 04.30 hours. He was snuggled down and warm and yearned to stay in bed. But no. Mother Nature called, he'd have to go. Well, so what. He was not on duty till 07.00. So, a quick slash and another two hours in bed. It was a nuisance but it would have to be. Dressed only in his pants he padded down the stairs. The latrine (and their escape route) was some little distance from the house. To hell with it. Why not use the steps? He hesitated. Captain Washington was fussy about little things like that. 'Well,' he thought. 'He's asleep and 'what the eye can't see . . . '

The door was just ajar. No one would be any the wiser. But the sooner the better, it was getting light. Looking past the door he fumbled in his pants. Then he froze. His heart began to pound. Two Japs in war paint were crouching by the fence! Worse, he could see another one in the trees. Ne Win felt sick. As quietly as he could he closed the door and dropped the bar, then scurried up the stairs to raise the alarm. Seconds later, consternation! Washington and his men were at the shutters, peering through the slats. For a moment, nothing happened. Then Washington spotted a trio with an LMG. They were steel-helmeted, their bayonets fixed. The machinegun was trained upon the door.

Ne Win called: 'Captain, there's more of 'em round the back.'

Washington sprang to life. 'OK, you chaps, move fast. Ne Win, send a May Day, then wreck the set. You two, burn the codes, the ciphers and the signal clips. And, all of you, into uniform. Quick.'

The three soldiers scrambled to obey. They had often practised this. Now it was for real.

Strangely, to Washington it seemed totally unreal. As if it was a play and he was watching himself perform. Most odd. Being taken prisoner by the Japs was something he'd always feared. Now it had come to pass he merely felt remote. He put it down to shock. Wryly, he hoped it would stay that way.

In next to no time everything that could be done was done. Still there was no reaction from the Japs. Washington realized that the sooner they packed it in the better. Give themselves up before the machine-gun raked the house and turned them into mincemeat.

His eye swept round: the set was dead. All the signals were burned. The rifles stacked to make a tripod, were well in view. He drew his .38, threw away the bullets and placed the gun on top. He fought a rising panic. Then he shook each man's hand. 'Remember,' he said. 'It's just name, rank and number.' An encouraging smile. 'OK?'

Ne Win raised a thumb. 'OK it is,' he said.

The captain took a long deep breath. 'Now hands above your heads and follow me.'

The four or them with hands on heads, stepped out into the dawn.

★ ★ ★

Meanwhile twenty miles away, Lieutenant Watanabe trained his glasses on the house. It looked and, to the anxious Watanabe, felt deserted. There was no sign of life at all. He looked around. The moon had long since gone. The stars had dimmed and the greying night gave promise of the jungle green to come. He sucked in the morning air. The humidity of the night had gone. Now a breeze caressed his face, ruffled through his hair and whispered to the trees.

He began to wonder if the birds had flown. Angrily he dismissed it from his mind. No chance of that. Everything had gone to plan.

He and his men had ghosted forward in an ever tightening ring. Unseen, unheard. Now, silent and alert, they merged with all the other shadows of the night.

'Ah!' Watanabe grunted with relief. There was movement from the house. Two shutters were being pushed apart. A match flared briefly. A wait. A cigarette glowed from time to time, then the butt came curving out.

Ten minutes ticked away. The house had settled down with the shutters still ajar. There came no further sound or movement. He buttoned his binoculars away. It was now light enough to see. It was time.

Watanabe finger-snapped a signal to his men, then loped swiftly and silently to the door. Gently, he tried the latch. He clicked his tongue — the door was barred. He finger-snapped again and three of his soldiers joined him. Tapping one of them on the arm he pointed to the open shutters just above. The man acknowledged with a nod. The pin of a grenade came free. To the other men he mimed a *breaking down the door.* Two understanding nods acknowledged his gesture. The soldiers crouched, bracing themselves to hit the door. A last look round, then Watanabe drew his automatic. 'Now,' he hissed.

The soldiers hit the door with all their weight. It splintered, crashed apart and they were in the house, fanning out and shooting as they went. The grenade went curving up. A flash. A crash. Cries of fright and pain. Shutters crashed apart and two men hurtled out. Landing on the run, they raced towards the trees. Tracer streaked and a machine-gun cut them down. Tumult. Children screamed. The village dogs went mad. Voices ricocheted from house to house.

Abruptly, the shooting stopped and the Japanese were swarming in and around the house . . .

Watanabe summed things up: The radio was wrecked. A man, an Anglo-Burman sergeant, was slumped against the set, dazed, blood pouring from his jaw. The two men who had made a run for it proved to have been sergeants too. Both had been shot and finished off with bayonets. Just one thing was wrong: the officer he'd been after wasn't there.

Dismayed, he thought of Mutaguchi's wrath. There was no time to lose. Grabbing the sergeant by the hair he rasped in English: 'Officer where?'

Gasping, nursing his shattered jaw, the sergeant shook his head.

A scream. But again the sergeant shook his head.

'Officer where?' Watanabe punched the sergeant's jaw.

41

A scream. But again the sergeant shook his head.

Watanabe raised his fist to strike again. But the man had had enough. On the verge of passing out, he was gurgling through his blood, stabbing a finger at the world outside.

'Officer where?' This time the question was a yell.

The sergeant closed a fist and pumped a finger in and out. Then he gestured towards the shutters.

Watanabe cottoned on. A quick command and the sergeant was hustled down the stairs. Across the fallen door and out into the open.

Again the question came. 'Officer where?' but this time in a normal voice.

With his hands clasped to his jaw the sergeant staggered along for fifty yards, then halted. Crazed with pain and fear, swaying and whimpering, he pointed to a house. Instantly the house was ringed by troops.

Everywhere there was a panic. One sight of the marauding Japs and an exodus began. Grabbing what they could, the villagers made a beeline for the trees.

Watanabe cupped his hand. 'Englishman come,' he yelled.

No reply. He shouted it again. Still no answer. Turning to the machine-gun crew he pointed to the house.

The machine gun opened fire. Shutters danced, chunks and splinters flew, water-pots exploded as the bursts tore though the walls. The LMG cut off. Still there was no reaction from the house. Led by Watanabe, the Japanese stormed in.

The house was empty. A search revealed a tumbled double bed, its mosquito net awry. By it were tumblers and a bottle of English whisky. A set of teeth were grinning from a glass. Shot through with bullet holes was an over-bright green uniform. With it, a baseball cap and a pair of jungle boots. Beneath the bed they found an American lightweight carbine. There could be no two ways about it, the two in the bed had left in quite a hurry!

Watanabe took in the jungle-covered hills. He cursed his luck. The bird, the bloody randy bird, had flown. Even now, albeit plucked of all his feathers, the 'bird' was flitting somewhere in that endless stretch of green.

He looked around. 'Flown' applied to the people too, for by now the village was deserted. Poor devils, he thought. Not surprising after what had happened at Thandaung. Despite Mutaguchi's claptrap about Asia for the Asians it was not their war. But then, an order was an order and had to be obeyed. He shrugged. It was not for him to reason why.

So, as ordered, Watanabe put the village to the torch.

★　★　★

Major Willis was striding out and he had less than a mile to go. It was already the morning of the tenth and SEAC must be told at once how well the cloak-and-dagger thing had gone. There had been no need for the courier or the timber-raft. General Aung San had got the message. He was not a fool. He had realized that the mountain no longer needed to journey to Mahomet. 'Mahomet' had come cap in hand, instead. Beside himself with joy, the major punched the air.

Then he sobered up. Just ahead was the ruined pongyi temple. No point in taking further risks. He turned on to a secret path that led to the headman's house. Unslinging his rifle he pushed one up the spout and slipped the catch to 'Fire'. Better safe than sorry!

He trained his binoculars on the village down below. The people were going about their everyday affairs. The scene was one of village peace. Old men sat and smoked cheroots and watched the world go by. Children scuffled happily in the dust. Pi-dogs were dozing in the shade. And, just below, laughing and chattering, women in gaily coloured clothes were returning from the wells, gliding along with earthenware water-pots balanced on their head. From where he was, he could see the headman laughing with his wife. Saw him playfully slap her bottom. Willis returned the catch to 'Safe'. Yes, it was safe all right.

The headman was glad to see him back. 'Bad news, Major. Very bad indeed.'

Willis learned about the happenings at Thandaung, and of the threats the Japanese had made. He was also told that a party of Kempetai had been spotted in the hills. Just three of them and fairly close at that. But, happily, they were bound for the Salween ferry.

'It is all very worrying, Major.'

'It certainly is, Min Taung. Tell me. What if they try a 'Thandaung' here?'

'We have made our plans, Major. If the Japanese soldiers come we will leave the village. In the jungle we have hidden weapons and supplies. Enough to keep us going till the British come.'

'And if the Kempetai burn the village?'

The headman shrugged. 'We will build again,' he said. 'Soon the British will be back and we will have no worry.' Then, anxiously: 'How soon will the British soldiers come, Major?'

Willis clapped him on the shoulder. 'Sooner than you think, Min Taung.' He was aching to tell the headman what he'd learned about the so-called patriot Aung San, the leader of the Burma National Army. But no. The Japs were on the warpath and the Japs played rough. *Least said* . . . he thought.

But now he must be off. He still had nearly a mile to go before he reached the hide-out and the signal to SEAC couldn't wait.

★ ★ ★

Mutaguchi knew exactly where to go and when to strike. It wasn't all that far but he had played it safe. They had marched in a sweeping circle and approached the hide-out from the rear. Earlier on and heading east, they had passed a bullock cart. The driver had confirmed that they were on course for the Salween ferry. They had then turned north. Then west and, finally, due south. Apart from the driver of the bullock cart they hadn't met a soul.

There were just the three of them — Mutaguchi, Stevens and Sergeant-Major Ekesta, the 'Gorilla'.

The hide-out had been difficult to find but luck was with them. Quite by chance they stumbled on a narrow path that led to a latrine. The path went on to finish in the hills. They recognized the path for what it was — an escape route to the jungle. Retracing their steps they stopped at the latrine. Here, Ekesta was told to wait and deal with anyone who came. The 'Gorilla' grinned. Drawing his sword he vanished into the scrub.

The other two carried on. Suddenly, Mutaguchi pricked his ears and stopped dead. Then he dropped into the scrub, pulling Stevens with him. He held a finger to his lips. From ahead came a tuneless whistling. It heralded a British soldier who came strolling up the path. He was hatless, his shirt was flapping wide and he was carrying some scraps of paper and a book. Mutaguchi let him pass.

Still whistling the soldier arrived at the latrine. The seat was in the shade. As he let his trousers down he felt the breeze's caress. With his eyes half-closed he surrendered to its touch. The whistling stopped. He murmured: 'Oh, lovely, lovely, lovely.' A split second before he died he thought he saw a shadow. Thought he heard a swish.

Mutaguchi and Stevens were back upon the path. They turned a bend and there it was — a bamboo hut on stilts. Again they ducked into the scrub, silent, still. Mutaguchi's eyes were fixed upon the hut. Then: 'You stay here,' he hissed. With his automatic in his hand he walked quite brazenly to the hut, climbed the creaking stairs and pushed through the open door.

There were two men in the room, both in shorts and vests. One of them was fiddling with a radio, the other was asleep. Engrossed, the man at the radio did not look up. 'You were quick,' he said.

Mutaguchi put a bullet through his head and shot the sleeper too. He went to the door and beckoned his interpreter to join him. Then, pointing to the bodies, he said: 'Get rid of those, then tidy up the mess. When you have finished, make some tea.'

With his pistol on his lap and his feet up on a box he settled in a chair . . .

The major was almost there and he was in a hurry. Again he checked his watch. They were due to come up on the air in fifteen minutes. The message would take some time to code. No time to lose. He broke into a run.

The steps creaked beneath his weight. Then suddenly he stopped. It was like running against a wall. Something was wrong. What it was he didn't know. Could be the silence. Could be imagination. But no, it was more than that. The hairs on his neck stood up. Alarm bells were ringing in his head. With only four more steps to go, his head was level with the gap beneath the door. That was it! Despite the heat the door was closed. His skin began to crawl. During the day the door was never closed. Was that a shadow just behind the gap? It moved. It was!

It was time to leave. With his eyes glued to the door, he descended backwards, step by step. Each step creaked. He could feel the sun, hot upon his back. Could feel the silence, the menace in the air. Just two more steps to go. He sensed just the slightest movement. It caught his eye. It was the muzzle of a pistol sliding through a slat. It was pointing to his head. Instinctively he twisted round and hit the ground, turning over in a roll that took him sideways, then back on to his feet to go scurrying crabwise in a crouching run. A shot. A bullet nicked his head. Then he was haring along the escape route, blood pouring down his face.

The 'Gorilla' heard the shot. Heard the pounding steps. Cocking his captured Thompson he stood squarely in the path.

An Englishman came hurtling round the bend. Seeing him, the Englishman, plunging sideways, grabbed for the pistol on his belt. The 'Gorilla' felt the Thompson vibrating in his hands. Smelt the cordite. Saw the amazement on the bearded English face as the bullets smashed his chest.

He heaved the body over with a foot. Gave a nod of satisfaction at a job well done. Quickly and efficiently he searched the corpse. He took both the rifle and the pistol and, with a grunt of pleasure, the Rolex 'Oyster' watch. Then having changed the magazine, he strode towards the house. There would be no more trouble in the Toungoo hills.

6

Watanabe emerged from the debriefing with a feeling of relief. Although it was not his fault he had expected an onslaught on the officer's escape. But no, Mutaguchi was on a 'high'. Promotion to an even more important post was in the air. It appeared that his achievement in nipping the insurrection in the bud had gone down well with the Nippon high command. Not only for the military success but for political reasons too. So much so that he had received a personal call from the C in C. As the Commander in Chief had put it: 'It is an oasis in a desert of defeat.' He had gone on to say that, because of the disaster at Imphal, a number of Burmese 'bigwigs' were threatening to rat. That even General U Aung San, the commander of the Burma National Army, was having second thoughts. No fool, he had realized that fighting fellow-nationals would be a political disaster. To offset this the Nippon high command had promised that the Toungoo problem would be solved in fourteen days. Mutaguchi had made his mark. He had brought it off in six. A warning to all

51

fair-weather friends of the speed and ruthlessness of Nippon retribution.

So now he made no fuss about the officer's escape, saying: 'One man, naked, in the jungle cannot be a threat.' Elated, he had decreed three things. One, that the 'carrot' would replace the 'stick'. Two, that soldiers captured in uniform would not be treated as guerrillas. Three, that if the villagers proved their loyalty, there would be no further sanctions.

Most surprising of all he had entertained the captured captain to a meal. Stevens was there as well but strictly as an interpreter, not a guest. It was then that Washington learned the extent of the disaster. Encouraged by Mutaguchi's warmth he asked who had betrayed them. The Jap laughed, saying, 'Walls have ears, Captain. Burmese ears.' Then, clearly embarrassing Stevens, he added: 'And our mixed-race friends can be relied upon as well.'

'So, it was you, you renegade sod,' Washington muttered to himself.

Inevitably the whereabouts of the dump cropped up. By then Mutaguchi had had too much to drink and, on learning that only the officers had known the location, he shrugged it off. 'So what,' he said. 'Without anyone to use them the store will wither on the vine.'

He gave an expansive, drunken smile. 'Sooner or later the dump will be betrayed to the victorious Nipponese. Like a fallen apple it will drop into our lap.' Drunk with wine and triumph, Mutaguchi dismissed the dump as 'unimportant'.

Washington returned to the lock-up a relieved but thoughtful man. He couldn't believe his luck. He was not a particularly religious man but he offered up a prayer that his luck would hold.

He was right to have his doubts. In a matter of hours it all went sour . . .

It was sometime in the night. Washington was woken by the clump of army boots, keys rattling in the lock. The door swung wide to reveal two Jap soldiers, one big one small, grim, steel-helmeted with bayonets fixed.

The big man stabbed a finger. 'English come,' he said. Washington made to dress but, put out, the big man went into a rage and slapped his face. Barefoot and in just his vest and pants he was hustled across a courtyard and into a darkened shuttered room. The only light was from a naked bulb suspended from the roof. From its double-socket another wire snaked off to join a small black box.

Mutaguchi was sitting at a desk, with Stevens in Japanese uniform standing at his side. A huge sergeant-major closed the door. Then, expressionless, he stood with his feet astride, his thumbs hooked round his belt. Washington licked his lips. This must be the infamous 'Gorilla'.

The 'Gorilla' pointed to a chair and, still expressionless, nodded towards the small black box. Washington's stomach lurched. Despite the stickiness of the night, he shivered. Please, God, no, he prayed.

Mutaguchi had sobered up and was now aloof, as if the two of them had never met. Stevens's eyes were flickering round the room, flickering everywhere but at the British captain's face.

Mutaguchi tore a signal from a pad and handed it to Stevens. The sergeant cleared his throat and read it out. It was from Burma Army GHQ and addressed to Mutaguchi. It was brief and to the point: 'Major Mutaguchi to report forthwith to C in C Burma Army Stop He will attend Burma National Army briefing Stop He will bring captured British/ guerrilla stores for hand over to Burma National Army Stop Acknowledge Message ends.'

Mutaguchi retrieved the signal, placed it on the desk and, very carefully, smoothed it out. A pair of ice-cold eyes came up. 'Captain, you will lead me to the dump,' he said.

Washington was taken by surprise. 'The dump is unimportant, Major. You told me that yourself.'

He listened to Stevens relaying his words in Japanese — cool, quick, efficient. Treacherous bastard though he was, the sergeant knew his stuff.

The ruthless eyes flicked to the signal on the desk, came back. 'You will lead me to the dump,' Mutaguchi said again. A pause, then, with a gesture to the box, 'Or else.'

Suddenly, Washington found it difficult to breathe. He had heard about these things. Heard about the Kempetai. Stories that had chilled. But this was not a story, this was real. The room was deathly quiet. Blood hung heavily on the air. Fear sucked away his strength. Now what?

Icily. 'I'm waiting, Captain.'

Hiatus. Then Washington had the same uncanny feeling he'd had just before his capture. As if this was just a play and he was watching himself perform already written words. He felt remote. All his fears had gone and he knew, quite simply, that come what may he would not betray the dump. No rhyme or reason, for, as this sadistic sod had said, the dump was 'unimportant'. But that was just the point. Not betraying it was important. Not betraying the dump was why he had struggled out to India. Why he had parachuted back into the hills. Why he was sitting here right now. It was not just a matter of betraying the dump, but that in doing so he would be betraying Gordon Willis and all the others. Surrendering to this shit would mean betraying everything he believed in, stood for. No, come what may, he would not give in.

His mind made up, he said, quite calmly: 'All I'm obliged to tell you is that my name is Washington. My army rank is captain and my number is 235797.'

In a strange euphoria he watched the interpreter's lips translating what he'd said. Watched the reaction in the hard, cold eyes. Heard yet another: 'You will lead me to the dump.' Heard his answer, first in English and then in Japanese. A simple 'No.'

The Jap stalked round the desk and looked down at him with a pitiless gaze. Washington faced him out. Saw the gaze begin to burn. Felt the sting as Mutaguchi slapped his face, *crack-crack*, like pistol shots.

'You. Lead me to the dump,' Mutaguchi hissed in English.

'You. Get stuffed,' came back. It needed no translation.

For a moment time stood still. Then Washington saw stars. The Gorilla's fist had smashed into his face. Had sent him sprawling to the floor, stunned and bleeding from his nose and mouth. In a daze he felt his pants being ripped. Felt pain in his arms and wrists. Was aware that he was spinning and that he couldn't feel the floor.

His head began to clear. With handcuffed wrists he was dangling from a beam, completely naked. Blood from his nose and mouth was trickling down his chest.

Mutaguchi was back behind his desk. The Gorilla's hitherto impassive face, was distorted in a grin. He was holding two electrodes. Stevens had moved close enough to touch.

Mutaguchi spoke. 'Captain, for your sake. For your men's sale. For the sake of the villagers involved. You will lead me to the dump.'

Stevens translated. Humiliated, in pain and hardly listening, Washington spat into his face and shouted: 'NO, NO, NO.'

Instantly he exploded in a shattering white-hot pain. His knees jerked up and hit his chin. Every muscle cramped and agony filled the world. From a long way off he heard a thin demented scream . . .

The agony ebbed away and left him all atremble. His joints were burning. Every muscle ached. Like a close-up in a film the

57

interpreter's face loomed up. Washington saw that he had a little pustule on his chin, smelt a whiff of curry on his breath. When he spoke the words boomed and faded like a radio badly tuned. The voice was saying: 'Captain, lead him to the dump.' Then, more loudly: 'Captain, for God's sake tell him or he'll kill you.'

But the words were pushed aside. At the edge of Washington's mind he could see, or sense, or both, a little *no*. It was no bigger than a pin-point but black and sharply clear. Like magic, it grew and grew until it filled his head, grew bigger than the room, bigger than the Toungoo hills, bigger than the whole wide world. Somewhere a voice was screaming: '*No*, you fucking bastards. *No*.'

Instantly there was another searing shattering explosion. His body jerked like a frantic marionette, sinews cording, eyeballs popping out. Again he heard the thin demented scream.

Then it was back to the aching burning; back to the close-up face demanding: 'Captain, lead him to the dump.'

But again the tiny *no* came burgeoning like the genie from the lamp. Again he heard the sound of someone screaming, 'No. No. No.'

Again. And then again. And yet again, with every fibre of his body willing him to tell them where it was. To tell them anything to stop this searing, hammering pain. But all he could see and hear, remember, was the burgeoning of the jetblack no. Then there was just the black. Then nothing . . .

★ ★ ★

When he came to, the sun was shining through the bars. What time, or even day, it was he didn't know. His watch had gone. Now it would be on a Japanese soldier's wrist: a minor spoil of war.

Vaguely he began to wonder where he was. 'Why was he lying naked on this blanket-covered bunk. Why was his head hammering and why did he ache in every limb? Then, *crash*, it all came back — Mutaguchi, the renegade Sergeant Stevens, the Gorilla and his box. Whimpering, he shrank into himself: those Japs, those fucking Japs. They'd do anything, anything at all, to get their way. Would just keep hammering on until he broke or died. His body tightened at the thought. What now? He shuddered. One thing was for sure, he couldn't, he simply couldn't face that agony again. Suddenly he fell apart. He began to shake. His teeth were chattering and he could hear the gasping of his breath. A moan of abject terror bubbled up. He gave a silent scream. 'Dear God, no more, no more,' he gasped. Then his face screwed up and he was sobbing, the tears streaming down his face. 'Dear God,' he prayed, 'please help me, please. I couldn't bear it, I simply couldn't bear it any more.' His knees came up and touched his chin and he curled into a ball, lay terrified, dreading the sound of footsteps. He knew now that he would tell them anything they asked, anything at all to avoid that pain. He felt a sense of both relief and shame. Then panic. His stomach fell away. Dear God, what if they asked for something he didn't know!

The day dragged on, turned into night. Then he heard the clump of footsteps on the path. Again his stomach lurched. He was almost sick. What now?

Keys rattled in the lock. The door crashed wide. His heart pounding, he pressed against the wall. It was the same two soldiers, one big, one small. The big man was carrying a bowl of water, soap and a towel, his comrade a tray of food. The big man grinned, and pointing to the food, he rubbed his belt. 'Good, English, good,' he said.

Not to be outdone, the little man produced a pack of cigarettes, took two out and placed them on the tray. Then, from a jar, he decanted two red matches. He too was smiling. He held the packet up and said, 'Senior Service' in a funny sort of way, then added: 'English. Very good.' and gave a little bow.

Washington was euphoric with relief. He knew just one word of Japanese *arregeto*: thank you: '*Arregeto*,' he said and smiled. Instinctively he returned the little bow.

Delighted, the soldiers took it up, bowing to him to each other and everything in the room, saying '*arregeto*' in different tones of voice. For all the world like knockabout comedians they imitated waiters as they laid out the washing-things and food. '*Arregeto, arregeto, arregeto* . . . ' Then, chuckling, they gave a special double bow and left. He could hear them laughing and *Arregeto-ing* as their footsteps died away.

Washington shook his head in disbelief. It takes all sorts, he thought, even with the Japs. Gratefully he had a wash and lit a cigarette. He realized he was hungry and the food looked good. His spirits rose. No two ways about it, things were looking up. He crossed his fingers and hoped it was the same for his three sergeants.

'Mutt and Jeff' were back as soon as it was light and again later in the day. Each time the pantomime was the same. But it left him wondering whether the cheerfulness would last. Or would the sods revert to type?

Sometime in the evening the soldiers came again. This time they were armed and formal, bayonets fixed. Washington was tense. Was this an interrogation ploy, the good guy and the bad? The sort of thing you saw in films.

'English, come,' the big man said, and with one of them on either side he was hurried across the courtyard to the interrogation room.

Relief. The shutters were apart and the sun was streaming in. Mutaguchi was propped, half-sitting, against his desk his polished riding-boots stretched out. Stevens was there as well but there was no sign of the Gorilla, no black box.

The Jap waved Washington to a chair and, to his astonishment, not only offered him a cigarette but lit it for him too. On the desk he could see two glasses and a bottle of Black and White.

'A drink,' Mutaguchi said in English.

Washington shook his head. A cigarette was one thing. drinking with this sod was something else.

The Jap was not put out. Through Stevens, he said: 'But I insist, Captain. This is a celebration.' Saying this he poured two drinks and handed one across. He raised his glass and, in English, said: 'Good health.'

Good health! Washington thought of the previous night. Drink it? He'd sooner throw it in the bastard's face. But the Jap was looking down his nose, put out. Washington took the drink. 'A celebration?' he enquired as stiffly as he could.

'Yes, Captain, we have found your dump. We can now be friends. There is no need now for pressures. Not for you, your men, or any of the people in the hills.'

'You are bluffing.' He had almost said *lying* but had changed it just in time.

Mutaguchi sat with a hand supporting himself on either side. At ease, he crossed his boots. 'No, not a bluff, Captain. The stores have just arrived. They will be photographed for the South East Asia press. Finish your drink and come with me.'

Washington put his whisky down untouched. Not much but in his plight it was the best that he could do. Then, escorted by the Jap, he went outside.

Four captured Bedford three-tonners were standing side by side, their tailboards down. Jap troops were busying around, unloading and piling the stores in groups. Photographs and newsreel men were busy too.

His spirits sagged. They had found the dump all right. He cursed. All that work and planning gone to waste. Lives had been

63

wasted, too. Dejected, he asked: 'And who betrayed it?'

Mutaguchi said in English: 'Sergeant Stevens.' Then through Stevens: 'But not betrayed, Captain. It was his duty to Nippon. The English are not loved, Captain. Not by the Burmans and certainly not by the mixed-race people they despise. These people's time has come. Through Nippon and the Burma National Army they will kick the English out.'

Washington struck back. 'And the hill tribes, Major? The Karens? The Nagas? The Kachins and all the rest. Do they prefer you to us?'

Mutaguchi pulled a face, saying frostily: 'Nippon discipline will alter that.'

Just then the Jap was called away to be photographed with the stores. He left Stevens to interpret what he'd said.

Washington heard him out. Then, through set teeth, he said: 'Sergeant Stevens, when we win the war there'll be a reckoning. I will see that you, Mutaguchi, and that 'Gorilla' shit will swing.' He began to shout. 'Do you hear me? Swing. Swing by your fucking necks until you're dead.'

Before Stevens could reply Washington was summoned to be photographed with the spoils. He looked them over. The stores were neatly stacked. He could see that everything was there: weapons, ammo, radio spare parts, batteries, rations, uniforms and boots. Everything that was except the cash, the bags of silver. Someone had got their fingers in the till! Washington was tempted to mention this and take a little of the sunshine from Mutaguchi's day. After all he'd probably pinched it for himself. But on second thoughts, no. Sadist though he was, that somehow didn't fit. Then who? The joker who had found it? The recovery party? Stevens? Or would it be the villagers? For his money (for his money!) it was almost certainly Stevens. But with all his heart he hoped it was someone from a village, preferably Thandaung.

His thoughts were interrupted. He was being chivvied into line. Cameras were whirring. Reporters crowding round . . .

Back in his cell he had time to think. On the whole it was not too bad. He had Mutaguchi's assurance that he would be treated honourably as 'a prisoner of the Emperor', whatever that might mean! Whilst being photographed by the press, Mutaguchi had said: 'You are a brave man, Captain Washington. Most men would have talked. It took great courage. For that I salute you.' And the oddball had done just that! It could have been for the benefit of the press. But no, it had seemed more genuine than that. He had even promised that his three sergeants would be treated in just the same way. Well, he hoped Mutaguchi would keep his word. One thing was for sure. He Washington, would keep his word to Stevens that all three of them would swing. It was a thought that was to keep him going through the difficult times to come. Keep him going till two unbelievable puffs of smoke set him, and thousands like him, free.

In the meantime he prayed that Po Kyin would make it back. His chances were not too good, but, as his poker-playing friends would say, he was a right tough cookie. If anyone could make it, Po Kyin would. He raised a glass of beer that 'Mutt and Jeff' had brought and wished the Burman luck . . .

PART TWO

COURT MARTIAL

7

Colonel Young looked up and smiled. 'Morning, Robbie, sit yourself down,' he said. He produced a file. 'I've got a job for you. Court martial.' Another smile. 'Big stuff. Right up your street. The JAG's branch is sending someone up from Army.' A quick reference to the file. 'A Major Ledward. He's nominated the members of the court. They're listed in the file. The president is from the Service Corps. Colonel Perceval. I think you know him?'

'I do indeed, sir. I'm in his mess.'

'Good. Watch your p's and q's though. He's a bit pedantic. Goes strictly by the book.'

Captain Roberts nodded. He knew the colonel well. 'Pedantic' was right. It accounted for his nickname: 'Pompous Perce'.

'You'll need to fix a venue and the witnesses will need watering and quartering. You'll be needing interpreters too. Get them from the BIC. Quote me if there's any trouble over this. There are two main witnesses. A Brigadier Po Kyin and a Captain Washington. They will be guests of the GOC so you can leave that side of things to the 'A' Mess Sec.'

'Transport, sir?'

'OC Provost, Captain Fletcher. He's been warned. You know him too, I take it?'

Captain Roberts grinned. 'I most certainly do. We're both in the colonel's mess.'

'Good. Fletcher will produce the accused as well. He's holding him in his cage. A Sergeant Stevens. An Anglo-Burman by the way. Deserter.' The colonel pulled a face. 'Worked for the Kempetai.' He flourished the file. 'It's all in here: summary of evidence, list of witnesses and make-up of the court. They've all been warned but you'll need to check. Case shouldn't take long. A couple of days at most. It's all pretty much cut and dried.' He passed the file to Roberts, saying good-humouredly: 'What you press wallahs would call an open-and-shut case.'

Roberts took the file. 'Anything else, sir?'

'Yes, just one more thing. Sergeant Stevens's father lives in Toungoo. He's something on the railway. Wants to know if he can see his son. Be a good chap. Pop along and tell him that the answer's no. He can attend the trial of course.' A wintry smile. 'Then have a few last words before he's hanged.'

* * *

70

Roberts let the file fall on his lap. Colonel Young was right. If ever there was an open-and-shut case, then this was it. Leaning back, he went over in his mind Stevens's appalling record as one of the TUT: the deaths of first-class blokes like Major Seagrim and Major Willis and so many of their men. Torturing Captain Washington. Murdering all those villagers, especially at Thandaung. Betraying the guerrilla dump and swiping all that silver coin as well.

And all of it was backed by unimpeachable witnesses. Brigadier Po Kyin DSO, MC and bar, no less! And there was the tortured Captain Washington and three Burmans who had actually seen the sergeant applying the electrodes. Christ, what a charmer this Stevens was!

And for the defence? The only witnesses to be called were a Burmese muleteer and a Roman Catholic priest. They would appear, no doubt, to say that, apart from pulling wings off flies and chopping off people's heads, he was a decent sort of chap!

No, Stevens hadn't a cat in hell's chance. He might as well plead guilty and save them all a lot of fret.

Well, there was a couple of weeks before the trial took place. Right now it was almost time for tiffin. But first, a long cold glass of

71

beer. He rang the bell.

The day was hot but a fan was swishing just above his head and the shutters tamed the sun. He took a sip, let the beer roll round his mouth and gave a grunt of satisfaction. Life was good. After tiffin he would have a snooze, then go along and break the news to Stevens's father. Probably as big a bastard as his son. After that a shower, a change of uniform, then dinner with Fletch and Marie at the club. Yes, life was good. Taking a swig from time to time he let memory hold the door.

Barely a couple of months ago the div had been slogging up that dreadful Mawchi road. And, God, what a road it was! Narrow, completely hemmed in by jungle. In fact, an elongated death-trap that wound through the Toungoo hills. With those fanatical Japanese bastards at every twist and turn it was a death-trap right enough. But it was not only the Japs. There was the pissing non-stop rain, the knee-deep mud and the bloody awful flies. Three-inch mortars planted on every available bit of ground, their bombs hurtling skyward, a cascade in reverse. Murderous treebursts as the Japs replied. Flooded foxholes. Leeches. Everyone unwashed and stinking. Blood forming patterns in the slime. Always a lack of sleep with the Japs jittering in the night. A dank closed world of blood, weariness and pain with never an end in sight.

And then? And then a bloody miracle! Two waves of a magic wand. Two incredible puffs of smoke. And suddenly, unbelievably, the war was at an end.

From then on it had been roses all the way. With the regiment disbanded, he'd got this cushy job at Div HQ. Just three more months to go and he'd be on his way to England, home and beauty and the job on the local rag. By then he would have gone full circle: from press reporter, to soldier, to press reporter. But it had encompassed six long years of war.

His mind went back to 1939. The change from working on a paper to becoming a man at arms had been a jolt. But he had taken it in his stride. Becoming a wartime soldier had opened new horizons, for, being a reporter, people were his life: how they lived, what made them tick, the stupid and, yes, the wonderful things they did. He'd always gone along with Shakespeare that all the world was a stage, and that he, Robbie Roberts, was both a spectator and player. Yes, and often a critic too! In particular he had relished attending and reporting trials. To him, it was not a chore, it was real-life theatre. OK, so the lines and pace were not as slick as in the playhouse, but the courtroom cut and thrust could be as good as any play. So much so that he'd often wished he could have taken up the law. He had had many a daydream of being in wig and gown, clutching his lapels and winning a case against all odds. But of course it would always be a dream. An elementary education and a father on the dole had seen to that. However it gave a new dimension to this court martial of Stevens. 'Right up your street,' Colonel Young had said. Robbie Roberts drained his glass. Colonel Young was right.

★   ★   ★

From her bedroom window Angela saw a jeep turn into Station Road. Or rather what was left of Station Road, for the RAF had cratered it like the surface of the moon. Scarred and patched, the Stevens house was one of the few that had survived. The jeep rocked slowly down the pockmarked road as the driver, an English officer, peered out. Looking up, he caught her eye and coasted to a halt. 'That eighteen?' he called.

She nodded.

'Stevens?'

Another nod.

Angela heard the brake rack on. She saw the officer dismount and, giving his cap a tilt, come sauntering up the path.

Panic. She smoothed down her dress (oh dear, no bra!). She glanced into the mirror, ran a comb through her hair and changed quickly out of sandals into shoes. Then, having pinched her cheeks to make them glow, she met him at the door.

The officer, a captain, smiled and casually brought his fingers to his cap. 'Miss Stevens, I presume,' he said.

The girl's heart missed a beat. That horoscope was right. It had said that one day her prince would come. And come he had. He was everything she had ever dreamed about: crisp green uniform; shining pips; tall; a sun-tanned face; an English officer's clipped moustache; white and even teeth and grey-blue eyes. And oh, that hair curling from underneath his cap! Her knees went weak. If only she'd had time to change her frock and do her face and lips. But it was too late now. Nervously, she primped her hair.

'Miss Stevens?' Again the smile.

The smile went like an arrow to her heart. He was just like the illustrations in her magazine. A *Real Romances* hero come to life.

'Miss Stevens?' Now he gave her a puzzled look.

Angela pulled herself together. Whatever would he think! 'I am indeed,' she said. Then: 'Have you come about my brother Andrew?' (His mouth and chin, so firm. His eyes so blue).

'If Andrew is Sergeant Stevens, yes. Is his father . . . is Mr Stevens in?'

A spate of Bombay Welsh. 'No, Daddy is at the yard. But, Captain, how dreadful of me to keep you standing at the door. Will you please join me in our house and I will get you something cold to drink.'

With this she turned and ushered him to a large and darkened room. It smelled unused and musty but she flung the shutters open and let the sun stream in.

Roberts caught his breath. The sun was shining through her dress. Under the dress she had nothing on at all and for one delicious moment she was naked, absolutely starkers! Unaware (or was she?) she bent to plump the cushions on his chair. The shapeliness and nearness of her bottom made him gasp. Long time no see, he thought and, down in the forest, something stirred.

All smiles, she handed him a somewhat dog-eared magazine and said: 'Please make yourself at home, Captain, whilst I prepare your drink.' As she spoke she touched his hand. Still smiling she walked self-consciously but gracefully through the door.

Roberts shook his head and grinned. 'Down boy,' he told himself, then 'made himself at home'. The room had a high-days-and-holidays-only feel and was clearly seldom used. But it was clean and tidy and, with the shutters open, the mustiness had gone. The magazine was a thing called *Real Romances* and was dated October 1939. He knew it well. Flicking through, he stopped at a feature headed 'Cupid's Dart', edited by a Prudence Heart. Small world, he thought. He'd known 'Prudence' well. His name was Harry Turner and he had made a fortune with this *Real Romances* rag. Roberts leafed through the pathetic pleas for help. He sighed. How innocent the pre-war years had been.

Then Angela was back with an earthenware jug and a pair of crystal tumblers, good ones too. The jug had a muslin cover edged with beads. On it was embroidered: *The Lord helps those* . . . .The girl had changed her dress and put a flower in her hair. It suited her, as did the dress. The top two buttons had been left undone and a little gold-chained crucifix dangled in the gap. And what a gap! When she leaned to pour the drink he found himself looking down the happiest little valley he had seen in years. Steady boy, he thought, and took a long deep breath. Whatever

Sergeant Stevens was, his sister was a peach. Yes, and a ripe and willing peach at that. She knew the score. He felt a desperate need to touch but there was the sound of someone moving in the hall and a tall, thin, greying man came in. He was dressed in oil-stained dungarees, British army boots and an army webbing belt. Around his neck was a rather sweaty scarf. The man looked tired and old and was revolving a somewhat battered topee in his hands. Roberts clambered to his feet. This must be 'Dad'.

It was. 'I take it you have called about my son,' the man said.

'Yes, sir, I have.' Roberts told him of the GOC's decision.

The man absorbed it like someone reconciled to the short end of the stick. He raised just an initial spark of protest. 'Is that not inhumane, Captain?'

'That I'm afraid, applies to the whole sorry business, sir,' said Roberts as gently as he could.

Mr Stevens sagged. Then: 'Tell me, Captain, will you be one of the English gentlemen who will judge my son?'

'No, my job is administration only.'

'But you will ensure that Andrew is treated properly. That his trial is just?'

'I'm afraid that is outside my remit, sir.'

Mr Stevens then surprisingly, and embarrassingly, gripped Roberts by the arms and peered into his face. His hands were trembling and all the misery in the world was in the look. He licked his lips and said: 'I think you are a good and honourable man, Captain. I beg of you to see that my son is treated justly. He is not a bad boy, Captain. Whatever he did, it was for us. No son could have done his duty to his family better.'

The old man's eyes had filled with tears. Embarrassed, he turned away and stood gazing through the shutters. Roberts waited. How many parents throughout the world are saying things like that, he thought. But parents are not the best judges of their sons. The war had seen to that. Many, guilty of the most appalling crimes, had been loyal and loving to their folks at home. For many of them it had been a case of far too much too soon. Now had come the reckoning. He remembered a phrase he had heard in court. Some kind of proverb: *Take what you want, said God. Take it and pay for it.* Taking was one thing, paying the bill another.

Mr Stevens turned. 'You will excuse me, Captain, if I leave Angela to see you out. I have many things to do.' He had retrieved his hat and, still turning it in his hands, stood waiting by the door. Roberts was moved. The old man was pathetic in a way but he had the dignity of one who had said his piece and had nothing more to add.

Well, that's a bit abrupt, thought Roberts wryly, but I can take a hint. Donning his cap, he said: 'Then I'll be off.' Then, on an impulse, he gave the old man an 'Aldershot' salute and said: 'Mr Stevens, I will do everything I can. You have my word on that.'

The old man turned and left but Roberts had seen hope kindle in his eyes.

At the jeep, Angela was all apologies. 'Daddy really is in a hurry, Captain. In an hour he has to drive a train to Mandalay.'

Roberts brushed it off. 'Not to worry,' he said. He meant it; he had other things in mind. What a cracker, he was thinking. Definitely the answer to a sex-starved captain's prayer. And, as the embroidery had said, *The Lord helps those* . . . .So why not help myself? He went to work.

Seated in his jeep, he took her hand. 'Would you be my guest at the Officers Club tonight?' He gave the hand a squeeze. 'Please say yes.'

She took his hand in both of hers. 'Oh yes, Captain, yes,' she breathed.

'Good. My name's Roberts by the way, but it's 'Robbie' to my friends. So let's drop the 'Captain', shall we?'

Her hands clasped tighter still. 'Oh yes, Robbie, yes.'

Raising her hands, he touched them with his lips and said: 'Right then, it's dinner at eight. I'll pick you up at seven.'

As he drove away he blew a kiss and waved. Entranced, and with her hands clasped to her breast, she watched him out of sight.

Angela was on cloud nine. And why not? she thought. Other girls had made it, why not she? After all, she could pass — well almost pass — as white, and Robbie was falling in love with her. The way he had smiled and held and kissed her hands was proof of that. And he'd been so kind to Daddy and he'd promised to be kind to Andrew too. Her *Real Romances* horoscope was coming true. Dear, kind, darling Robbie. Angela's wishful thinking soared. If she was nice to him he would marry her and take her home to England where everyone was rich. Take her away from Toungoo and all its dirt and smells and coloured people. She would live in a luxury bungalow, wear fine clothes and have servants to do her work. Later on, Daddy and Andrew would come to England too. Robbie would have many influential friends who would find them both a job. It would be better for Daddy if he came to live with her. He was getting old. He and Robbie would get on well together. There would be no problem there. Angela felt like dancing round the room. She had never been so happy in her life. Now she must get ready. It would soon be seven. A tremor of joy — the Officers Club! It could not be soon enough . . .

Her 'Prince' was also on a high. Clearly his hair shirt period was coming to an end. And what an end! She really was a cracker, no two ways on that. And if she was anything like Fletch's Marie Gomez it would be Christmas every day.

The evening at the club went well but ended suddenly when Captain Fletcher had a brush with 'Pompous Perce'. Colonel Perceval was dining with his po-faced second-in-command, a Major Smith. Leaving the dance floor mellowed by far too much to drink, Fletcher introduced the nubile Marie Gomez to the colonel. It was not a good idea. By now Marie was not too steady on her feet and when she leaned across to say hello she lost control and kept on going down, subsiding, giggling helplessly and bottom up, across the colonel's lap.

Fletcher had clicked his heels. 'Colonel,' he said formally. 'May I introduce Miss Marie Gomez, the toast of Mandalay.'

For a moment Fletcher wondered where 'the toast of Mandalay' had gone. In his fuddled state, all he could see was a very shapely bottom, the tops of two suspendered stockings and a look of outrage on the colonel's face. The colonel's hands were raised above his head as if to stop them getting soiled.

Fletcher was confused. Somehow the bottom looked familiar. From somewhere a muffled voice was giggling. 'Fletch, you silly bugger, help me up.' The voice was familiar too, especially when it became a little more shrill. 'Fletch, for Christ's sake, lift me up.'

The penny dropped. The bum belonged to Marie. It was Marie's voice as well. Marie was a fallen woman. The phrase amused him. She was that all right!

Squaring a massive pair of shoulders he shot his cuffs, then with a ''scuse fingers, Colonel,' he heaved her to her feet. Sensing a need to ease the situation, he wagged a finger, saying roguishly: 'If you've finished with the lady, Colonel, I'd be glad to have her back.'

Speechless and with his hands still held above his head, the colonel gave a nod. Fletcher acknowledged it with an old world bow. Then, with the same old-fashioned charm, he offered the 'toast of Mandalay' his arm and they wove their drunken way to join the other two.

But the other two had gone. Seeing what

was happening Roberts had sounded the retreat. Not that either of them had disapproved. They had fled because they had other, as yet unspoken, things in mind.

Their jeep crunched across the gravel and swung into a soft and gentle night. A huge full moon lit up a cloudless sky, mellowing the broken buildings, rounding off every edge, casting shadows that melted the paddy fields and the jungle into one. Here and there it picked out a ghostly white pagoda as it reached towards the stars. It turned the river into a strip of molten steel.

Soon the tyres were whirring on the smooth macadam road and, with the windscreen down, the rush of air was toying with their bodies, pulling at their clothes. A polished metal sheet came shining through the trees. The lake. The jeep slowed down, turned off the road and coasted to a halt.

For a while they sat, untalking, side by side, glorying in the magic of the night. The air was fragrant, softly warm. Fireflies sprinkled fairy lights across the night and a line of palm-trees spiked a hard black fringe against the sky. Now and then a meteor flamed its way across the heavens. On the isle a white pagoda reared, stood stark, erect. The moon mirrored its face upon the stillness of the lake. Then a breeze came whispering through the reeds and teased the surface into little silver fires that darted, dazzled briefly and were gone. The only sound was the dainty slap of wavelets at the water's edge.

Angela took his hands in hers and shook her head to free her hair. Released, it cascaded down to swamp her neck and breast and shoulders. Robbie caught his breath. The moonlight gave her hair a sheen that made it blacker still. He thought of it tumbled on the whiteness of a pillow, setting off that oh so pretty face. And yes, those oh so soft and lovely breasts as well. His craving flickered into flame and made him weak and full and strangely light. He knew full well that an ecstasy was in, or almost in, his grasp. Silently, hand in hand, they wandered to a knoll that overlooked the lake. They sank down. Their hands were busy but gentle, then they were lying naked on a blanket on the grass. Firmly but gently he took her in his arms, turned her face to his. Softly, oh so softly his lips came hovering down to touch her brow, her eyes, her lips, floating on the sweetness of her breath. Then the fullness of a kiss with lips that brushed and pressed and brushed again. Tongues that pierced and probed. Hands that fondled, oh so tenderly, the exciting heaviness of her breasts, the softness of her bottom, the silky smoothness of her thighs and, finally, the alien bushy roughness of her bush. Thighs, oh so gently moved apart and fingertips exploring. There came little gasps and murmurings, little sighs. A tongue flickered fire and sparked a quivering that was followed by a frantic: 'Oh Robbie, oh Robbie darling, love me Robbie darling, love me now . . .'

But Robbie was in heaven too. Deep down, at the very core of life, he felt the dam go down. Then the torrent broke and the flood came swirling, roaring, carrying them both away. A mutual pinpoint shock of joy and they were lost in the timeless scalding ecstasy of melting into one.

8

At tiffin the happenings of the previous night still rankled with Colonel Perceval. More than ever he regretted having Captain Fletcher in his mess. Officers, whatever their origins, should at least behave like gentlemen. But Fletcher did not behave as such. Fletcher was an oaf. His carrying on with that dreadful half-caste tart was one more proof of that. Such behaviour was not expected of the OC Military Police. He, of all people, should be an example to the rest. True, he had apologized at breakfast and had been suitably contrite, but Colonel Perceval knew that, inwardly, the man was laughing up his sleeve. But then, what could one expect from a constable off the beat? The man should never have been commissioned in the first place. Not that all ex-rankers were the same. They weren't, not by a long chalk. Major Smith his second-in-command who, as usual, was sitting by him, was a case in point. Not a brilliant man, but sound. Did his job efficiently and had a proper regard for rank.

The colonel took in the others sitting round the table. There was Second-Lieutenant Johnson.

Fresh from home, he had the respect and shyness that matched his nineteen years. The lad had breeding. Not surprising. He had an impressive family background. His father was quite something in the city. The family had a house in town and a country seat in Surrey. Johnson's father a man of influence, a man of means. A man who could be a very useful contact when retirement time came round. Yes, a regular officer of colonel rank could be quite an asset to a man like that. Perceval caught Lieutenant Johnson's eye. He gave him an approving smile, a nod. He was a gentleman. He cut so-called officers like Fletcher down to size.

Then there was Roberts. A reasonable sort of chap. From what he'd heard his Military Cross had been a good one. What did he do in peacetime? Some sort of position with the press. Not an ideal background but on the whole he, like Major Smith, warranted his commission.

Right now, Smith and the odious Fletcher were discussing the half-caste accused of waging war against the King. And from what the JAG had said, he was as guilty as they came. But then, what could one expect of men of mongrel breeding? It was in the blood. They combined the very worst of east and west. Bad mixture. The man would be innocent until proven guilty of course. British justice would see to that. But 'waging war against the King' was a very sorry business and not to be bandied round the mess.

'Gentlemen, please, no shop,' he chided. 'Remember, I have been appointed president of the court. The case is now *sub judice.*' The colonel revelled in the phrase. It had a pleasing legal ring. He rolled it round his tongue. 'Yes, *sub judice,*' he said again.

The conversation stopped. Two faces turned, amusedly rebellious, then looked away. Fletcher muttered something and Roberts laughed. Major Smith gave a tut of disapproval. The colonel frowned. Whatever had been said would not be complimentary. Best ignore it. As a peacetime policeman, Fletcher would be demobilized quite soon. He would go back home to plod his beat. A consummation devoutly to be wished, he thought and preened himself at his knowledge of the bard.

Nevertheless, the attitude of the officers had stung. The mess steward was hovering close at hand. 'Corporal Jenkins, I'll have my coffee in my office.' The colonel dabbed his lips. Carefully he arranged his napkin along its original folds. He placed it neatly by his plate. His chair scraped back. 'Captain Roberts,' he said coldly, 'when you've finished sniggering with Fletcher, see me in my office. I want to check your arrangements for the trial.'

Some time later, having reported to the colonel, Roberts had made his way to Fletcher's office. He was amused to find that Fletch was ensconced on a simply magnificent, plush cushioned and canopied throne. Almost certainly looted from Mandalay. He could see him through the thrown-back doors: huge, black-haired, black-jowled, he had a boxer's flattened nose. What looked like a coiled hair mattress was spilling from his shirt. His uniform was green and crisply starched. Belt buckles gleamed. Brass pips shone from each broad shoulder. A brassard of red and gold proclaimed 'MP'.

Roberts summed him up. Fletch was a man of violent likes and dislikes. A man who had no time for those he considered fools. And, like all policemen, he saw everything in black and white, no greys. But, overriding that, he was a firm believer in taking care of number one. 'Don't do as I do but as I tell you' was very much his creed.

Seeing Roberts, Fletcher beckoned him in and waved him to a chair. 'Sit yourself down,' he said. Gesturing to the throne he grinned and added, 'My crown's in the post.' Then, cranking a telephone, he ordered tea. That done, he asked: 'And how was Pompous Perce? Happy with your arrangements, or did he slap your wrist?'

'He seemed happy enough, Fletch.'

'Was he now. Well that's a change.' Fletcher grinned his distaste. 'Pompous old fart,' he said. 'But enough of Perce. What can I do for you?'

'I need your help Fletch. You're holding Sergeant Stevens. I'd like to borrow him. Is that all right with you?'

'All right with me, old son. You've already borrowed Angela, why not brother Stevens too?' Shrewd calculating eyes gimleted into him. 'But, just for the record, why?' A grin. '*Cherchez la femme*, old son?'

Roberts laughed. 'No, nothing to do with Angela. He's asked for a couple of witnesses. A local RC priest and a Burmese muleteer. The priest's no problem but I haven't the foggiest where the muleteer hangs out. It'll save me a lot of sweat if Stevens takes me to him. Save bothering with interpreters, too.'

Fletcher gave a nod. 'Sound reasonable,' he said. Then a finger stabbed. 'But bring the bugger back. Lose him and you'll land me in it. Perce'd have my guts for garters. Delay my demob.' A laugh rumbled round the room. 'Can't have that, old son. Soon as my replacement's here you won't see my arse for dust.'

'And how soon's that?'

Fletcher shrugged. 'Can't say for sure. He's in Singapore. Involved with some resistance jokers. War crime case. It'll be a week or two before the trial takes place.'

'As with Sergeant Stevens.'

A nod. 'As with brother Stevens.'

An orderly with a tray interrupted the conversation. On the tray was a bone china teapot with the rest of the set to match. There were apostle teaspoons and an exquisite silver-and-china cake-stand complete with sandwiches and cake. There were linen table napkins too.

Roberts had been expecting army cha in mugs. All this was something else. He half-expected Fletch to ask, 'Will you be mother? Or shall I?' But the orderly swiftly and efficiently poured the tea and left.

'You do yourself well.' He smiled.

Delicately, Fletcher raised a cup and pointed to other, clearly looted items in the room. 'The Lord helps those . . . ' he said and, with little finger out, he took a sip.

Roberts took an inventory of the room. He thought of the self-same slogan on Angela Stevens's jug, and of his taking of her on the previous night. He considered the stolen bags of silver, and all the other fiddles he had heard were going on. He dismissed them with a shrug. It had been a jungle war and the law of the jungle still prevailed. It always would. He too sipped his tea.

In the event, the trip to find the muleteer was never made. Colonel Perceval saw to that. As 'President of the Court' he put his foot down and, with the approval of the JAG, he decreed that: 'Under no circumstances will the accused be allowed to swan around the countryside. He will remain strictly under lock and key.' He gave Captain Fletcher, the OC Military Police, a written order to ensure that this was carried out.

He also ruled that responsibility for procuring the witnesses rested with the officers for the prosecution and defence. Finally he made it clear to Captain Roberts that his duties were administrative only. 'The cobbler to his last, Captain Roberts. The cobbler to his last.'

Roberts took the order in his stride. It was no skin off his nose who did or didn't, notify the witnesses. After all, the case was all over bar the shouting. It would be, largely an utter waste of time. And, as he pointed out to Fletcher, Pompous Perce had a point. There'd have been hell to pay if Stevens had escaped.

As it was, the admin was not too arduous. Mainly he had to find a venue and then prepare it for the trial. That was not easy. With so much destruction, all the intact buildings had been grabbed. Eventually he settled for a bomb-wrecked school. It was not ideal but, through Pompous Perce, he pressed the CRE to restore the place to shape. The sapper colonel waved a magic wand and the building was transformed. It became more than adequate for the staging of the trial, with all the personnel involved: the members of the court, the witnesses, the various clerks. Then there were the interpreters, the orderlies and the guards. And, most important there was provision for any local people who wanted to attend. For, as Colonel Perceval had said: 'Not only must justice be done. It must be seen to be done.' This he uttered in his usual pompous way. But again Roberts had to agree that 'Old Pompous' had a point.

In the meantime, the mills of the law ground on.

★　★　★

The trial was due to start the following day. Roberts's job was finished. Everything he had to do was done, and done well, at that. From now on he would be just a looker-on.

But, for the moment, he had pushed the

94

court martial from his mind. He was with Angela at their secret haven by the lake. Naked, they had finished making love and Angela was asleep. He stretched luxuriously, his hands behind his head and let his mind run free. Life was good. No two ways on that. Not a cloud was in sight and that applied to every meaning of the phrase for, at last, the skies were clear and, freshened by the monsoon rains, the land was bright. Now, from dawn to dusk, the sun, as yet still muted, shone from a dome of blue, picking out the snowy-white pagodas with their golden spires and the multicoloured blossom of the trees. Away from the town new growth had covered the scars and skeletons of war as if the war had never been. In the town, rebuilding had begun and, in the reborn streets, gaily coloured longyis and the saffron robes of monks relieved the drabness of the army's jungle green. Chattering and bargaining, the townsfolk thronged the markets. Everywhere, children scuffled happily in the dust, dogs lay dreaming in the shade. Bullock carts creaked and groaned and the old men sat behind their huge cheroots and watched the world go by.

Roberts blessed his luck, marvelling at the contrast between all this and the shortages and the bitter winter that people were enduring back at home. Yes, life was good.

He gazed across the lake. Lily-blossomed, it sparkled in the sun. Little wavelets lapped and tiny movements rustled in the reeds. Here and there, long-legged birds stepped daintily, absorbed in their own affairs. Fish plopped. Biblical palms stood stark against the sky. A breeze began to whisper through the trees, fondling his naked body and rippling the surface of the lake. Cool and caressing it rolled green waves across the rice-fields, then wandered off to climb the distant blue-green hills. Roberts lit a cigarette and drew the smoke deep down. Yes, life was good all right.

Then a shadow fell across the day. It was not so good for Stevens and his family! True, Angela was on cloud nine, for Angela was 'in love', besotted. Besotted with him, besotted with her *Real Romances* dreams. ('You *do* love me, Robbie darling? You're not just saying so to please me?' She would raise two anxious, pleading, dark-brown eyes. 'Please tell me again you love me, really love me.' He would silence her lips with kisses, avoiding the dark-brown eyes, saying, as gently as he could: 'Of course I love you, darling. I'll always love you. I'll love you for ever and a day.' Then would come complete and sweet abandon. 'Oh, Robbie, I love you so. Oh,

Robbie darling, love me. Love me, Robbie darling. Love me, love me now . . . ') Poor, pretty, trusting Angela. All that would turn to ashes when it was time for him to go. For her, what then? He felt a sudden wave of shame for the way he'd used her, led her on.

And what about her brother? Well, the future for him was grim. At best it would be many years in gaol. At worst he would end up dangling from a rope.

That was food for thought. A week or so ago he would have joined the chorus of: 'And a bloody good job too!' But now he was not so sure. Angela had bent his ear quite a lot on what a good man her brother was. How he had been forced to join the dreaded Kempetai. It seemed that before the war he had worked for a transport company run by the Japanese and had learned to speak their language. He had learned to read and write it too. Then, when the Japs attacked, he had been pitchforked into an auxiliary transport unit. Within a week, he had been made a sergeant. Within two weeks his war was done. Or so he thought. Mainly through desertion his largely Burmese unit fell apart and he and the few remaining men were told to go back home and wait for the British army to return. This he did. But so did his pre-war boss! It turned out that his pre-war firm had been a

Japanese army 'front'. His boss, a Mr Mutaguchi, was now Major Mutaguchi of the Japanese Kempetai. Without as much as a by-your-leave Stevens had been enrolled as a Kempetai interpreter and, as Angela phrased it: 'Andrew's nightmare had begun.'

Well, Roberts could go along with that. As everyone now knew, the Japanese played rough. But then, by all accounts, that had applied to Stevens too. Not surprisingly he must have thought the Japs had won. He had certainly dropped a bollock over that. Or had he? As Angela had told him, it meant that Andrew's kith and kin were saved from the depredations of the Japs. Other Anglo-Burmans had been treated badly, especially when the war turned sour. Angela had been vehement that; 'Andrew would never harm a fly.' That: 'All those dreadful accusations are a pack of wicked lies. Andrew had no choice.'

Again, what she had said was food for thought. Families were no longer the most reliable judges of a man. The war had applied so many strains, temptations; had probed so many weaknesses; had caused a people to react in so many dreadful ways. Let's face it, Roberts thought, people guilty of the most atrocious crimes had often been devoted family men. Yes, and loyal and gallant soldiers too. It was said that circumstances alter cases.

That was often true. There was a number of things that he himself would not like broadcast to the world.

And what about British rule? Angela and 'Daddy', like most Anglo-Burmans, had a touching faith that, with the war now over, everything would turn out right. But Roberts knew that such hopes were built on sand. At this very minute that tergiversating sod Aung San was being wined and dined in London and being pandered to by the new socialist government. A government who were anxious to flush the Empire down the drain. Who were falling over themselves to give away our hard-won victory. What was more, to give it away to a man who had sided with the Japs. Ay, and a man who was a cold-blooded murderer too.

Poor family Stevens. They and their kind were outcasts. Not fish nor fowl nor good red meat. Their day was done. Aung San and his British socialist pals would see to that. Roberts's lips drew back. So three cheers for our brave new socialist masters. Three more for our brave new socialist world where everyone was slated to be equal. But some more equal than the rest!

And what of the Stevens's faith in British justice. Roberts thought of all the prejudiced and prejudged comments he had heard (and made) on Stevens's guilt. He compared the lot of Stevens with that of the arrogant Aung San. Not much chance of Stevens being wined and dined in London! He thought of the dilemma faced by a frightened half-caste youth. It raised a searching question: Put in his position, what would you do, chum?

A saw was hovering in Roberts's mind: *To know all, is to forgive all.* Well there was a lot of truth in that. It could well apply to Stevens. It probably did. Suddenly he hoped with all his heart that, whatever it was, the truth would out. That justice, genuine justice, would prevail. What Pompous had said was right. Justice must be done and, equally important, be seen to be done. Well, that now depended upon the court, on Pompous Perce. The colonel must put his principles where his mouth was.

His gaze turned to the naked sleeping girl. Poor, lovely, but pathetic Angela. She was probably dreaming that sad little Anglo-Burman fairy tale of going 'home'. Of going 'back' to England. A country they had never seen and, almost certainly, never would.

She must have sensed his gaze. Her eyes were open and she was sitting up. Then, suddenly, he didn't know whether to laugh or cry. Smiling, she had gestured to the lake. 'Just as I remember Lake Windermere,' she'd said.

His eyes were pricking. He couldn't trust his voice. Tenderly, and with all lust gone, he took her in his arms.

9

After having been delayed by a puncture, Roberts led Angela to their seats. The court had now convened and Major Ledward, Judge Advocate General was heaving himself to his feet.

Seeing them sidling in, the colonel pursed his lips and, uncapping his Parker 'visi-ink' fountain pen, he made a note. From a position by the door Fletcher had seen their arrival too. His mouth widened in a grin and, catching Roberts's eye, he mimicked the colonel's frown and mimed the slapping of a wrist.

Unlike Roberts, the colonel was not amused. Again he pursed his lips. Again he made a note. Then, very carefully, he screwed the top back on his pen. Equally carefully he placed it parallel to his pad. With that now safely done he gave his full attention to the waiting JAG.

Curtly, the lawyer indicated that the accused should stand. The sergeant scrambled to his feet and stood rigidly to attention.

Roberts leaned forward in his seat. So this was Angela's brother. Like her, the sergeant could almost pass as white. He was well turned out: brand new jungle-green fatigues, blancoed sergeant's stripes, gleaming polished boots. Buckles shone on his webbing belt and gaiters. Clearly, the sergeant was trying to impress. His jet-black hair was over-long and he looked just like his sister. But that was not surprising, they were twins.

There was the rasp of a throat being cleared. Then, begowned and wearing a small grey wig, the JAG took them through the charges. His voice was deep but clear and Roberts was fascinated by his bobbing Adam's apple. There followed a seemingly unending stream of jargon and then, at last, the emptiness of a quiet.

Roberts had taken notes to condense the legal jargon. Under an umbrella of 'Waging war against the King', there were five main accusations. He ticked them off:

1) Desertion.
2) Acting as an enemy interpreter.
3) Giving information of value to the enemy.
4) Inflicting actual bodily harm on an officer of His Majesty's forces. This was potentially, the most damaging charge of all.
5) Stealing army funds.

6)

With one exception, Stevens had given a firm: 'Not guilty,' the exception being: 'Acting as an enemy interpreter.' To this he had replied: 'Guilty, but under duress.' *Duress.* For an Anglo-Burman, this was quite a word.

The JAG now indicated that the accused should sit. Bolt upright, Stevens sat. With a slight inclination to the court, the lawyer sat down too. Two green-clad interpreters then took the stage and commenced translating the charges into Karenni and Burmese.

Roberts made a hissing through his teeth. The defence would have its work cut out to talk Stevens out of this.

The interpreters droned away. With an MP by his side, Stevens was sitting out in front. Roberts could see that his eyes were flickering, flickering everywhere but at the members of the court. Spotting Angela, he half-raised a hand and smiled. Angela did the same, then gave a sob. Her eyes had filled and were glistening, wet with tears. Roberts's heart went out to her and, under the cover of his cap, he squeezed her hand. At this she moved up close, took his arm and, with the tiniest of handkerchiefs, dabbed the tears away.

Roberts surveyed the scene and was

impressed with what he saw. Apart from Major Ledward, the JAG, no one wore wigs or gowns or anything like that. But the simple trappings, the layout and the general atmosphere was right. As with the pre-war courts he'd seen, there was an exciting sense of theatre. Delighted, he drank it in:-

The five members of the court — Colonel Perceval, three majors and a captain, were seated centre stage. All were beribboned and uniformed in impeccable jungle green. Upright to a man, they sat in line at a blanket-covered table, upon which were laid carafes of water, tumblers, blotting-paper, sharpened pencils and ink. On each blotting-pad lay an army-issue notebook with elasticated straps. On the wall behind them was an outspread Union Flag.

The JAG was sitting at a separate wooden table, upon which were law books, a red-tabbed pile of briefs, a water carafe and a tumbler.

Out in front sat the accused and a military policeman escort. To the right sat the officer for the prosecution, a Keren lieutenant, young and nervous, looking almost Mongolian with his close-cropped skull. He too was campaign-ribboned and wearing pristine green. Facing him, and as alike as a carbon copy, sat the officer for the defence. The two were identical, two peas from the same green pod.

Roberts's eyes continued round. Further back, at other blanket-covered tables, sat the interpreters and the clerks. Dotted here and there, and a pleasing contrast to the all-pervading green, could be seen the splash of an MP's cap and the gleam of blancoed webbing. Overhead, four-bladed ceiling fans turned in lazy circles.

A silence. The interpreters had finished with the charges. The JAG now took centre stage. Turning to the judges and the outspread Union Flag he made the suggestion of a bow. Then, with both hands gripping his lapels, he addressed them with his dark-brown voice.

'May it please the court,' he said. A pause. The page of his brief flicked over. 'Before the trial begins I will explain, in strictly layman's terms, the background to the case.' Another pause as if he was assessing the intelligence of the five behind the bench. Then: 'The events you will hear described arise from the activities of British units operating behind the enemy lines and the efforts of the Japanese to have them killed or captured. Such activities are not illegal in themselves but are justified acts of war. Note that carefully, gentlemen, justified acts of war for, with all civilized nations, a line is drawn between what is and what is not a justified act of war. Sadly, as we now all know, it is not an easy line to draw. In this modern age war is no longer confined to armies in the field but extends to the very fabric of the lands involved. The sorry happenings of the past six years are proof of that. However, even so, a line is and in fact must be drawn. Therefore murdering soldiers and civilians as an act of terrorism and or retribution must be on the wrong side of the line. As is the use of torture, or even the threat of torture, to come by information. By international law all that is required of a captured soldier is that he gives his name, his rank, his number. Nothing more. Broadly the same applies to civilians who find themselves subject to enemy authority.'

A pause whilst another page of the brief was turned.

'Japan is not a signatory to the Hague Convention. Therefore members of the Japanese armed forces cannot be held legally responsible for any breaches of its rules. However, and this is why we are gathered here, this does not give the Japanese forces the right to flout the laws of civilized humanity. There must be depths to which civilized men and nations must not descend. Such depths may be plumbed only at the perpetrator's peril and in the certainty of eventual retribution. Pleading expediency, obedience to the orders of superiors, or giving way to *force majeure*, are no excuse. This is such a case. It will therefore be the responsibility and the duty of this court to decide whether or not the acts you will hear described were crimes against humanity.'

The JAG paused to refresh himself from the water carafe on his table. Delicately, he dried his lips. Then once more his hands were gripping his lapels.

'In the course of this trial you will learn of acts, brutal, even barbarous acts that were carried out by members of the Japanese Kempetai — A Major Mutaguchi and a Sergeant-Major Ekesta. Judgment on these two is not within the province of this court. Mutaguchi is already facing trial at a Rangoon war-crimes court for these and other acts. Ekesta is beyond the jurisdiction of any human court. He was killed in the closing stages of the war.'

Another pause whilst he flicked over yet another page of his brief. Then his eyes locked on to the eyes of Sergeant Stevens. Roberts was reminded of a rabbit held spellbound by a snake.

'The only concern of this court is with the actions of the accused, Sergeant Andrew

108

Stevens.' The eyes bored in. 'As a member of the British armed services, Sergeant Stevens had sworn allegiance to His Majesty the King. As such he was, and is, subject to British military law.'

The JAG moved his gaze from Stevens and turned it on the bench. 'He is also, and members of the court I cannot stress this fact too strongly, he is also subject to the laws of decency, of civilized humanity.'

Again he took a sip of water and performed the meticulous drying of his lips. Once more his fingers gripped his lapels.

'Finally, I must make it clear to the members of the court that the judgment will be theirs alone. My sole responsibility is to give guidance on points of military law. This guidance will apply to both the prosecution and the defence.'

Once more he gave the suggestion of a bow, then the lawyer swirled his gown around and took his seat. Roberts was filled with admiration. The man had style.

The first witness for the prosecution was the Thandaung village headman. A Keren, a Christian, he took the oath upon a Bible. His evidence was given in Kerenni and then, sentence by sentence, translated into English.

The headman pulled no punches and a

shocked and silent court heard how Thandaung had been invaded by the Japs. The court
heard of Mutaguchi's threat and bombast, of
his cold-blooded murder of the headman and
of how Ekesta had chopped off the heads of
four of the village elders, two of them were
well over ninety years of age. They heard of
Sergeant Stevens, armed and in the uniform
of the Japanese, efficiently and arrogantly
translating every order, every word. Finally
they heard of the sacking and then the
burning of the village.

The prosecution officer let the evidence
hang heavily on the air. The only sound was
the swishing of the fans. Then came his
examination of the witness:

The PO: (In Kerenni, then in English.)
Did the accused make any protest on what
was taking place?
Witness: No.
The PO: Did the accused give the people
of the village any comfort or assistance
whilst this was going on?
Witness: No. At the start, he told us that
Mutaguchi wasn't bluffing and that we
should do what we were told. That it was
the only way. After that he spoke only
when he was translating. He was like a
machine. He even copied Mutaguchi's

tone of voice.

The PO: Thank you.

Sweating, the prosecutor sat. His counterpart, the defending officer took over. He too began to sweat.

The DO: Apart from the interpreting, did Sergeant Stevens take any part, any physical part that is, in any brutal act?

Witness: Not that I saw.

The DO: When the beheading took place was Sergeant Stevens sick?

Witness: Caustically. Stevens *is* sick. Sick in his head. *The witness struck his breast.* In his heart.

The DO: I mean did Sergeant Stevens vomit?

Witness: I know I did. I wasn't watching Stevens.

The DO: Thank you. No more questions.

The defending officer wiped his sweating face and then sat down.

Three headmen from other villages followed. With each of them the story was the same: the brutality of the Japanese and the cool efficiency of Stevens.

The court then adjourned for tiffin. However, before they left, the colonel had both Fletcher and Roberts on the mat. Had them standing to attention whilst he tore them off a strip.

'I won't mince words,' he said. 'I appreciate that neither of you has even the makings of a gentleman. However, unfortunately, you are officers of His Majesty the King. I regard it as my duty to tell you that a court martial, especially one as serious as this, is not a matter for levity. Particularly when the eyes of our subject people are upon us. I warn you both, if there is any more levity, unpunctuality and, in your case, Roberts, conduct more suitable to the back row of a cinema, you will find yourselves in front of General Rees.' Then, with a gap between each word: 'Do I make myself clear?'

Two red-faced officers assured him that he did.

Coldly. 'Right. Dismiss.'

Normally both men would have resented being spoken to like that. But, after the morning's evidence, they were genuinely contrite. Even Fletcher had admitted, 'Old Pompous has a point.'

★ ★ ★

'Call Brigadier Po Kyin.'

There was a buzz of anticipation. It was

112

14.00 hours. The court had reconvened and well in time Roberts and Angela were in their seats. The space allocated to civilians was filled with ex-guerrilla fighters, all chattering, all anxious to greet their war-time hero, U Po Kyin. A cheer. Hands were clapping as the soldier took the stand.

Roberts was impressed. Although a wreck of what he had once been, the brigadier had presence. Tall and on the slim side for a Burman, military moustached and uniformed in red-tabbed jungle green, he had an array of ribbons on his chest. Roberts could see the DSO, MC, and what was possibly the MBE. He looked every inch the jungle warrior.

Roberts felt a wave of pity. He'd been in the wars all right. His medals were endorsed by wounds. A patch blacked out an eye. From this an ugly scar ran down to meet his mouth. Judging from the way he walked he'd lost a leg and in place of his right hand was a hook. Roberts shook his head. Medals or not, sooner you than me, he thought.

Po Kyin took an oath and then gave his evidence in a clipped and forceful voice. He told the court of his arrival in the hills. Of joining the legendary Major Willis and, almost immediately, being betrayed. How, sleeping away from his HQ, he had heard the Japs attack. How, stark-naked, he had to

113

make a run for it to the trees. 'Caught with my trousers down. Not good. Not good at all,' was how he phrased it.

The PO: And then?
Po Kyin: It was clear that my men were either dead or captured. I decided to make my way to the unit dump, re-equip myself and get a warning to Major Willis and the others. It proved to be a waste of time. Whoever had betrayed us had done a thorough job. Willis was dead, Washington was a prisoner and the Japs had found the dump.
The PO: Please tell the court about the dump.
Po Kyin: When the Japs had gone I went back to the village. They'd burned it to the ground. However, I salvaged some Burmese clothes and set off for the dump. It was a case of best foot forward, for I had thirty miles to walk. When I was almost there I stumbled across some Japs. I turned a bend and there they were. About forty of them with a string of mules. They were taking it easy. Having a meal.
The PO: And did they stop you? Question you at all?'
Po Kyin: No. Surprisingly, they took no heed at all. They were busy eating and I

walked straight past. (*A shake of the head at the memory*). It was a nasty moment, though.

The PO: What then?

Po Kyin: I realized they were heading for the dump. Once out of sight, I ran. I had to get there first.

The PO: And did you get there first?

Po Kyin: No. A Japanese sergeant and a Burman were already there. They had a mule. A big one. About eighteen hands at least.

The PO: And then?

Po Kyin: The sergeant told the Burman to go back and tell the officer that they'd found the dump.

The PO: And did he?

Po Kyin: Yes he walked back along the track.

The PO: Without the mule?

Po Kyin: (*A nod*). Yes, without the mule.

The PO: Please tell the court what happened then.

Po Kyin: As soon as he had gone the sergeant loaded the mule with silver rupees. They were from the drop. In canvas bags. He then led the mule around a bend. He was back in no time at all He must have dumped the money in the jungle. In all he made five trips. Six bags each trip. He was clearly in a hurry.

The PO: Thirty bags in all.

Po Kyin: Yes, he took the lot.

The PO: And?

Po Kyin: The Japanese arrived. The sergeant spoke to the officer, a lieutenant. He was pleased. Very pleased indeed. The sergeant then led him to the dump.

The PO: Could you hear anything they said?

Po Kyin: No. The only word of Japanese I know is *arregeto* — thank you. (*A rueful smile*). I've had little cause to use it.

The PO: What happened then?

Po Kyin: They cleared the dump. Loaded it on the mules. It took many trips. They must have had lorries waiting further down the track.

The PO: Please tell the court about the sergeant.

Po Kyin: He was in Japanese uniform but he was not a Japanese. He was a man of mixed race. What the court would call an Anglo-Burman.

The PO: Brigadier, could you recognize this sergeant if you saw him?

Po Kyin: (*An outraged snort*). I not only could, I can! (*The hooked arm stabbed. The one eye blazed*). The man I saw was Sergeant Stevens, the accused.

The PO: You have no doubts on that?

116

Po Kyin: None whatever. (*Sardonically*). I had *two* eyes then.

Dumbfounded, Stevens was staring at the brigadier as if he'd seen a ghost.

The PO: And then, Brigadier?
Po Kyin: When the Japs had gone I found that they had taken everything. What little they didn't want, they'd burned. (*Suddenly, his face was grim, the hook thumped down*). I made up my mind that, somehow, I would get back to India. Report what had taken place. Bring the betrayer, whoever he was, to justice.
The PO: (*All smiles*). And you did get back. (*It was a statement not a question*).
Po Kyin: I did. (*A deprecatory shrug*). But that's another story.
The PO: One final question, Brigadier. Have you any idea who betrayed you to the Japanese Kempetai?
Po Kyin: Nothing I can prove. But, either directly or indirectly, it must have been our friend here, Sergeant Stevens.
The PO: Thank you, Brigadier, no more questions.

The brigadier fixed the defending officer with his single eye. It was a challenge.

117

Embarrassed, the defending officer said: 'No questions, sir, no questions.'

Suddenly the hitherto silent court was buzzing. The ex-guerrilla fighters clapped as, limping, Po Kyin left the court.

Again Angela was in tears. 'It isn't true. It just isn't true,' she cried.

But Roberts was remembering what she'd told him earlier on. How her brother had been desperate to get some cash together to bribe their way across the Siam border.

Yes, it all tied in. The only query now was why he hadn't used the money to do just that. Perhaps someone else (the muleteer?) had pinched it? Perhaps Stevens had decided to save it for a rainy day? Perhaps? Perhaps?

So far, the evidence had been very black for Stevens but, from what Fletch had told him, there was worse, a whole lot worse, to come.

10

Fletcher was right. Captain Washington's evidence was very bad indeed for Sergeant Stevens. It chilled the blood of everyone in the court.

Clearly and concisely he gave details of his life in peacetime Burma. Of his service with Major Willis in the hills, his betrayal and unavoidable surrender. He spoke of the surprisingly friendly attitude of his captors. 'The lieutenant and his men treated us like fellow-front-line soldiers. We even had a meal together before we left,' he said.

'But then, Captain?' asked the prosecuting officer.

'When we got to Toungoo I was told of what had happened to Major Willis and the others,' Washington replied. 'Mutaguchi was overjoyed. Not surprising in the circumstances. At first he treated me more like a guest than a POW. I gathered that by wiping us out he had become the blue-eyed boy. That he was being promoted to bigger and better things.'

The PO: 'You said, 'at first', Captain,' prompted the PO.

'Yes. But then, suddenly, it all went wrong.' Washington gulped. A shudder rippled through him. His mouth began to work. Both his fists clenched up.

'Just how wrong, Captain?' the PO asked, quietly.

But Washington was very close to tears. He couldn't trust his voice. For close on a minute he struggled for control. He took a long deep breath. Another. And then another. Then his story tumbled out.

Appalled, the courtroom heard the dreadful details of his torture: of how he had been stripped stark naked and suspended from a beam. The humiliating handling by Ekesta. Of how an electrode had been thrust into his rectum and another fastened to his penis. He described his body jumping, whipping, arching; his knees jerking up and crashing against his chin. He told of a searing, hammering, excruciating pain, of agony beyond belief. Of how he had heard himself screaming, screaming, screaming. And through it all, seeing the interpreter's face an inch or two from his; seeing the pustules on his chin, smelling the curry on his breath. Through it all, the interpreter's mouth demanding: ' . . . tell him, Captain, tell him . . . ' Always the excruciating hammering pain, the interpreter's face, his mouth. Always through the agony his voice: ' . . . tell him, Captain, tell him, tell him . . . tell him . . . ' Then the captain's voice became like a gramophone winding down . . .

Washington looked up with vacant eyes. He was tired, so tired. Oh, to go to sleep. But he couldn't, for the Keren lieutenant's face was coming up a long, long tunnel and the face was getting bigger all the time. He could see that the lieutenant's lips were moving, could even hear his voice but, somehow, he couldn't grasp the words. He must try to listen harder. But he was tired, so tired. He'd rather go to sleep. But the words were filtering through: ' . . . just take it easy, Captain. Captain, take a sip of this . . . '

Washington was bemused. What does he mean: 'take it easy Captain'? Why take a sip? A sip of what? Then there was a burning in his throat and the mist began to clear. The court came back. Now it was Stevens's face that loomed, just as it had all that time ago. For a moment they were eye to eye. Then Stevens dropped his gaze and Washington knew a hatred that almost stopped his breath. He struggled to his feet. His voice came out, strangled: 'Yes, hang your head, you sod. We'll hang the rest of you later on.'

He was aware of restraining hands. From somewhere he could hear a chorus of approval. Then Captain Washington simmered down and shook the hands away.

Almost dispassionately, he told the court of being present and being photographed when the betrayed and captured stores arrived.

The PO: Did you see any sacks of silver being unloaded?
Washington: No. Everything else was there but not the cash.
The PO: Have you any idea of how they found out about the dump?
Washington: Well at first I thought they'd captured Po Kyin and knocked it out of him. (*Set teeth*). I wouldn't have blamed him. (*A shudder*). I know that, any more rough stuff, I'd have told them. Told them everything I know. Told them anything at all to stop the pain.
The PO: Major Willis perhaps?
Washington: (*Vehemently*). No. Never. No matter what they did. No. Never, never.
The PO: Have you any idea where the silver went?
Washington: At the time, I thought it must be Mutaguchi who'd taken it. The lieutenant wouldn't have dared. But, on reflection, no. Mutaguchi was a sadist but not, I think, a thief. It would have gone against *Bushido*. Gone against his code.

The PO: Who then?

Washington: (*Pointing*). Almost certainly that bastard over there.

JAG: That remark is merely supposition. The court will strike it from the record.

The PO: Thank you, Captain, no more questions.

The DO: (*A helpless shrug*). No questions.

The President: Before you go, Captain Washington, may I say on behalf of my fellow officers and, I have no doubt, of everyone in this courtroom, just how much we admire your fortitude and courage in such appalling circumstance. I will, personally, bring this to the attention of the C in C.

Washington: Sir.

The President: The court will now adjourn for half an hour. We can all do with a breath of air.

It was the waterworks again. Angela was distraught and her face was wet with tears. Grabbing Robert's arm, she sobbed: 'It isn't true. It just isn't true. Andrew would never do a thing like that.' Roberts winced. Her fingernails were digging in. 'I know Andrew. He wouldn't hurt a fly.'

Roberts's eyes went up. She'd said all that before. But, he thought, for a man who 'wouldn't hurt a fly', he hadn't done poor

Washington any good!

'Please take me home, Robbie. Take me home. I'm not going to listen to any more dreadful lies. Please take me home.'

Poor suffering humanity, Roberts thought. Well, he'd better humour her before she caused a scene. The last thing he wanted was to cross swords again with Pompous Perce. First making sure that 'Perce' was out of sight, he took her in his arms. Gently, he fingered away the tears and brushed her lips with his. 'OK, Angie, I'll run you home,' he said.

On his return he was buttonholed by Fletcher.

'What have you done with Angie?'

'I've run her home. She's in a state.'

'Just as well. The next witnesses will crucify the sod.' Then, with relish, he added: 'They'll put a rope round brother Andrew's neck.'

'More so than Washington already has?'

Fletcher grinned and drew a hand across his throat. 'To quote Al Jolson, 'You ain't heard nothin' yet',' he said.

Later, Roberts had to admit that Fletch was right. Two Burmans who had been and still were, prisoners in the makeshift gaol, described how they had seen Captain Washington being tortured. How they had seen the 'Gorilla' *and* Stevens bash him and

124

apply the electrodes. How they'd heard and seen the captain's screams.

True, the Burmans were two nasty bits of work (they were awaiting trial for rape) but they were adamant that they had seen it all from across the courtyard of the gaol. It was true also that they had no personal axe to grind. Without any sign of rancour they made it clear that they didn't care whether Stevens lived or died.

At the defending officer's request (it was just a request, no more) the court adjourned to check the viewpoint for themselves. On their return the president made it known that, whilst there, they had carried out a reconstruction of the crime and that, as the witnesses had claimed, they had been able to see what happened very clearly.

Stevens blanched at this. Jumping up, he rounded on the defending officer. Vehemently, he referred him to his notes. But it got him nowhere. The court waited patiently whilst the embarrassed officer ummed and ahed. Waited patiently even when the idiot, fumbling, dropped his notes and scrabbled about to put them back in order. However, they drew a line when Stevens, incensed by the officer's dismissive shrug, began to lose his temper.

As Fletcher described it later on: 'The

bugger got really stroppy.' He then added: 'Not that I blame him. That so called officer's a twat.'

The president intervened, speaking coldly. 'The accused will settle his differences with his defending officer when the court adjourns.' He glanced at the old-fashioned clock. 'I think we have all had enough to think about for one day. The court will now adjourn. It will reconvene at O nine hundred on the morrow.'

'On the 'morrow'!' Fletcher raised his eyes in disbelief. The defending officer wasn't the only twat in court!

Roberts too had had enough. He felt weary and depressed. Depressed for Angie. Tonight he would give seeing her a miss. It would save him having to tell her how badly things had gone. So, a shower, a drink or two, supper in the mess and then he'd be off early to his bed.

But it was not to be. Roberts got precious little sleep that night.

A military policeman was at the door. He gave an Aldershot salute. 'Captain Fletcher's compliments, sir, and would you join him at his office. I'm to tell you it's important.'

Roberts groaned. He'd been half-way up the stairs. Goodbye to an early night. 'OK, Corporal, I'll be there right away.'

'Sir.'

His office, not the club. Now what was all this about?

Fletcher was waiting in his jeep. He gave a friendly grin. 'Sorry to spoil your beauty sleep, old son. It's brother Stevens. He's had an up-and-downer with that twat of a defending officer. They nearly came to blows.'

'Did they, now. But what's that got to do with me?' asked Roberts, none too pleased.

'Brother Stevens spotted you with Angie. Says he doesn't know you but he's got to see you. I'd have told him to get stuffed but,' he gave a knowing leer, 'I didn't want to queer the pitch with Angie.'

'It's something to do with Angie?'

'No, it's about his case. I've brought the DO in. He's inside now with Stevens. Name's Bo Taik. Prize twat. Bone from the neck up. But it's better that he's there or we'll have Perce breathing down our necks. I'm off but Sergeant Hicks'll take care of anything you need. If you want me, I'll be up at Marie's.' Fletcher screwed his mouth up and made a raunchy gesture with a fist. ''Up' is right.' He grinned. Angling his cap Fletcher gave a wave. Then, with a scrunching of tyres, he disappeared.

Roberts followed Sergeant Hicks into Fletcher's office. Stevens and his Keren DO

127

were sitting there, silent, the atmosphere thick with hate. Again Roberts was aware of Stevens's likeness to his sister: he had the same finely chiselled features, the skin that almost passed for white, alert, dark eyes, long-lashed, and glossy jet-black hair. He was almost effeminate, in fact. Roberts suddenly had a yearning to be with Angie by the lake. With a pang he pushed her from his mind, for having seen him, the sergeant was scrambling to his feet. Capless, he gave a Hollywood-type salute. Bo Taik, the Keren lieutenant, seemingly bewildered, followed suit.

Roberts was both irritated and amused. *Christ, we've got a right pair here*, he thought. Raising his hands he beckoned them to sit. 'OK, you two, relax.' He smiled.

He sat himself at Fletcher's desk and, stretching out his legs, he said: 'Right now, what's this all about?'

Bo Taik looked at Stevens. Stevens looked at Roberts. Neither of them spoke.

Roberts broke the spell. 'Well, one of you say something, even if it's just hello,' he said.

A spate of 'Bombay Welsh' gushed out as Stevens opened fire. There was nothing effeminate about the sergeant now.

'Captain Roberts, sir, I am needing help.' Stevens flicked a hand towards Bo Taik. 'This man is a fool who will get me hanged. He has no brains at all . . . '

The fat-faced Keren sat stolidly silent, his mouth agape. Roberts was reminded of a goldfish peering from a bowl. Stevens had a point.

' . . . I expected to be treated fairly but I have been given this moron to defend me.'

'Oh? And what do you expect me to do?' asked Roberts nastily, 'Stick an electrode up his arse?'

Stevens flinched as if Roberts had struck him in the face. 'That was most unkind, unjust,' he said.

Once again Roberts inwardly conceded that Stevens had a point. 'Well, what is it you want?' he asked more kindly.

'Hear me what I have to say, Captain. I must speak to someone.' He cast a look of withering contempt at his DO. 'Not this fool. He does not listen. He asks no questions. He accepts everything a witness says as . . . ' Stevens searched for the apposite word. He found it: ' . . . as gospel.'

'Now take it easy, Sergeant. Firstly, just remember you're referring to an officer. Secondly, so far he hasn't had much to challenge.'

'But he has, Captain. Brigadier Po Kyin was mistaken that I took the silver. It must have been another man he saw.'

'I trust there's not another man like you.' Roberts observed, thinly.

The irony was wasted, for Stevens took him at his word.

'But there is, Captain. For instance, a Sergeant Anderson, an interpreter like me, is awaiting trial at Kynmauk. But this foolish lieutenant did not challenge the brigadier on this. Nor that the brigadier has only one eye to see with. And there is something else.'

'What else?' Roberts questioned curtly.

'The two Burmans,' Stevens answered excitedly. 'They are bad men. Dishonest men. Liars. They said they had seen me torturing the captain. This they could not have seen.'

'Oh, and why is that?' Roberts showed some interest.

'Because I didn't,' Stevens answered bluntly.

'No? Any other reason?' Roberts's tone was sceptical.

'They could not have seen into the room. This can be proved. I have explained just how to this foolish man but he has done nothing. Said nothing.'

'Oh?' Roberts turned to the defending officer. 'Is that so, Bo Taik?'

The officer gave a dismissive shrug. It was like the shrug that had nettled Stevens in the court. It nettled Roberts now. It nettled

Stevens too. Furiously he said: 'You see, Captain, he just doesn't want to know.'

Roberts was now very interested. 'Then you'd better tell me what it is, Sergeant. I'd certainly like to know.'

Stevens leaned forward, his fists, separate, clenched upon the desk, his eyes aglitter. Again the 'Bombay Welsh' gushed out . . .

What Stevens had to say was startling but through it all Bo Taik sat staring at the floor and, damning though it was, he made no comment.

'There is another matter, Captain,' said Stevens. 'A very serious matter. Something far, far worse.'

'Oh, and what is that?'

'Witnesses, Captain,' said Stevens vehemently. 'Five witnesses can prove me innocent of all these dreadful things. But the lieutenant here is only calling one.'

'That so, Bo Taik?' asked Roberts.

There was no reply. The lieutenant's gaze stayed riveted to the floor.

'Lieutenant, I asked you a question,' said Roberts sharply.

A wait, then two bleary eyes came up. So that was it. The man was not only stupid, he was drunk. Any questions would be a waste of breath. Roberts pulled him to his feet. Again he met the vacant goldfish gape.

'Now listen to me, Lieutenant. I'm going to get the MPs to run you home. When you get there go straight to bed. Nothing more to drink. Nothing, do you understand? You're going to need a clear head in the morning.'

There was no response. Just the same out-of-focus stare. Roberts curled his lip. As the 'Eskimo Nell' ditty had it: — 'Eyes like pools of piss'. No wonder Stevens was upset. Roberts called the MP sergeant and within a minute Bo Taik was on his way.

Roberts closed the door. He lit a cigarette and placed the packet and his matches on the desk. 'Help yourself,' he said. With a white-toothed flash of gratitude Stevens lit up too.

For a while they sat there quietly smoking. Then Roberts settled in his chair, linked his hands across his stomach and put his feet up on the desk. He gave a nod. 'OK, Sergeant. Shoot,' he said.

Stevens poured his heart out and Roberts heard a whole lot more of the Stevens family and their pre-war years. Heard of the coming of the war and the way it had so quickly ruined their lives. Of Mrs Stevens being fatally injured by a mine — a British mine, at that. Stevens described the shambles of the 1942 retreat, and how he had been ordered to go back home, where he came upon the metamorphosis of his pre-war boss as the head of the Kempetai. Roberts heard of Stevens's conscription and his being forced to interpret for the Japs. Of Mutaguchi's reign of terror in the hills. In particular, he heard Stevens's version of the ritual beheading and the sacking of Thandaung. The betrayal and wiping out of Major Willis and his group. The torturing of Captain Washington. He heard how the dump had been discovered and the part that he and the muleteer had played.

Roberts listened well into the reaches of the night. He found himself believing (and liking) Stevens more and more, and knowing in his gut that what the sergeant had to say was true. That, although no angel, Stevens had been more sinned against than sinning and that, so far, the trial had been a farce.

He watched the sun reclaim a wakening world, holding a steaming mug cradled in his hands. 'Help yourself,' he said. 'There's plenty in the pot.'

Stevens joined him at the window and together they sipped and shared the glory of the dawn. He and Stevens and the whole wide world were one.

Roberts went back to his seat. Tomorrow Bo Taik would have to pull his finger out. And if he didn't? The injustice took him by the throat. He punched a fist into a palm. In that

133

case, he would see that the truth came out and that justice would be done. After all, he had promised this to Angie and their father. After what he'd heard last night he wouldn't, couldn't, let them down.

Convinced of the rightfulness of his cause he braced himself for battle.

11

When Roberts arrived he found a queue snaked round the building, of Burmans and Kerens anxious to be there at the kill. But already the public area was packed and buzzed with a chattering that drowned the swishing fans. Looking around, he was swept with a sense of theatre. Through an open shutter a shaft of sunlight lit an ancient clock that ticked ponderously above the courtroom door, its hands at three minutes to nine. Overture and beginners. Almost time for curtains-up, for the 'star', the audience and the supporting cast were all in place. Behind the blanket covered table stood five empty chairs. Seated, the JAG was sharpening a pencil. Behind him an interpreter mined for something deep within his nose. Another scratched his crutch. Clearly to them the trial was no more than a play. Bo Taik seemed to have sobered up and was sitting at his table gazing at the floor. Catching Roberts's eye, Stevens gestured to him and raised his eyes to heaven. Roberts smiled and acknowledged the gesture with a thumb.

Then, as he took his seat, the MP

sergeant-major closed the doors. Turning on a heel he barked: 'Quiet.' Instantly the buzz cut off. Now the only sound was the swish-swish of the fans. The hands of the clock read two minutes to nine. All eyes were on it. Just two minutes to the off.

A click, a jerk. Thirty seconds later it clicked and jerked again: one minute to the hour. Two more clicks to go. Everyone was hanging on the clock. Click. Just one more click to go. Time stood still and Roberts began to wonder if the clock had stopped. Then a click and with it the sergeant-major's: 'The court will rise.'

Everybody stood as the president led his fellow-judges to their seats. Everybody, that was, except the young Keren officer for the defence, Bo Taik. He remained seated, gripping his chair-arms, gazing into space.

The colonel raised an eyebrow. But, he thought, an indigenous officer, what else could one expect? He decided to let it pass and gave a signal to the waiting Judge Advocate General.

'The court is now in session,' announced the JAG. 'Officer for the defence, you have heard the case for the prosecution. You will now produce your evidence in rebuttal.'

All eyes now focused on Bo Taik, who was still sitting upright, his body rigid, still with his hands clasped tightly to his chair.

Bo Taik was soaked in sweat. He could feel it running down his neck. He was cold and clammy. His mind was cold and clammy too. So much was expected of him but his head was full of soggy cotton wool. He couldn't think. No matter how hard he tried he simply couldn't think. He could feel the eyes boring in upon him, but he pushed them from his mind. His hands gripped more tightly still. One thing alone was clear. If he could hold on tight like this he'd be all right. He concentrated on his grip. Whatever would he do without the chair to hold on to. His knuckles gleamed.

The JAG looked puzzled. 'Lieutenant?'

No reply. Just a silence broken by the swish-swish of the fans.

'Lieutenant,' the JAG spoke sharply. 'Your evidence . . . '

But still there came no reaction. Still the knuckles gleamed. Walking across, the JAG put a hand on Bo Taik's arm. He sucked in a breath. The man was rigid, almost as if he'd turned to stone. He lightly slapped the downturned face but that was rigid too. The man was breathing in little jerky gasps, for all the world like a railway engine panting up a hill, and he was gripping his chair so tightly it was creaking with the strain.

Turning, the JAG gave a helpless shrug. 'The man is ill, sir. Some sort of fit I think.'

The MP sergeant-major took command. 'With your permission, sir,' he barked. He barked again. 'Corporal Saunders. Smith. Bell.' Then, expressionless: 'Take this officer gentleman to the quack.'

A corporal made to loose the grip.

'No. Leave the officer gentleman in the chair.' Still expressionless. 'He's become attached.'

'S'arnt-major.'

Chairborne, in a parody of a Bisley champion shot, Bo Taik was carried out.

A whispered exchange ensued between the colonel and the JAG. Then the president announced: 'The court will recess.'

Followed by the JAG, the colonel led his fellow-judges out and once more the buzz of chattering drowned the fans.

My, oh my, what now? thought Roberts. Certainly there would have to be a new defending officer. Someone a lot better than Bo Taik, poor sod. Someone whom he would tackle about the uncalled witnesses. His thoughts were interrupted. A stir. The prosecution officer had been summoned from the court . . .

Again the MP sergeant-major took the stage. Again he barked: 'Quiet!' Once more

138

the chattering was hushed as the judges, the prosecuting officer and the JAG filed back to their seats. Once everyone was settled the president addressed the court.

'The case for the prosecution is now complete. The defence have called two witnesses. A character witness and the accused himself. They will now be heard. However, in view of the defending officer's retirement from the case, they will be taken through their evidence by Major Ledward here, the Judge Advocate General.' Then, carefully: 'In the circumstances this will be to the advantage of the accused.' The colonel then addressed himself to Stevens and, even more carefully, said: 'I am sure the accused will agree with that.'

Stevens looked across at Roberts. Roberts shook his head.

'No, sir. I do not agree with that,' said Stevens firmly.

All the judges' jaws had dropped. Roberts was reminded of a Bateman drawing. What now? he wondered. For the moment the court registered complete astonishment.

'What do you mean, 'you don't agree with that'?' the colonel spluttered.

'With respect to you and the other gentlemen, sir, I demand a proper defending officer.' A long deep breath. Then: 'I demand a proper trial.'

Flabbergasted, the colonel gestured to the assembled officers of the court. 'But you're having a proper trial,' he said.

'No, sir, I am not,' said Stevens doggedly.

Outraged the colonel spluttered: 'You're not? What do you mean, you're not?'

'Sir, apart from anything else, I asked for five witnesses. Only one of them was called.'

'That was a matter for your defending officer, not the court.'

Stevens answered him coldly. 'As you have seen for yourself, sir, my defending officer was a fool.' Then, through set teeth, he added: 'No, not a fool, a moron.'

The colonel's hackles rose. He opened his mouth to speak but the lawyer intervened. 'If I may be permitted, sir,' he said. He turned to Stevens. '*I* have read the summary of evidence, sergeant, and you can rest assured that *I* am not a fool and certainly not a moron.' The suggestion of a sneer. 'And where, at this stage, would you find another officer capable and, if I may say so, willing to take your case. You are not,' he added cuttingly, 'exactly the flavour of the month, you know.'

Stevens flushed. There was a silence. Then: 'I think I know of someone,' Stevens said.

'Oh. And who would that be?'

It was the moment of truth. Roberts was seething at the 'flavour of the month' jibe. It summed up everybody's attitude towards the case. 'Me,' he said, standing up.

Sensation! A buzz went round the court. 'Quiet,' barked the sergeant-major.

The colonel was bewildered. 'You, Captain Roberts? Why you?'

'Quite simple, sir,' said Roberts briskly. 'I think Stevens could well be innocent. That, given the chance, I could prove it.'

'Before you commit yourself, Captain, I suggest you read the summary of evidence. I think it would change your mind,' said the JAG.

'I have read it,' replied Roberts shortly. 'What's more I spent all last night discussing it with Stevens. I heard his side of things. I believed every word he said.'

The JAG looked worried. He rubbed his chin and flicked a page or two. Then he turned to the colonel. 'Sir, I suggest we recess to talk this through.'

A nod, then it was the same rigmarole again. The audience was getting its money's worth. The courtroom buzzed.

Roberts crossed to Stevens and grabbed his arm. His voice was urgent. 'Sergeant, you must tell me before they return. About what you told me last night — now you could have been telling me the tale. If you were, admit it. Tell me now. There'll be no hard feelings. I would understand.' His grip grew tighter. 'But I've got to know for certain what you said was true. If it was, I'm with you all the way.' Roberts's face set hard. 'If I find you've let me down . . . ' He clenched a fist and shook it, 'by Christ, your feet won't touch. So tell me, tell me now.'

Stevens faced him out. His eyes had filled with tears. 'Captain, everything I said last night was true. On the memory of my mother you have my word on that.'

For almost a minute they were eye to eye. It was quite emotional and Roberts's eyes were pricking too. Then he punched the sergeant on the arm. 'OK, you're on,' he said.

The court had reconvened. The colonel cleared his throat and waited till the murmurings and shuffling died away. Then, reading from his notes, he gave the court's decision.

'After due consideration of all the facts pertaining to this case, and with the interests of the accused in mind, Captain Roberts will take over the duties and, may I add, the responsibilities of defending officer . . . '

The ensuing stir was flattened by the sergeant-major's: 'Quiet!'

' . . . however, the court has ruled that, in accordance with the rules laid down, the trial will proceed as scheduled. These rules require that a) No prosecution witnesses may be recalled and b) Only the defence witnesses already subpoenaed will give evidence.' Carefully, the colonel placed the note aside and placed his pen on top.

Roberts could not believe his ears. Springing to his feet he said: 'Sir, with respect, that's a nonsense.'

The JAG answered him icily. 'Captain Roberts, it may be a nonsense to you but it is still the law.'

'I was referring to justice, not the law,' Roberts insisted hotly. He dredged up a summary of something he had read. 'If that is justice, then the law's an ass.'

'Not an original thought, Captain,' said the JAG, drily, 'but the law is still the law.'

Roberts appealed to Colonel Perceval direct. 'Sir, before the trial commenced, you said, and I quote: 'Not only must justice be done, it must be seen to be done'.'

The colonel nodded gravely. 'I did indeed.'

'Then, sir, hear me out.' Roberts hurried on. 'I'm not a lawyer but from what I've seen and learned, this trial is a travesty, a farce. It's obvious that everyone's so convinced he's guilty they haven't done their homework.

Witnesses, vital witnesses have not been called. Those who have, have not been properly questioned. What's more, whoever appointed that poor lieutenant should be thoroughly ashamed.'

The colonel looked uneasy. 'So what is it you want?' he asked.

'I want time to prepare my case. Time to find my witnesses. The opportunity to question the brigadier and the others we have heard. In fact, go back to square one. Start again.'

There was an intervention by the JAG. Clearly he was not too pleased. 'It is not only a question of law, Captain, it's a question of practicalities as well. There are so many cases pending and many witnesses are time-expired and are going home. We have got to clear the decks. We've only so much time. I know you mean well, Captain . . . ' The JAG turned towards the bench. ' . . . but I must insist sir, that the case proceeds not only in keeping with the law but in view of sheer necessity too.'

The colonel felt relief. All this fuss about a half-caste renegade, he thought. He nodded to the JAG. 'I fully concur,' he said. 'The case will now proceed.'

Roberts clenched his fists. In for a penny, in for a pound. His voice was steel. 'Then, sir,

144

as defending officer I must request, no, not request, demand that the court records that you, sir, as president of the court, have refused to hear witnesses who could prove the innocence of the accused.'

Faces tightened. The colonel licked his lips. The JAG looked sour. He looked worried too. But Roberts hadn't finished.

. . . I will then demand an interview with the C in C. Give him all the facts. Tell him there's been a travesty of justice meted out to a Burmese national.'

The colonel blanched. 'But, Captain Roberts — '

But Roberts had got the bit between his teeth. 'Having seen the C in C, sir, I will then contact that U Saw chap and give him the facts as well.'

Puzzled, the colonel asked, of no one in particular: 'Who is this U Saw chap?'

The major sitting to his left replied. 'He's a politician, sir. A rabble-rouser. Once a friend and now an enemy of General U Aung San. A shit. A dangerous shit at that.'

Aung San! Suddenly the colonel smelled danger, a personal danger, in the air. This was blackmail, throwing mud. It was unforgivable, but when mud began to fly it stuck. Stuck to the guilty and the innocent alike. With the war now over the army was shrinking fast. He couldn't afford to risk his chances of promotion. The approach to the C in C would be bad but to become embroiled in Burmese politics would be worse. He would become a pawn in this rabble-rouser's game. He was on thin ice. He'd have to watch his step. For a moment he considered appealing to Roberts to change his mind. Then he thought of pulling rank. But no, one look at the captain's face precluded that. If ever a man meant business Captain Roberts did. It would go against the grain but he would have to go along with the captain's demands. Put on the best face that he could. The need for self-preservation honed his wits. But then, why not? He was there to ensure justice for the accused. It was his duty, yes his duty, to show the subject races what British justice meant. Show them that everyone, however guilty, would get a fair unbiased trial. And if the JAG proved awkward? Well, with justice and not the law in mind, he would put him in his place. Dammit, he'd point out that the army's honour was at stake. That justice was more important than the letter of the law. That good, conscientious, officers like Roberts should be given every help. Yes, why not?

He gave a placatory smile. 'Captain Roberts, I admire your spirit. It is in the best tradition, the very best tradition. If I may say so it's above and beyond the call of duty. Believe me, Roberts, I am as keen as you to see that justice is carried out.' He rubbed his hands and gave the court a smile. 'The court will adjourn,' Another smile, this personal to the JAG. 'You will agree with that Major will you not?'

There was a sullen nod of agreement from the JAG.

He rubbed his hands again. 'Good. Then we'll now adjourn to decide how much time the defending officer needs.' He began to suit action to his words.

The MP sergeant-major — 'The court will rise.'

It was agreed that Roberts would recall the brigadier and the two Burmans at the gaol, since their evidence had not been sifted or challenged in any way.

Roberts decided that there would be no need to recall Captain Washington and the village headmen since the defence had no argument with what they'd said. The headmen had all agreed that Stevens had interpreted, nothing more. As for Washington, well, under such appalling pain he, quite understandably, could not have appreciated the predicament that Sergeant Stevens faced. Equally understandably he would have an overwhelming hatred for all the three men involved.

It was also agreed that the defence could have two weeks in which to find their witnesses and prepare their case.

For Roberts it was a hectic fourteen days. The witnesses he wanted, five in all, were first, Thein Maung the muleteer, who had been last heard of as hiding somewhere in the Toungoo hills. Second, Tun Oke, the custodian of the Toungoo gaol. Third, Mutaguchi, currently facing a Rangoon war-crimes court. Fourth, Lieutenant Watanabe. His present whereabouts, if he had in fact survived the war, were as yet unknown. Lastly, Mother Theresa, the Mother Superior of Toungoo's Roman Catholic convent. And Father Gregory the Roman Catholic priest.

It took four days to find the muleteer's hideout in the hills and another day to convince him that he was not being arrested for working for the Japs. Playing safe, Roberts brought him back and had him locked up in the MP cage. Thein Maung was not pleased!

It turned out that Tun Oke, the Burmese gaoler, was piqued that he had not been called before. He was more than ready to have his say. And a very good say it proved to be.

With Mutaguchi Roberts came unstuck. He found him easily enough. He was in a death cell in Rangoon's Insein gaol. (And that's where the bugger stays till he's hanged in three days' time,' the Provost Marshal said).

He had better luck with Watanabe. It was not all that easy though, for it seemed that finding a 'Watanabe' in the Japanese army was like finding a Jones or Morgan in the Royal Welsh Fusiliers. Luckily, however, Mutaguchi's defending officer turned up trumps. Watanabe had been cleared of any war crimes and had been a witness for Mutaguchi at his trial. Roberts was only just in time, though, for the lieutenant, due for repatriation, had been about to board a boat.

Watanabe took the postponement of Nippon, home and beauty in his stride. As he put it: 'I've survived China, Malaya, Singapore and Burma and now your war-crimes courts. Anything that happens now I look on as a bonus.' What he went on to say about the case was gold, pure gold. With this however, there was food for thought. Would a British court believe a Jap? Well, be that as it might, Watanabe joined the muleteer in the MP's cage.

Roberts knew the mother superior well. At Christmas he had provided the convent with a Christmas tree he'd brought from the Chinese border, four hundred miles away.

Since then he had been the mother superior's blue-eyed boy.

It turned out that Mother Theresa had known Stevens all his life. In fact she had helped to teach him at the Roman Catholic school. In Roberts's book she was the most worldlywise person he had ever known. No two ways about it, in the mother superior, Stevens had a friend. That went for Father Gregory too.

By now Roberts was cock-a-hoop. Everything was going better than he had ever dared to hope. However, there was one black cloud: Brigadier Po Kyin's insistence that Stevens had been the Anglo-Burman sergeant at the dump. But, thought Roberts, it was a cloud with a possible silver lining (*silver* lining!) In an almost identical case, an Anglo-Burman sergeant was being hunted by the Kynmauk military police. Almost certainly he was the Anglo-Burman the brigadier had seen. If that proved true, Stevens could well be home and dry.

Roberts knew that he owed a debt of gratitude to Fletch. Despite having received strict orders to the contrary Fletch had put the sergeant in his charge. Without the sergeant's help he would never have found the muleteer or understood what the various witnesses had said. No wonder the Japs had used him. Interpreters like him were scarce.

Fletch, being Fletch, had shrugged it off. Said he regarded it as a smack at Pompous Perce. 'So what, old son,' he'd said. 'On Saturday it's my farewell piss-up at the club. Then I'm off. If anything hits the fan it'll be the new bloke who cops it. I'll be on that boat.'

12

The news that the brigadier would be giving evidence again swept through the town. Again a queue formed. Again the public seats were full and, when Po Kyin appeared, many exguerillas crowded round him, all anxious to be remembered, all eager to wish him well. It was some time before the MP sergeant-major gained control. Clearly, the prosecuting officer thought so too. Playing to the gallery, and this with the approval of the court, he would bring out Po Kyin's odyssey after the Japs had cleared the dump.

First however, Roberts had his say.

Roberts: Brigadier, in your earlier evidence you said that you recognized Sergeant Stevens as the sergeant at the dump?
Po Kyin: I did indeed.
Roberts: How far away were you at the time?
Po Kyin: Forty yards or so. Fifty at the most.
Roberts: A long way to see and remember someone's face?
Po Kyin: No, not really. My eyesight was

excellent, still is.' (*He turned his solitary eye on the clock above the door.*) 0 nine fifteen hours and thirty seconds. (*Then with just the suggestion of a squint,*) Maker's name: Ram Singh. Clockmakers. Madras'. (*A mischievous grin*). And that with one eye, Captain.

A ripple of laughter ran around the court. 'Oh.' Deflated, Roberts changed his tack.

Roberts: That was over two years ago. Surely a long time to remember someone's face?

Po Kyin: Not for me. I've always had a memory for faces. It was Stevens right enough.

Roberts: (*Persevering*). After all that time?

Po Kyin: Yes, Captain, after all that time. In fact I can clearly remember the Burman who was with him too. A little man with a very wrinkled face. If I'm not mistaken I passed him in the ante-room just now. (*Again the mischievous grin*). Am I right?

Roberts: (*None too pleased.*) Yes, Brigadier, you're right.

Po Kyin: (*Turning and speaking directly to the judges*). I can assure you, gentlemen, that the man I saw was Stevens and that the man outside is the Burman who was with him. The man he sent back to the Japs. (*Then, almost as an afterthought,*) I could recognize the Jap lieutenant too.

For a moment Roberts was tempted to ask if he could recognize the mule as well. He decided, no. The brigadier almost certainly could! He bit it back and changed his tack again.

Roberts: What did the man you saw say to the Japanese lieutenant? Or were you too far off to hear?
Po Kyin: (*Amused*). Nice try, Captain. Shall I say that I was close enough to see but not close enough to hear. In any case they must have spoken Japanese.
Roberts: You do not speak any Japanese?'
Po Kyin: (*Patiently*). As I said before; like Captain Washington, the only word I know is *arregeto* — 'thank you'. (*Deadpan*). I never had cause to use it.

Again the laughter rippled.
Roberts was getting nowhere. He began to scrape the barrel but it did him little good.

Roberts: Had you ever seen Sergeant Stevens before the events in question? Or have you seen him since?

Po Kyin: (*Grim-faced*). Never before or since. And never again, I trust.

Roberts: And yet it was you, I understand, who had him arrested?

Po Kyin: Yes. Washington told me what had happened. Told me that Stevens was strutting around in British uniform saying he had been coerced by the Japs. (*A pause. A sneer*). But then of course he would.

Roberts: (*Discomfited*). Thank you, Brigadier, no more questions.

Roberts resumed his seat. He avoided Stevens' eye. It had not gone well.

The PO: Brigadier, to make things absolutely clear, have you any doubt, any doubt at all, that the man you saw was the accused?

Po Kyin: (*Firmly*). None whatsoever.

The PO: Thank you, Brigadier. Now, with the indulgence of the court, I would like you to tell us what happened to you after the Japs had cleared the dump.

Po Kyin: (*Clearly pleased*). It has no bearing on the case. But if the court insists?

The PO: (*After seeking confirmation from the judges. Smiling*). Yes Brigadier, the court insists. (*The smile was transferred to the public seats*). I'm sure your ex-comrades-in-arms will be pleased with that.

They were. Their clapping and buzzing of approval had to be silenced by the MP sergeant-major's 'Quiet.'

Po Kyin: Well, to use your English slang, I was 'up the creek without a paddle'. I only had the clothes I stood in. No weapon of any sort. No money. (*Dramatically, his eye swept round the court*). So what to do? Not easy, gentlemen, not easy. Pegu was over a hundred miles away but I had some contacts there. People I hoped would shelter me from the Japs. I managed to get there safely. (*A reminiscent smile*). For most of the way I hitched a ride in a Japanese army truck. My contacts did not betray me to the Japs. However, playing safe, they reported me to U Aung San, the Burmese commander of the Burma National Army. His headquarters were in Pegu. As you know, at that time, the BNA had sided with the Japs.
The PO: Did you know Aung San?
Po Kyin: No, but I knew of him. Before leaving to join the Major Willis group I had been told about him. That he was a traitor and very anti-British. That he had gone to

Japan for training as a soldier. He and thirty others. They were called the Thakins. All young zealots. Not one of them was over thirty. After the British had been driven out they formed the BNA and fought for the Japanese. When I was brought before Aung San he was wearing the uniform of a Japanese major-general. I thought I was done for. I thought he would hand me over to the Japs. But no. Swearing me to secrecy, he told me that it was now clear that the Japanese would lose. That when the time was ripe he would abandon them and take the BNA over to the British. He went on to tell me that less than a week before he had had a secret meeting with Major Willis. They had agreed that Major Willis would inform British GHQ and then act as go-between in settling the details. (*Po Kyin shook his head sadly*). It was then that I learned that Willis had been killed before he could contact GHQ. (*Again he shook his head*). It was a dreadful shock. Everyone had looked upon Willis as indestructible. Then I got another shock. Aung San asked me to take Major Willis's place.

The PO: And I understand you did?

Po Kyin: Yes. I realized that this was something big. That if the BNA defected it

157

would make things a whole lot easier for us. Not only from the military point of view but politically as well.

The President: And how did you get back to GHQ?

Po Kyin: (*A grin*). Part of the way — in fact most of the way with Aung San in his staff car. I was dressed as an officer of the BNA. (*An even wider grin*). The car was flying a general's flag. We went through Toungoo and all the Jap troops we saw saluted us as we passed. Then at a village occupied by the BNA I changed into civilian clothes and went the rest of the way on foot.

The President: Was it difficult crossing through the lines?

Po Kyin: It certainly was. It was what the RAF would call a 'dicey do'. First a Jap and then a British patrol took me for a spy. (*A laugh*). Which, in a way, I was. However, I talked my way out of it and got to GHQ.

The PO: And then?

Po Kyin: At GHQ they made it clear that they didn't trust Aung Sun. That, as far as they were concerned Aung San and his BNA could go to hell.

The PO: In the circumstances, not surprising.

Po Kyin: (*A shrug*). They didn't altogether trust me, either. I began to wish that I'd said no.

The PO: What happened to you then, sir?

Po Kyin: General Slim thought differently. He even put me forward for a gong. He ruled that we should give the BNA a try. Said it would make things smoother when we'd beaten the Japs in Burma and were heading for Malay and Singapore.

The PO: (*Enthralled*). And then, sir.

Po Kyin: I became the link between Aung San and General Slim. I made many trips across the lines. At first I was parachuted in. Later I was allocated my own L5. This then flew me in and out. (*A laugh*). First class.

The President: The Japs never cottoned on?

Po Kyin: Possibly. But they didn't want to believe it. Apart from anything else it would mean the Japanese C in C losing face. (*A grim smile*). He lost face all right. As you know, the BNA did come over, just before the end. Just before the two atomic bombs were dropped. Aung San had timed it well. He had finished on the winning side and now the Burmese looked upon him as their leader. As soon as the war was over he formed his anti-fascist party. Now, despite some pretty virulent opposition in high places, he is in London demanding an independent Burma.

The President: (*Huffily*). Surely you are not in favour of that, Brigadier?

Po Kyin: (*A shrug*). The tide is coming in, Colonel. Remember King Canute.

The PO: (*Impatiently*). But you, Brigadier, what happened to you?

Po Kyin: On my very last trip my luck ran out. The L5 crashed. The pilot was killed. I survived. (*A rueful smile*). At least, most of me survived. When they had put me back together I became military adviser to General Aung San.

The President: (*Reproachfully*). A traitor who fought against us. Fought for the Japanese.

Po Kyin stood silent for a while. Then said, simply: 'Aung San fought and fights for Burma, Colonel. As soon as he gets back from meeting your socialist prime minister, Mr Attlee. I will be meeting him at Mingaladon. If the court wants me any further I am to be found at the secretariat in Rangoon.' He gave a bow. 'May I thank you, Colonel, for looking after me so well. May I also commend the prosecuting and defending officers for their courtesy. I know that, between you, justice will be done.' He drew himself erect. 'And now, Colonel, with your permission, I must be off.'

160

As he turned to go, the MP sergeant-major carried out an audit of the medals on his chest. 'The court will rise,' he barked. Standing like a ramrod, he gave the brigadier an Aldershot salute.

It was acknowledged by the hook.

Still standing to attention, the MP sergeant-major watched him go. He turned to the MP on duty by the door. 'There goes a man,' he said.

★   ★   ★

Roberts was depressed. A crack had opened in Sergeant Stevens's story. It had been a mistake to recall the brigadier. It had done his case more harm than good. His only hope now was that the Kynmauk police would apprehend that other Anglo-Burman sergeant and that, seeing him, the brigadier would change his mind. Despite his growing doubts he would pin his faith on that. He crossed his fingers. Now for those two lying bastards at the gaol. He thought of what the prison gaoler would tell the court. His doubts began to fade.

13

Roberts took the two gaolbirds through their previous evidence. The court heard them repeat that they had seen Captain Washington being tortured, with Sergeant Stevens manhandling him and applying the electrodes. All this they had seen across a courtyard and through an intervening room. Roberts pinned them down to detail, ensuring there could be no recantation later on. Then, having set the trap, he sprang it.

'I now require the court to see this for themselves. On site,' he stated.

The PO replied starchily. 'May I remind the new defending officer that we've already had such a reconstruction. We found we could see everything quite clearly.'

'Yes, but you saw it far too clearly,' said Roberts.

'Too clearly, Captain?' the President intervened. 'How could it possibly be seen too clearly?'

'I will demonstrate that on site, sir,' Roberts answered.

The president checked the time and said rather wearily: 'If you must.' He began to

collect his bits and pieces. Then, this accomplished, he announced: 'The court will adjourn to the Toungoo gaol. It will reconvene, here, at fourteen hundred hours.'

In a matter of minutes everyone had assembled at the gaol. Here, Roberts took command. 'Will the prosecuting officer, with Sergeant Stevens, please stand where the torturing took place.'

The PO gave a shrug and, with Stevens, went inside.

Roberts spoke again. 'Will the members of the court now position themselves where the two witnesses claim they were when they saw what happened.'

The members of the court moved smartly. It was almost one o'clock. They were hungry. As soon as this nonsense was completed they could get away to tiffin.

Roberts addressed the colonel. 'Right, sir, now what exactly can you see?'

The president exploded. 'Dammit, man, whatever are you playing at? The shutters are closed. How can we possibly see anything?'

'Exactly, sir. That's just my point. I have witnesses who'll give evidence that when any torturing took place the shutters were always closed.'

The colonel splattered testily: 'Then this case must have been an exception.' His irritation was plain. 'Now stop playing silly buggers, man, and open the shutters.'

'Certainly, sir.' Roberts crossed the courtyard and flung the shutters wide. 'Any better now?' he called.

The answer was a no. A mosquito net completely blocked the view. 'What the devil are you playing at, Roberts?' the colonel asked.

'Simply, sir, that this was Sergeant Stevens's bunk. He was living there when the torturing took place. I've got the gaoler to dress the room exactly as it was. When you came the other day the shutters were open and the intervening room was bare. No wonder you could see.'

One of the judges intervened. 'But the torturing took place in the middle of the night. With the lights on it could make all the difference.'

'It could but it doesn't. I've checked. Just bear with me, gentlemen. I'll prove this to you later on.'

The colonel was looking thoughtful. 'Most interesting, gentlemen,' he said. 'Let's go inside.'

Inside, the room had all the appurtenances to be expected in a soldier's bunk. A mosquito net was nailed to both the charpoy and the wall. By the look of it, it was a permanent fixture. The walls and door-hooks carried various pieces of equipment. Roberts proceeded to demonstrate, beyond all doubt, that whether spread or folded up, the net completely blocked the view.

Now all the members of the court were looking thoughtful.

'Most interesting, gentlemen,' the colonel said again. 'And now, I think, it's time for tiffin.'

★ ★ ★

It had just gone two o'clock and the court had reconvened. Tun Oke, the gaoler, having established his credentials, had taken a Burmese form of oath. It involved setting light to a piece of paper and letting the ashes fall upon the floor. A whispered: 'Must be burning to tell the truth,' just carried to Roberts' ears. It had come from a dead-pan Fletcher.

Tun Oke had the attitude of a man who had seen it all. He looked every inch a gaoler. Bad-toothed and mean, he wore a ruby-coloured *longyi* and a shirt of dazzling white. Despite his teeth, he looked something of a dandy. His face was smoothly yellow with jet-black porcine eyes. and a shining hairless skull. Fletcher was

165

reminded of a well-groomed pig. He whispered this impression to Roberts. Roberts hoped with all his heart that Pompous hadn't heard. Or, even worse, Tun Oke.

Roberts: Please tell the court what your duties were during the time of the Japanese.
Tun Oke: (*Rattling off the information*): Custody of civilian prisoners. Records of civilian prisoners. Feeding civilian prisoners. (*Then, po-faced at the memory*). Cleaning for the Japs.
Roberts: You had, and still have, custody of prisoners, San Win and Ba Pe?
Tun Oke: (*Slapping down some sort of record book*). It's all in there.
Roberts: (*Flicking the pages. A meaningless sea of squiggles. Handing the book to Stevens*). Both there? he asked.
Stevens: (*Searches and gives a nod*). Both there.
Roberts: From where these two were housed, could they have seen Captain Washington being tortured?
Tun Oke: No.
Roberts: Can you confirm that the intervening room is now furnished exactly as it was when Captain Washington's

torturing took place?

Tun Oke: Yes.

(*By now it was clear that Tun Oke did not believe in wasting words*).

Roberts: So, even with the shutters open, could they see across the room?

Tun Oke: No.

Roberts: When torturing took place, were the shutters closed or open?

Tun Oke: Closed.

Roberts: Always?

Tun Oke: Always.

Roberts: (*to the prosecuting officer*). Your witness.

The PO: Are you absolutely sure the shutters were closed when Captain Washington was tortured?

Tun Oke: I closed them.

The PO: Were the charpoy and the mosquito net and the furnishings always there?

Tun Oke: Yes.

The PO: What, even when the net was being washed?

Tun Oke: It was never washed. (*Then sourly*), I am a court official, not a washerwoman.

The PO: Were you present at other Japanese interrogations?

Tun Oke: Yes.

The PO: (*A shot in the dark*). At Captain Washington's?
Tun Oke: Yes.
The PO: (*Astounded*). Why didn't you tell the defending officer that?
Tun Oke: He didn't ask.
(*Roberts clicked his tongue. Damn. He hadn't asked. It hadn't crossed his mind. Damn. Damn. Damn*).
The PO: Did the accused take any part?
Tun Oke: He interpreted.
The PO: Did he take part in any violence? Beating for instance, or applying the electrodes?
(*The court was deathly quiet. Everyone was hanging on the answer*).
Tun Oke: No.
(*A communal sigh gushed out*).
The PO: (*Annoyed and disappointed*).
Did you?
Tun Oke: No.
The PO: Were you — in fact, are you — a friend of Stevens?
Tun Oke: (*Getting tetchy*) No. He means nothing to me.
The PO: Did you want the Japs to win the war?
Tun Oke: (*Tetchier still*). I didn't care who won as long as I was paid.
The PO: (*To the court*). No more

168

questions. (*Then to Roberts*). Your witness.
Roberts: The other interrogations you were present at. Was Sergeant Stevens there as well?
Tun Oke: Yes.
Roberts: Did he at any time do anything but interpret? Use any violence?
Tun Oke: No.
Then there dropped a bombshell.

Roberts felt Stevens's hand upon his arm. On turning round he could see that Stevens was holding Tun Oke's book and Roberts's copy of the charge-sheet. Stevens's trembling finger was pointing to a date: the date of Captain Washington's interrogation. The finger moved to a page of Tun Oke's squiggles. 'The date, Captain, the date,' said Stevens almost in a whisper.

'What do you mean: 'the date'?'

Stevens could hardly get his words out. 'According to this, those two were not even in the gaol when Captain Washington was tortured. They were admitted two days later!'

A buzz drowned out the fans and even the MP sergeant-major's 'Quiet.'

The court adjourned whilst the dates were checked. Stevens was right. There could be no mistake. Tun Oke's book was a pre-printed daily diary. Every day was neatly filled

169

in. Even when there was nothing to report the diary clearly said so. In fact any suggestion that the dates were wrong touched the gaoler on the raw. He was quite voluble on this. 'I have entered my diary daily for the past ten years. Every entry is checked and initialled by the policeman who brings a prisoner in.'

When asked if there could, just possibly, be an error, he exploded with a 'No.' Then, with his feathers thoroughly ruffled, he stormed off with his book.

Roberts was on cloud nine. The gaoler had done him proud. His evidence had partly made up for his failing with the brigadier. Now, the accusation of Stevens causing bodily harm to Washington was looking pretty thin. In fact, in tennis parlance, the score was 0–6, 6–0. This with three more sets to go — the muleteer, Mother Theresa and the Japanese lieutenant. And what *they* had to say was good, was very good indeed.

Roberts crossed his fingers. Right, now for the most important witness of them all: Sergeant Andrew Stevens.

Sergeant Stevens took the stand, defiant, standing upright and looking straight ahead. He was promptly greeted by a low-pitched hiss, which was silenced by the knee-jerk reaction of the MP sergeant-major's 'Quiet.'

Roberts pulled a face. Clearly, as far as the

gallery was concerned, the gaoler's evidence had been a waste of time. But then, so what? he thought, a gaoler was not likely to be everyone's cup of tea and, in any case, he knew that with the judges, Tun Oke's testimony had gone down well.

Heartened by this he took Stevens through his background during the pre-war years: — his gift for languages; his employment by a Japanese concern. ('Not a crime gentlemen, not a crime'). Then came the bloody onset of the war; his joining up; the shambles of the '42 retreat; his mother's death; his orders ('Please note, gentlemen, his orders,') to go back home and wait. His subsequent conscription ('And I stress conscription, members of the court,') by Major Mutaguchi. Roberts emphasized the impossible situation that Stevens had been in. 'Put in the same position, would anyone here today have had the courage to spit in Mutaguchi's face? Have told the Kempetai to go to hell? Have put their kith and kin in mortal jeopardy? I think not, gentlemen. This was the judgment for a Solomon. Stevens was not a Solomon, gentlemen, Stevens was a frightened Anglo-Burman youth.'

Roberts then took Stevens through his part in Captain Washington's interrogation. Stevens began with a fierce rebuttal that he had ever

171

taken part in causing any hurt. Not to Washington. Not to any villager. Not to anyone at all. 'As far as I dared I even altered answers to avert the worst of Mutaguchi's wrath.'

Then Stevens told the court of the fateful night when the Willis group had been betrayed. He told them of the scene reflected through the fanlight, of the betrayal he had seen and heard: the map, the mutilated hand, the whisky, and, of his overhearing that the betrayer did not know the whereabouts of the dump. Then he told of the Japanese expedition to the hills, which had been quick, savage and totally successful. Totally absorbed, a stilled and silent courtroom heard of the bloody wiping-out of Major Willis and his men.

It was then that the president intervened. 'Captain Roberts.' He gave a glance to left and right. 'I think I speak for my fellow members of the court when I say that the business of the reflection through the fanlight is rather much. Most ingenious but a bit Agatha Christie, wouldn't you say?'

'That was my first impression too, sir. But, believe it or not, that is what actually happened.' Roberts crossed his fingers. 'What's more, I'm going to prove it.'

Colonel Perceval leaned forward. 'I take leave to doubt that, Captain.'

'But I can. With your permission, sir, I intend to reconstruct it all. In detail. On site.'

'You mean where we were this morning?'

Roberts nodded. 'Yes, but this time after dark.'

Glancing again to left and right, the colonel said resignedly: 'Gentlemen, I'm afraid we must forgo our evening at the club.' Then, to Roberts: 'Would twenty-one hundred hours, after dinner, be suitable?'

'It would indeed, sir.'

The colonel gathered up his bits and pieces. 'The court will now adjourn. It will reassemble at the Toungoo gaol at twenty-one thirty hours.' Coldly he added: 'Captain Fletcher, you will make the necessary arrangements.'

'Sir,' said Fletcher through his teeth. And I must forgo my evening on the nest, he silently mourned.

Assisted by Roberts, Stevens laid out the scene as it had been all that time ago. Everything was there — the lighting as it was, the map room desk, a map, the whisky bottle, tumblers, a Japanese officer's tunic. Robert had even found a patient at the CCS who had recently lost a finger. What is more, Fletcher had agreed to wear the tunic and act as Mutaguchi.

The little ante-room was dressed as it had

173

been earlier in the day. Stevens had put down on paper as near as he could remember what Mutaguchi and the other man had said, in English of course, not in Japanese.

Then, stage-managed by Stevens and with Roberts on the bed, Fletcher and the injured soldier played their parts.

Roberts was amazed. He could see and hear everything so clearly. In no way could this have been invented. It was too far-fetched for that. It had to be seen and heard to be believed. In fact, it was so outlandish that it had to be the truth. His spirits soared. 'Fletch,' he called, 'come in and change places. You've got to see this for yourself.'

This Fletcher did and he was equally impressed. His attitude towards the case was changing. From what he had seen and heard — the gaoler's evidence and now all this — Stevens could be innocent after all. Well, well, he thought, bully for the sergeant and bully for Robbie Roberts too. 'Sergeant,' he said, 'I think I owe you an apology.'

★ ★ ★

Taking it in turns the judges positioned themselves upon the bed whilst Fletcher and the soldier played their parts. They too were mightily impressed. 'Colonel you were right,' said one, 'This is really Agatha Christie stuff.' 'Yes, a case of truth being stranger than fiction,' agreed another.

Colonel Perceval had decided to be last. The scene was acted out one more time. It was a repeat of all the times before, but with one small difference. Just before the 'Japanese' officer's hand withdrew, two fingers gave the age-old gesture of contempt.

However Roberts's euphoria at the brilliant outcome received a jolt. For on arriving back at the Mess after a celebratory nightcap or two he found a nun waiting for him with a message. It was from Mother Theresa to tell him that her fervently desired but long delayed repatriation to Italy had come to fruition. That she and Father Gregory had been allocated two miraculously available places on an RAF flight to India. A flight that would link up with an ongoing flight to Rome. A flight that was leaving Mingaladon Airbase the following day. A boon that had been instigated by the Vatican. The nun went on to say that a letter would follow once she had settled down in her new vocation.

The letter was destined never to arrive. In fact it was never written. For the clapped-out Dakota of Air Transport Command came down in a storm over the sea. There were no survivors.

14

At the opening of day four the JAG gave a resumé of what had happened at the gaol. Not surprisingly, it caused a stir. As well it might, for the scales of justice had begun to tilt. Despite the shock of the unexpected departure of his unimpeachable character witnesses, Roberts was cock-a-hoop. There was a sniff of victory in the air. Now it was time to take up the cudgels once again.

'The defence will continue with its case,' announced Major Ledward.

At a nod from Roberts, Stevens took the stand. This time, the people in the public seats stayed quiet. Roberts smiled. The truth was getting through.

Roberts: Sergeant Stevens, will you please tell the court everything you know about the dump. When you first heard about it and the part you played in revealing its location to the Japs. (Then, turning to the court). Gentlemen, what the accused will tell you is the truth, the whole truth and nothing but the truth. But I must ask you to hear it in the context of the times in which it happened. Not with the benefit of hindsight.

There were nods all round. The underlying antipathy towards the accused had gone.

Roberts: Sergeant Stevens, when did you first know about the dump?
Stevens: To start with I knew nothing. Of course, I realized that the British party must be building up their stocks. That was common sense. And in any case Mutaguchi said as much.
Roberts: I'm referring to a specific dump. The one that has led to all this trouble.
Stevens: The very first time was when I was listening through the fanlight. The traitor, whoever he was, marked on Mutaguchi's map where the British radios were. There were three. Mutaguchi then asked him to mark the dump as well. When the man said he didn't know, Mutaguchi told him to find out and let him know. The man promised that he would.
Roberts: What happened then?
Stevens: Within twenty-four hours all three radios were captured. Most of the British group were dead and Captain Washington and three of his men were locked up in the gaol.

Roberts: And how were these prisoners treated?

Stevens: At first, quite well. Mutaguchi was a very happy man. He even had the captain to a meal.

Roberts: Were you there too?

Stevens: Yes, but only as an interpreter. (*A wry smile*). Not much more than a fly on the wall, really. I remember that Mutaguchi was very drunk.

Roberts: Was the dump mentioned at all?

Stevens: Yes, but Mutaguchi said it was no longer important. Said something about it withering on the vine.

Roberts: But it seemed that something changed his mind?

Stevens: Yes. He received a signal from Japanese HQ. It said that the captured stores and the prisoners were to be filmed and photographed for propaganda. Then the stores were to be handed over to Aung San's BNA. This caused Mutaguchi to change his mind. He now insisted that Captain Washington told him where it was. Captain Washington said no.

Roberts: The court knows only too well what happened. Now I know this may be painful for you but what part did you play in his interrogation?

Stevens: (*Swallowing hard*). I interpreted

what Mutaguchi said. Nothing more.

Roberts: Nothing?

Stevens: No, not quite. (*A shudder*)

Roberts: What then?

Stevens: Mutaguchi then told Ekesta that come what may they had to find the dump. (*Another shudder*). I knew what the two of them could do. Especially Ekesta. Ekesta was an animal. A sadist. He was capable of anything, anything at all.

Roberts: Captain Washington told us that you kept on shouting at him to tell them where the dump was. Is that true?

Stevens: Yes, in a way. At first I only translated, but Ekesta was at his worst. Enjoying it. I knew that if the captain didn't talk they would kill him, torture his men, torture the people of the villages too. Do anything that might possibly lead them to the dump.

The President: But we know that Captain Washington didn't talk.

Stevens: No, he kept on shouting No, no, no. He was a very brave man. Foolishly so, I think.

Roberts: And then?

Stevens: He became unconscious and they couldn't bring him round.

Roberts: Does 'they' include you?

Stevens: No, Ekesta and the gaoler. When

they couldn't bring him round, Ekesta was told to 'let him stew' then work on him again. (*Stevens was trembling, his eyes had filled with tears. Almost shouting.*) It wasn't worth it. All that courage. But it wasn't worth it. I knew that Ekesta would break him or kill him in the end. Kill and hurt many other people too. (*Stevens blew his nose and wiped his eyes*) It wasn't worth it.

Roberts: What then took place?

Stevens: Thein Maung, the muleteer was waiting in the compound. He had already told Mutaguchi that the British, at gunpoint, had commandeered his mules. He didn't know where they'd gone or what they'd done. I told him that the Kempetai were on the warpath, that they were determined to find the dump and, if necessary, torture everyone involved. Thein Maung included.

Roberts: And what was the muleteer's reaction?

Stevens: He was very frightened. He said he didn't know of any dump but there was just a chance that he could find it. I asked him how and he told me that his lead mule was very intelligent. So much so that he often used it on regular runs with no one with it. Apparently all he had to do was to load it up and then point it down a track. Then, provided the mule had already done the journey several times before, it made its own way there. It could even make its own way back as well.

Roberts: What then?

Stevens: I took Thein Maung to Mutaguchi and he decided it was worth a try. Lieutenant Watanabe was ordered to load the mules — there were six of them, on to trucks and take them to Thandaung. He was then to point the lead mule along the most likely track and see what happened. He promised Thein Maung a beating if it failed.

Roberts: And what did happen?

Stevens: It worked. It worked very well. The lieutenant radioed back that the mule had led them to it. In less than a day they had cleared the dump and brought the stores back to Kempetai HQ.

Roberts: And did you and the muleteer go with them?

Stevens: Thein Maung did. I didn't. As usual, Mutaguchi wanted me at his beck and call. He always referred to me as 'Sergeant Mouthpiece'.

Roberts: And did you see the stores being unloaded from the trucks?

Stevens: Yes, we all did. Captain Washington was there as well.

Roberts: And did you see any bags of silver rupees amongst the stores?

Stevens: I didn't know of any silver. I don't think anyone did. At least no one mentioned it.

Roberts: Not Mutaguchi? Watanabe? The muleteer?

Stevens: No one. The first I knew of any silver was when I was charged with stealing it from the dump.

Roberts: Yet Brigadier Po Kyin says he saw you at the dump. Saw you with Thein Maung. Saw you take and hide the money. What do you say to that?

Stevens: He couldn't have seen me. He simply couldn't. I didn't leave Toungoo.

Roberts: Then whom did he see?

Stevens: I don't know, I just don't know. All I can tell you is that it wasn't me.

Roberts: (*Turning directly to the court.*) I think I know the answer. In fact I'm sure I do. There was another young Anglo-Burman, a Sergeant Anderson, coerced into working for the Japs, for the Kynmauk Kempetai. Captain Fletcher has received a signal that he has been arrested by the Kynmauk military police. He must have been the man seen by the

182

brigadier.

The JAG: Will you be calling this Sergeant Anderson as a witness?

Roberts: I hope so, yes.

The JAG: Have you finished questioning the accused?

Roberts: Yes.

Roberts sat down and raised a thumb to Stevens. He was feeling pleased. In fact he was feeling very pleased, for the scales had tilted even more.

'The prosecution will cross examine,' announced the Judge Advocate General. Rising ponderously to his feet the prosecuting officer eyed Stevens with undisguised distaste. A studied wait whilst the gaze registered with the court.

Then he spoke:

Sergeant Stevens, on your own admission, in peacetime, you willingly worked for the Japanese. Learned to speak and even write their language. We now know that at this time the Japanese were building, or should I say 'spinning', a web of agents to help them in a war. I suggest that all your protestations that you were pressganged is a nonsense, designed to save your skin. I further suggest that you were such an agent and that you wanted the Japanese to take over Burma from the British. Is this not true?

Stevens: (*Firmly.*) It is not true.

The PO: I suggest that at this time you developed a respect, even a liking for the Japanese?

Stevens: In peacetime yes. Why not? They were generally affable, even kind. What's more they were very honest and very hardworking. Yes, I liked them.

The PO: And yet in your evidence you claimed that you were terrified of them. Terrified that these likeable friends of yours would harm you, harm your family. Surely you, of all people, had little cause to fear?

Stevens: The ordinary Japanese, even in wartime, hadn't altered all that much. There were bad people amongst them but then there were bad people everywhere.

The PO: So, despite the war. Despite your mother being killed, you still liked them?

Stevens: My mother was killed by a British mine, not a Japanese one. Yes, I still liked the Japanese, but not the Kempetai. The Kempetai were a law unto themselves. Everyone was scared of them. Even senior army officers.

The PO: But despite this fear, did the Kempetai ever treat you, or any member of your family, badly?

Stevens: No, not really.

The PO: Oh! And what exactly is 'Not really'?

Stevens: Once, just once, Ekesta got fresh with Angela my sister. But Mutaguchi slapped him down. Literally slapped him. Boxed his ears. Made his nose bleed.

The PO: (*Incredulous.*) And this hulking sadist, this so called 'Gorilla', let him?

Stevens: He had no choice. That sort of thing is normal in the Japanese army. I've even seen a general slap another soldier until the blood ran down his face. He just stood and took it. There was nothing he could do.

The PO: (*Sarcastically.*) You certainly knew how to choose your friends.

Stevens: (*Flaring up.*) That is insulting. I didn't choose them and they were not my friends. No one argued with the Kempetai.

The PO: You certainly didn't. Captain Washington did though, despite your help in trying to break him down. Oh, but I forgot. You were not trying to break him down. (*Even more sarcastically.*) You told us this yourself.

Stevens: (*Trying to control his temper.*) The Captain is a very brave man. I'm afraid I'm not. (*Then angrily.*) But I wonder how the captain would have reacted if his wife or mother had been tortured to make him speak? (*Now very angry.*) I wonder how sarcastic you would have been, Lieutenant, with Ekesta. I don't think even you would have kept your trap shut.

The PO: (*Stung.*) There is no call to be rude, Sergeant. That will get you nowhere.

Roberts: (*Springing to his feet.*) May I point out, Lieutenant, that rudeness is not the prerogative of prosecuting officers.

The President: Gentlemen, gentlemen, please.

Roberts was content. He had made his point. But even so, Stevens had better watch his tongue. He whispered this to Stevens.

The PO: About the dump and the missing silver, Sergeant. Is there anyone, anyone at all, who could back your story of this — how shall I put it — this almost human mule? That and your claim that you never left Toungoo?

Stevens: Yes, Mutaguchi. Thein Maung. Lieutenant Watanabe.

The PO: Well, well, what have we here? (*He held up a finger.*) One, a war criminal who, I am glad to say, has just been hanged.

(*Another finger.*) Two, that particular sadist's right-hand man. (*Another finger rose.*) Three, a Burman who admits, like you, that he collaborated with the Japs. (*Sarcastically.*) Under duress of course. (*A pause, then,*) 'Duress', the escape-hatch of all traitors brought to book. (*Again the look of undisguised distaste, the studied wait.*) Sergeant, it is said that a man is judged by the company he keeps. In your case, most apt, I think. Would you not agree?

Stevens: (*Hitting back.*) It is also said that sarcasm is the cheapest form of wit. (*He took a breath.*) I think it should add, 'and from the cheapest form of twit'. Would you not agree?

The PO: (*A disparaging hand.*) I'll take that remark from whence it came. (*Shooting his cuffs.*) Now, regarding the stolen silver. May I put it to you that these two witnesses — these two *sterling* witnesses of yours, if the court will excuse the pun, are up to their ears in this as well. That the brigadier made no mistake. That the silver was stolen by you and/or the muleteer and/or the Kempetai lieutenant. That to use an American expression either you and/or they have stashed it away. Or that there has been, or will be, a three-way split. I even venture to suggest that your mutual friend

187

the Toungoo gaoler has had a cut as well?

Stevens: (*Hotly.*) That's not true, not true at all.

The PO: Well, of course, you would say that. However, I beg to differ. In fact I put it to the court that this is precisely what took place. It was all part of the pattern of . . . (*Turning directly to the court,*) . . . Cupidity. Loyalties trampled in the mud. Innocent people savaged. Brave men killed and hurt (*Then pointing to the Bible that lay upon the desk.*) Thirty pieces of silver. What crimes have been committed for that dishonourable fee. (*In a tone of harsh contempt.*) No more questions.

The courtroom was all agog. Roberts was cursing beneath his breath. What the PO had said could possibly be true. It certainly looked that way. Of course it couldn't be proved but proven or not it had completely undermined his case. Clearly that claptrap with the Bible had gone down well. With a sinking heart he sensed the scales of justice tilt the other way.

'The defence will re-examine the defendant,' announced the Judge Advocate General.

Although dispirited, and now assailed with

doubts, Roberts knew that he must endeav-
our to save something from the wreck.

Roberts: Were you trained as a pre-war
agent of the Japs?
Stevens: I was merely a pre-war employee,
nothing else.
Roberts: Is there any truth in the
suggestion that there has been a conspiracy
between yourself, Thein Maung and
Lieutenant Watanabe?
Stevens: (*Firmly.*) None whatsoever.
Roberts: This is a purely hypothetical
question. If you had stolen the silver, how
would you have used it?
Stevens: (*Straight from the heart.*) I'd have
bribed our way across the border. Into
Siam or China. Anywhere to be clear of
Mutaguchi.
Roberts: But, as we well know, you didn't.
Stevens: (*A wry smile.*) Hardly. Or I
wouldn't be standing here right now.
Roberts: The suggestion — no, the
accusation — has been made that even
before the war you conspired for a Japanese
victory if war ever came to Burma. Is there
any truth in that?
Stevens: (*Very firmly.*) None whatsoever.
Roberts: Am I right in saying that, despite
everything that has happened, despite the

fact that you are accused of waging war against the King, you did, and still do, commit your allegiance to the crown?

Stevens: Yes. With all its faults, we Anglo-Burmans have always been better off under British rule. We always will be.

Roberts: So it was always in your interest that British rule would stay? That Britain would win the war?

Stevens: Very much so. I only hope that they win the peace as well. That Aung San, having ratted on both the Japanese and British, will not succeed. If he does, I dread the future.

Roberts: For yourself?

Stevens: For all Anglo-Burmans. For Burma as a whole. If the Burmans ever hold power over all the other races, it'll tear the land apart. But Aung San claims to be a socialist and the British government is socialist too. I think he'll get his way.

Roberts: Thank you. No more questions. (*Turning to the JAG.*) And now, please, Thein Maung, the muleteer.

Bristling with indignation the muleteer stormed in. The court sat up. Took note. Thein Maung was small and thin, scrub-typhus thin. His head was a skull, his face a mesh of lines. The least said about the teeth

190

the better and his breath was like the plague. But, transcending everything, his eyes were alert and shrewd and full of life and fire. Sweeping round, they condemned the court as fools. No two ways about it: once seen, Thein Maung was not a man easily forgotten. No wonder the brigadier had recognized the man so easily, thought Roberts. It was a thought shared by everyone in court.

His evidence supported everything the accused had said. Yes, as a muleteer, he had worked for the British and the Japs. 'Of course. Why not? As long as I was paid.' No, he hadn't cared who'd win the war. It was not his war, or come to that, Burma's. It was a foreigner's war, so a pox on both their houses. Yes, the mule had led the Japanese to the dump. No, there was nothing strange in that. That mule of his had sense, it did it all the time. No, he had known nothing of the silver, nor, at the time, had anyone else. There certainly wasn't any when the dump was cleared or he'd have seen it. How would he have spent it if he got it? 'I'd have bought some surplus army trucks and not still be buggering about with mules.' No, Stevens was not with him at the dump. Just Watanabe and his men.

'Not a bad chap, Watanabe. Not bad for a Jap, that is.' Had he done any sort of deal with Stevens? Watanabe? Or the gaoler? No, but the opportunity would have been more than welcome. 'And talking of gaolers, what the devil do you mean by locking me up in that MP cage?' No he hadn't wanted to give evidence at the trial. He was far too busy a man to waste his time like this. He'd always believed in minding his own business and not that of someone else. He had enough worries of his own without this Sergeant Stevens. 'God knows how that stupid brother-in-law of mine is coping with the mules. My lead mule has more sense than him.' He cast a malevolent glare all round. 'In fact the mule has more between his ears than anyone sitting here.' Had he seen or heard of Brigadier Po Kyin? No, he hadn't. Another malevolent glare. 'And if he's anything like all these others sitting here, that's just as well.' It seemed that, in the muleteer's opinion, uniforms, of any sort, spelled trouble. And the fancier the uniform the greater the trouble. He cast another glare all round. 'Now, if there's nothing else you want I'll be on my way.'

There wasn't, so, still bristling, on his way he went.

On the whole, Roberts was content with what the muleteer had said. The scales were quivering. He must hope that soon they would son be swinging back. He turned to the JAG. 'And now please, Lieutenant Watanabe.'

Lieutenant Watanabe strode into the court. Arriving at the stand, he stopped. One hand came up in a curved-palm Japanese salute. He then stood easily to attention, the epitome of the Japanese warrior. He wore a khaki cap and tunic; white collar, open at the neck; Sam Browne belt and breeches; knee-length leather boots. All of his apparel was neat, but faded and showing signs of wear. Standing unblinkingly erect, he looked the colonel in the eye: a man personally undefeated and every inch the warrior despite the poverty of his dress. The lieutenant was typical of the toughest, bravest, cruellest troops on earth.

A Nisei, a Japanese/American interpreter, joined him at the stand.

Roberts: (*Through the Nisei*) You are Lieutenant Watanabe of the Japanese Kempetai?
Watanabe: (*A nod and, again through the Nisei,*) Yes.
Roberts: In the last year of the war were you engaged in dealing with British irregular forces in the Toungoo hills?
Watanabe: (*Another nod.*) Yes.
Roberts: (*Indicating Stevens.*) Do you

recognize this soldier?

Watanabe: Yes, his name is Andrew Stevens. At the time he was attached as a Kempetai interpreter.

Roberts: And what part did Sergeant Stevens play in your operations in the hills?

Watanabe: As I said, he was our interpreter. A very good one. He is fluent in many languages, including Nipponese. A very useful man.

Roberts: During these operations was any violence used?

Watanabe: (*Almost casually.*) When deemed necessary, yes.

Roberts: And did Sergeant Stevens take any part, any physical part that is, in any violent acts?

Watanabe: (*A snort.*) No. When it came to the realities of war, Stevens proved to be a woman. (*Cold contempt.*) At times he cried.

Roberts: Were you present at Captain Washington's interrogation?

Watanabe: No, but I knew of it. Knew the necessity for it. That at all costs we had to find the dump. This was a direct order from Army GHQ.

Roberts: If Captain Washington had died or managed to hold out under torture, would you, would the Kempetai, that is, have used violence on anyone else? Washington's men or villagers for instance?

Watanabe: (*Very matter of fact.*) If deemed necessary, yes. But that would be up to Major Mutaguchi. As it turned out, it wasn't necessary. We found the dump.

Roberts: Well at least that is an honest answer. Now tell the court just how the dump was found.

Watanabe: Stevens told us that one of Thein Maung's mules could probably lead us to the dump. We thought it worth a try. So we lorried the mules to Thandaung —

Roberts: (*Jumping in.*) We? Who were we?

Watanabe: Myself and my men. Thein Maung.

Roberts: Not Sergeant Stevens too?

Watanabe: No. I wanted to take him but the major couldn't spare him.

Roberts: What happened then?

Watanabe: (*Smiling at the memory.*) Thein Maung put the mules in line and pointed them up a track. A huge mule led the string for several miles, then led them off the track. We thought we'd found it. But no, the mule just circled round and then went back along the track. Then it turned off the track again and there, right in front of us, was the dump.

Roberts: As simple as that?

Watanabe: (*Smiling.*) As simple as that. It took us ten or eleven journey's to ferry the stores back to the lorries. Then we brought the whole lot back to Kempetai HQ.

Roberts: And was there any sign of silver. Silver rupees in bags?

Watanabe: No. Arms, ammunition, radio parts, food and petrol but definitely no silver.

Roberts: You are sure of this? Absolutely sure?

Watanabe: (*Dryly.*) Absolutely.

Roberts: Now, at the time of the Willis group betrayal —

Watanabe: Betrayal, Captain? It was not a betrayal, it was a justified act of war. Many Burmans wanted a Nippon victory, wanted us to kick the British out. They believed as we did in an Asia for the Asians; freedom from the white-man's yoke. Many, many Burmans had joined the BNA and were fighting on our side. The 'betrayer', as you call him, was such a Burman. A patriot.

Roberts: Do you know who this Burman was?

Watanabe: No, only that he was a member of the BNA. I had never seen him before. Neither have I seen him since. Major Mutaguchi kept this matter to himself.

Roberts: How do you know that this man

was in the BNA?

Watanabe: After he had seen the major I was told to drive him to Pegu. To BNA headquarters. This I did. I then drove back through the night and played my part in stamping out Major Willis and his group.

Roberts: (*Through his teeth.*) Very commendable of you, I'm sure. Could you recognize this man again?

Watanabe: Possibly. But it was a very long time ago and I only saw him in the dark.

Roberts: Was there anything special, anything unusual about him?

Watanabe: Yes, just one thing. On the way he asked if he could drive. I noticed his hand upon the wheel. The fore-finger was missing.

Robert: You say he asked you if he could drive. Do I take it that you speak Burmese?

Watanabe: No, he asked me in Nipponese. He had quite a foreign accent but for a foreigner his Nipponese was very good.

Roberts: Now back to Sergeant Stevens. Did he want to work for the Kempetai?

Watanabe: 'Want' never came into it. Nippon was fighting for its life. Any one not for us was against us. (*Lips tightening.*) And were treated accordingly.

Roberts: And if the sergeant had refused? Would he or his family have been made to

197

suffer?

Watanabe: (*Grimly*.) If deemed necessary, yes.

Roberts: No more questions.

(*The prosecuting officer rose to cross examine*.)

The PO: You told the court that the Kempetai resorted to violence when, to use your own words, it was deemed necessary. Did you approve of that?

Watanabe: I did not approve or disapprove. I was a soldier. I obeyed my orders.

The PO: Were you always present when Stevens was interpreting at interrogations?

Watanabe: No, very rarely. Interrogations were normally the province of Major Mutaguchi and Sergeant-Major Ekesta.

The PO: Then Stevens could well have used violence without you knowing. In Captain Washington's case for instance?

Watanabe: In theory yes but not in practice. Stevens just didn't have the stomach. (*Through set teeth*.) Sergeant-Major Ekesta did not need any help. Least of all from a 'girl' like Stevens.

The PO: You must have known that Stevens had known Mutaguchi before the war. That he was fond of the Japanese. (*Mock concern*.) Oh, I beg your pardon. Nipponese?

Watanabe: Yes, I was aware that he knew the major before the war. And why should he not like the Nipponese? Surely they preferred us to their English lords and masters?

The PO: Let us not play with words. I put it to you that Stevens was a pre-war friend of Mutaguchi. That when war came he became a friend of yours as well. I further put it to you that because of this you are doing your best to save his neck?

Watanabe: (*Coldly.*) We were officers. Officers of the Kempetai. Stevens was an NCO. There could be no question of being 'friends'.

The PO: To your knowledge, did Mutaguchi, or anyone else for that matter, even threaten Stevens to ensure his ... how shall I put it ... his co-operation

Watanabe: No. (*Then grimly.*) But Stevens knew which side his bread was buttered.

The PO: Now let us turn to this matter of the silver. Your journey to the dump. Did the muleteer, Thein Maung, at any time, go on ahead?

Watanabe: He stayed with the mules. There was no point in anyone going ahead.

The PO: Did your party take a rest *en route*? And whilst resting, were you passed by any civilians?

199

Watanabe: No we didn't stop. Why should we? It was no distance. No real distance at all. (*Cuttingly*.) We were soldiers, not boy scouts. Did any civilians pass us? Possibly, but it was a very long time ago. I can't remember.

The PO: And when 'Big Ears', the wonder mule, led you to the dump, you say you found no silver. In the circumstances not a likely story. I put it to you, most strongly, that you did find the silver and that you left it at, or near, the dump to be picked up later on?

Watanabe: (*Icily*.) I am an officer of his Imperial Majesty, not a thief.

The PO: (*Sneeringly*.) Other Nipponese officers have dipped their fingers in the till. Why not you?

(*Dipped their fingers in the till? Again Stevens came to the Nisei's rescue*.)

Watanabe: I will not demean myself by answering that.

The PO: Then the court must draw its own conclusions. Now. This fairy story of the missing finger. I put it to you that this is a fabrication to give credence to that pantomime about the fanlight. That in fact all your evidence is part of an overall conspiracy by you, Stevens, the gaoler and the muleteer. (*A pause*.) And not forgetting

200

of course, 'Big Ears' the wonder mule. All very clever. All very slick. But far too slick to be believed.

The PO: (*Flicking a dismissive hand.*) No more questions. (*He resumed his seat.*)

The JAG: The defence will re-examine.

However, Roberts decided to leave well alone. As far as he could see, on balance, Stevens had emerged on top.

'No more questions,' he said.

The president had his eyes upon the clock. 'I think we have heard enough for one day,' he said. 'The court will reconvene at 0 nine hundred hours on Tuesday.' He beamed a smile all round the courtroom. 'I think we've all earned a long weekend.'

'The court will rise,' pronounced the MP Sergeant-Major.

★   ★   ★

Roberts was standing by the window, looking out across the lake. The night was hot, without a breath of air. Angela had pushed the mosquito net aside and was lying naked on the sweat-damp sheet. The moon, glaring through the shutters, picked out the blackness of her hair against the pillow, the rise and fall of her daintily nippled breasts, the curving smoothness of her honey-coloured skin, the shadow of her jet-black bush.

But Roberts felt only the faintest stirrings of desire. Turning, he gazed across the stillness of the lake. His thoughts were not on Angela but on what had happened earlier on.

When he had left the courtroom he had been confident that, in spite of all that had been said, he was going to pull it off. But then, increasingly, a doubt came niggling in. Not about what his witnesses had said. No, on the contrary, for all four of them had turned up trumps. Each one's evidence and the demonstration at the gaol had dovetailed neatly into place. But that was what raised his doubt. In retrospect perhaps they had dovetailed far too neatly. The PO's words came back: *All very clever. All very slick. But far too slick to be believed.* Roberts now realized that the PO's scorn and reasoning had made an impression on the court. As well they might, for even he had begun to wonder whether he was being hoodwinked; whether the Stevens version was a carefully thought-out plot.

Then, just as he was leaving to spend the night with Angie, his suspicions had been confirmed. A bombshell.

He'd had a call from Fletch. 'Rob, old son, bad news.' Fletch had then read out a signal he had received from the Kynmauk military police. 'Ref enquiry Sergeant Anderson Stop On relevant date Anderson attending Kempetai conference GHQ Manila Stop Details checked and verified Stop Message Ends.'

Roberts had been shattered by the news. It meant that Stevens and not Anderson was the man the brigadier had seen. There couldn't have been three look-alike Anglo-Burman sergeants in the area. Even two had been stretching things a bit. The signal had driven a coach and horses through the Stevens version of events. If guilty of pinching the silver he was most certainly guilty of all the other charges too. Clever though his story was, Stevens had not bargained on the fugitive Po Kyin seeing him at the dump and living to tell the tale in court. This sighting had blown the conspiracy sky high.

Now Roberts' mind was in a turmoil. What a bloody fool he'd been. How Stevens and Angela must have laughed. So much for trust. So much for all that work, for all that devotion to the case. Even now he found it difficult to believe. He would have staked his life that Stevens — and yes, Angela as well, had been telling him the truth.

Well, tomorrow night he'd be drowning his sorrows at Fletch's farewell do. It would give him the chance to forget how Stevens had betrayed him. Betrayed Major Willis and all those others too. He smacked a fist into a palm. He'd sort brother Stevens out on Monday. Tomorrow, sister Angela was off to Mandalay with 'Pa'. Good riddance to them both. Well, as far as the Stevens family was concerned he'd get his money's worth tonight. The three of them had taken him for a ride. Had made him a laughing stock. Had cost him dear. Now sister Angela would pay her portion of the bill. Roberts set his teeth. There were one or two things he hadn't dared to do with her, with anyone. He licked his lips. Whether she liked it or not he was going to do them now, right now.

He stalked over to the bed and slapped her face. 'Wake up, you bitch,' he snarled.

15

The moon was riding in a cloudless sky and cast enough light to read by. Not that Roberts or Fletcher was capable of focusing on print. Both of them were drunk or as the MP on duty at the club had phrased it earlier on: 'as pissed as newts'.

Roberts was at the wheel. It had to be that way for Fletcher was sitting on the bonnet on a high-backed chair. He had a violin tucked beneath his chin and the strains of *Claire de Lune* were wailing through the night. It was nearly two o'clock and, bathed in the protective glow reserved for drunks, they were doling out their tribute to the moon.

It had been an evening to remember, no two ways on that. But by now, apart from the two of them, the revellers had staggered off to bed, and after a fruitless search, the club's musicians had sadly given their violin up for lost.

However, the musician's loss was Toungoo's gain. The jeep, having scraped across the bridge, was weaving along the bank. Fletcher, now inspired by the moonlit river, had changed his tune. Now, the ebb and flow of *The Blue Danube* swirled amongst the palm-trees and the silent bamboo houses, disturbing the patterns of the night. It invaded dreams. Copulations changed their rhythms to match the fiddler's lilt. Dogs stirred and pricked their ears. Those more musically inclined began to howl.

Roberts, with an unlit cigarette dangling from his lips, was on another plane. One hand grasped the wheel. In the other he held a bamboo slat that conducted Fletcher's beat. In keeping with the lilt, the jeep weaved harmoniously from side to side and the headlights waved their wands. And when the fiddler's elbow put on speed the swerves took up the pace. Faster. Then even faster. It was all too much. Abruptly, the music stopped. The jeep had left the road and was up to its hubs in mud. Still seated in the high-back chair Fletcher and his fiddle carried on. For a fleeting moment the headlights lit their passage through the air. Then with an oath and a splash, they disappeared from view.

Roberts sat leaning on the wheel; wondering at the quiet; bemused by the two white spots of light. He watched the river swirling by. It was all most odd. With his tongue he moved his cigarette from left to right and fumbled for a light. The matchbox slipped. It slithered across the bonnet and joined

Fletcher and his fiddle on their journey to the sea. Roberts sought his cigarettes. Found them. A fresh one joined the one already in his mouth. Now where were the bloody matches? He made a fruitless, fumbling search. He gave a sigh. Ah well, he'd sooner go to sleep. With the cigarettes between his lips he nodded off, his forehead on the wheel.

He was awakened by the sound of dragging footsteps. Then a huge black shape came squelching through the night. It was Fletch. It was good old Fletch. He hoped that Fletch'd have a match. He asked. Owl-like, he watched Fletch search his soaking pockets one by one. Fletch shook his head and without a word he climbed into the jeep.

For a time they sat companionably in silence. At long last Roberts broke the quiet. Gazing at the moon, he said in carefully spaced-out words: 'It's a lovely night. It's a really lovely night.' He thought deeply for quite a time then spoke again. 'Yes, a really lovely night.'

Fletcher mulled this over and then accepted it as true. But he too had something on his mind. He too stayed deep in thought: Then, in a disenchanted voice said: 'The Danube tastes like piss.'

Roberts nodded gravely at the news. 'Smells like it too,' he said. 'But it's still a

207

lovely night.' He shook his head in wonder. 'Who'd want to be in bed on a lovely night like this?' Then he chuckled as a piece of Shakespeare surfaced in his mind. Putting a hand on Fletch's arm he focused on his face. 'Fletch, old son,' he said, 'Gentlemen in England now a-bed will think themselves accursed that they're not here.'

Fletcher heard him out, then guffawed. He had been tickled by the 'now a-bed'. It reminded him of Perce. He repeated it several times and rolled it around his tongue. Then: 'Who's a-bed right now?' he asked. He answered it himself. 'Pompous Perce is now a-bed.'

Knowingly, Roberts dug him in the ribs. 'And so's the Toast of Mandalay,' he said.

They fell about at this, then, gravely, they began to name all those others 'Now a-bed'. They were saddened at how many were now a-bed on a lovely night like this.

Then Fletcher's mouth turned down. 'But they are all alone a-bed.' As he spoke he had a vision of the virgin Johnny Johnson sleeping solo in the mess. He gave the wheel a thump that rocked the jeep. 'Johnny's always been alone a-bed.' His face grew sadder still. 'It just isn't right,' he said.

Silently, they mourned for Johnny all alone a-bed. Then a thought ballooned in Fletcher's head. Towering to his feet he raised his arms towards the moon. 'Tonight, Lieutenant Johnson becomes a man,' he boomed.

Roberts was bewildered. 'But Johnny *is* a man,' he said.

Fletcher gave a seraphic smile. 'He'll not be a man till he's had it off with the Toast of Mandalay.' A pause for thought, then 'Marie, here we come,' crashed out and a great backside bundled Roberts from the wheel. Fletcher took it and slammed into four-wheel drive. A roar. With a scrunching of wheels, a shower of spray and mud they were back upon the road. A grunt. Another scrunching and the jeep shot off.

Roberts mind was cotton wool. 'Why Marie?' he yelled. He had to shout, for the jeep was roaring as it bounced along.

Another guffaw. 'Because she's got the biggest tits you've ever seen.' Fletcher released the wheel and made a cupping, lifting gesture with his hands. 'Like melons.' He turned to Roberts, his laugh booming out. 'When Johnny goes 'Brgggh' between those tits he'll be a man.' Saying which, he grabbed the wheel and avoided disaster by an inch.

They were now rocking along a pock-marked track. Mysterious in the moonlight, bomb craters fell away on either side. The

209

headlights caught them. Huge black-shadowed pits. They also caught the yellow splashes of two unexploded bombs.

Another great idea ballooned in Fletcher's head. He slammed the brakes on and as they slithered to a halt he made a grab at Roberts's arm. 'Pompous Perce, the president of the court, is all alone a-bed,' he said.

'So what? He should always be alone a-bed.'

Fletcher favoured his old friend Robbie with a grin. 'Yes, old son, but what if Perce was a-bed with one of those?' He pointed to the bombs. 'Can you imagine Perce waking up with one of those between his legs?'

Roberts could. It was a heady thought. 'Couldn't think of a better bloke,' he said. Climbing down, he posed in a 'strong man' bent-arm stance, then gave the bomb a heave. It hardly moved.

'Here, let's have it.' Without any sign of strain Fletcher picked it up and dumped it in the jeep. Then he brushed his hands together on a job well done.

Roberts cupped an ear. 'Shsssssh, I can hear it ticking.'

Again they fell about. This was the funniest thing yet. Fletcher picked up a rock and gave the bomb a bash. Still laughing, he said: 'Not any more, you can't.' Then his eye alighted on the other bomb. It seemed to bring him down to earth. He said: 'These bloody things are dangerous. No business near the road. Could blow innocent passers-by to buggery.' He wagged a reproving finger. 'Must clear the road.' He added primly: 'I'm a policeman. Remember that.'

He stopped to lift the bomb but Roberts, still chuckling about that *I'm a policeman* . . . stopped him. 'No,' he said, 'Jap bomb. Heathen. Never been christened. Never gone off bang. Must be christened before it goes off bang.' He fumbled at his fly.

Fletcher grinned and did the same. 'But first, a toast,' he said. He freed his cock and waved it at the bomb, then said solemnly: 'We name this bomb John Thomas.'

At this they raised their penises in salute and then, crossing swords, they pissed silver in the moonlight.

'Gee, I needed that,' said Fletcher. They buttoned up. Each then took an end of the wet and gleaming bomb. With a cheerful, 'One — two — Three,' they swung it down into a crater. A clunk, a silence, the scurrying of a tumbling stone. They peered into the pit. 'Bloody thing's a dud,' said Roberts in a let-down voice. 'No wonder the bastards lost the war.'

Fletcher, also disappointed, pondered for a

while. 'No, let's be fair,' he said. 'When we peed on it, it must have put it out.'

Then, back in the jeep and with the bomb rattling and bouncing in the back, they roistered through the night.

Marie heard them in the distance. Heard their happy song. Faint at first, the words grew even louder till they were ringing through the night. 'You put your left leg in, your left leg out, you put your left leg in and you shake it all about. You do the hokey cokey and you turn around . . . '

They were not only singing the words but going through the actions too. It gave driving a jeep a new dimension. At the speed they were travelling along the rutted tracks it was pretty dangerous too. They had just completed 'putting your right leg in' when they zigzagged to a halt by Marie's gate.

Marie, already dressed, stood smiling at the door. For her, getting dressed was simple. Sleeping naked, she had merely hurried on a *longyi* and a pair of flip-flop shoes. She knew, only too well, that when Fletch arrived it would save a lot of time. A lot of wear and tear as well.

Excited and warm with sleep, she met him at the gate. She flung her arms around him and wriggled close. She slipped a hand inside his fly. Then with a pseudo-shocked surprise she whispered 'What's that you've got down there?' Her breath was in his ear. A giggle. 'My, my Fletch, you're certainly glad to see me!' Her words were promptly followed by her tongue and Fletcher's bellow of delight. Whirling her aloft he made a beeline for her bed. A well-worn path. The bedroom door slammed shut. The slam was closely followed by a thud that shook the house, then came a groan of hard-pressed springs, a mutual giggling. Then, as she remembered her manners, came Marie's voice: 'Robbie, get yourself a drink.' Then a gasp. 'Fletch, you randy sod!' A happy shriek. A shrill; 'Oh Fletch!' Then a peal of happy laugher.

Roberts poured himself a drink. A big one, after all that singing he was running dry. Then, glass in hand, and ignoring the 'noises off', he wandered round the room. It was basically Burmese with a typical teak-planked polished floor. But it had been filled with odds and ends of furnishings clearly looted in the .42 retreat. He looked around. Along one side stood a gigantic sideboard with a badly mildewed mirror. There were a few wicker chairs and tables, a tiger skin complete with snarling head: real Theda Bara stuff. There was a garish cocktail bar, some tasselled standard lamps and an ancient grand piano with a tasselled stool. Spaced around the walls were some pretty dreadful prints: *September Morn, When Did You Last See Your Father?* and *The Stag At Bay*. One wall was given over to a flight of plaster ducks. Roberts shuddered. All in all, it would never do for the women's magazines.

On the piano was an array of photographs in silver frames. He poured another drink and studied them one by one. They were mostly of Marie; a very young Marie in Burmese dress; Marie with an elderly Anglo-Burman couple, almost certainly Mum and Dad; Marie the only female in a group of Anglo-Burman youths; Marie, (this a snap-shot) with a very handsome Burmese officer. Roberts looked more closely. Surprise, surprise! The soldier was Brigadier Po Kyin. But looking younger, somehow fresher. As yet unscarred, uninjured and wearing majors' crowns. Again, Po Kyin, lined up with others in front of General Slim: the general pinning a gong on Po Kyin's chest: Last of all, an over-the-general's shoulder shot of Po Kyin at a very smart salute. Stern-faced and looking every inch the warrior that he was.

Well, well, our Marie certainly puts it around, he thought.

At that moment from the bedroom came: 'Fletch, oh Fletch,' A grunt. A crash as of something, or someone, falling. A squeal of

214

joy. Roberts grinned. By the sound of it, Marie was 'putting it around' right now! The sounds were making him feel quite fruity. He'd be better off outside.

He finished off his drink, walked unsteadily to the jeep and climbed aboard. Suddenly, he was tired, so tired. Putting an arm around the bomb he nodded off . . .

A rumpled-looking Fletcher woke him up. Fletch had Marie's *longyi*, turban-like, around his head. The girl, stark naked, was cradled in his arms, her arms around his neck. She smiled and, reaching out, she ruffled Roberts's hair. Her smile was whitened by the moonlight. Her eyes were smiling too. Her hand slipped behind his head and pulled him forward for a warm soft kiss. 'Robbie, my sweet,' she cooed.

'My sweet' was most impressed. The words of an ancient ballad flashed across his mind: 'How the moon shines bright on pretty Redwing'. It was apt, most apt. In no way had Fletch exaggerated. If there were bigger and lovelier tits around he'd yet to see them. Johnny Johnson was in luck!

The two of them had collapsed, giggling, on the jeep's back seat. Roberts took the wheel. With a scrunching of burning tyres the jeep roared off. The bomb, propped against the windscreen, jumped and clattered as they bounced across the ruts. It was wearing Fletcher's cap.

Several close shaves later, Roberts cut the engine and the jeep coasted to a halt. The mess loomed stark and silent as if waiting for the bomb.

Fletch and Marie were still giggling in the back. Roberts frowned and clicked his tongue. That would have to stop if they were to achieve surprise. He took command. 'You.' His pointing finger was an inch off Fletcher's nose. 'And you.' The finger was now in Marie's face. 'Belt up.'

Fletcher came to attention and answered: 'Sir.' Marie took the finger in her mouth.

'Fletch,' ordered Roberts, 'You take the bomb. I'll take Marie.'

'Sir,' said Fletch again. He swapped Marie for the bomb. Marie was not displeased. Unbuttoning Roberts's shirt she stroked her nipples across his chest. 'Yes, you take me,' she said and kissed him on the lips.

'Duty first,' he said and scooped her up. Her body was soft and smooth and warm and he wondered how, with a bosom as big as this, she could be so light. She had that marvellous smell of musk. It brought a wave of lust. Suddenly, he wanted to take her, there and then.

It was not to be. 'Lead on, MacDuff,' said

Fletch, 'A standing cock awaits.'

A chuckle. 'At least it will when Marie gets a-bed.'

Marie's laugh pealed out. 'Yes, lead on MacDuff,' she said and again she kissed his lips.

'MacDuff' led on and, all of them giggling away, they struggled up the stairs. Roberts with Marie and Fletcher with the bomb.

Johnny's door was open and the room was drenched in moonlight. They could see him through the net, looking even younger than his nineteen years. He stirred and muttered something in his sleep.

'He's dreaming,' Roberts whispered.

Fletcher chuckled, whispering: 'It'll be a wet dream soon.'

Smiling, Marie eased away the net, turned down the sheet and pulled at the cord round Johnny's waist. Gently, oh so gently, her hand caressed. Then she eased herself against him in the bed. Johnny's breathing stopped. Suddenly he was wide awake. Or was it all a dream? There was an ecstasy of touch, a smell of musk, a cool and tender glide, a smiling face, soft breath. Softly parted lips were whispering: 'Johnny, love me. Love me, Johnny.' The lips came floating down. A heavy lightness pressed and became the whole wide world. From somewhere far away, a friendly laugh, the click of a closing door. Then Johnny's mind and body were melting in delight. The whispering, now urgent, was in his ear: 'Johnnee, love me. Love me, Johnnee . . . '

In the corridor, Fletcher grinned and hefted the bomb across a shoulder. 'Now for Pompous Perce,' he said and strode to the colonel's room.

The door was closed but, through it, they could hear the colonel's snores.

'Sounds like a porker on the job,' said Fletcher.

Stealthily they crept inside. The mosquito net was up and they beheld Pompous Perce, warts and all. Not a pretty sight, thought Roberts. The colonel was sleeping in the raw, exposed, his knees and forearms dark against the untanned skin. His small pot belly was quivering like a badly set blancmange. His mouth was open and his teeth were grinning from a nearby glass. An irregular wetness snorted past his toothless gums. He sounded like a badly tuned machine.

'Looks like a porker too,' said Fletcher in a whisper. Then he murmured 'Bombs away,' and put the five-foot monster in the bed. He regarded it with pride. Then, pulling down the net, he tucked it in.

The colonel stirred. Turning over in his

218

sleep he placed an arm and then a leg around the bomb. The snoring stopped and all was quiet.

'Sweet dreams,' mouthed Roberts. Then Shakespeare surfaced yet again. 'But in that sleep of death, what dreams may come once you have shuffled off that bloody bomb . . .' God, what would the Old Vic make of this!

As they tiptoed to the door the colonel smiled and hugged the bomb and murmured someone's name. Then the snores broke out again.

Once outside, they slapped each other's back and bundled down the stairs. Then switching on the lights, they skipped about in glee.

'What a night, what a bloody marvellous night,' Fletch was chortling. 'Not a thing went wrong.' He fell into a chair. 'Johnny's bum is wreathed in smiles.' He gave a guffaw. 'And Perce's balls are resting on that bloody bomb.' He slapped a thigh with joy. 'That calls for another drink.'

Roberts checked his watch. 'It's just gone four. Let's make it cha.'

Fletcher raised a thumb. 'Two chas coming up,' he said and ambled from the room.

Left on his own, Roberts lay back in his chair. He too was feeling fine. Fletch was right, it had been a marvellous night. He glowed and stretched his legs and felt as one with the whole wide world. The court martial surfaced briefly but he pushed it from his mind. That could wait till Tuesday. From somewhere there came the sounds of Fletch's search for cha. Fletch. What a crazy bloke he was. The way he carried on. Who'd ever dream he was a policeman? Roberts laughed aloud at the memory of him putting the bomb in Perce's bed. What an awakening there was to come! Suddenly he became aware that he was not alone for, standing at the door with a towel clutched round his waist, was the ghost of Pompous Perce!

The bomb had woven a spell. Perce's head seemed to have shrunken to a skull. His eyes were pools of fright. Soundless words were jerking from his ashen lips.

Pompous Perce came in and crouched, trembling, on a chair. He was doing his best to speak. Behind him, a grinning Fletcher was stabbing a finger at the stairs.

'Hello, Colonel, you're up bright and early,' said Roberts affably.

The colonel moved his lips but he was still unable to utter a sound.

'Can't hear you, Colonel.' Roberts screwed a finger in an ear and examined the tip for wax. 'No, can't hear a word you say.' He cupped a hand to facilitate reception. From just outside a thud informed him that the bomb was no longer in the bed! He hid a grin.

'A bloody bomb; huge thing, next to me in bed. Could've gone off. Blown us all to bits.'

Good, thought Roberts, sound has been restored. The frozen eyes were thawing and the words were tumbling out. Suddenly, Fletch was back. He clattered down three mugs of tea. The steam was rising in tiny columns that widened, joined, then gossamered away.

'The colonel's had a nightmare,' Roberts told his friend.

'A nightmare, Colonel?' Fletcher was all concern.

The colonel shook his head. 'No, not a nightmare. A bomb. A bomb next to me in bed.' The colonel's lips were trembling. His hands were shaking too.

Fletcher shook his head and said, as though consoling: 'That all Colonel? Not much of a dream to get all steamed up about.' He pushed across a mug. 'Here, sir, have some cha.'

The colonel spluttered, 'Not a dream. A bomb. A real one in my bed.'

'Oh come now, Colonel.' It was Roberts's turn to show concern. 'Don't let a nightmare get you down. Have some cha, like Fletch here said.'

'A bomb I tell you. Five feet long. I know, I've seen it. It's in my bed.' The colonel's voice was shrill.

'Colonel, please,' chided Fletcher, 'whoever heard of a five-foot bomb in bed? All this fuss about a dream.'

'It's not a dream,' the colonel screamed, 'It's real.' He took in the two patronizing grins and shouted: 'Come upstairs, I'll show you.' He scrambled to his feet, and still clutching at his towel he scurried up the stairs. Two great big grins were following close behind. Crashing back the door, the colonel flung a hand out and bellowed: *There*.

'There', was an empty rumpled bed.

★   ★   ★

'Time Cinderella left the ball.' Fletcher drained his mug and made for Johnny's room. Marie heard the latch and, seeing Fletcher beckon, she slid from Johnny's side. Johnny murmured in his sleep and, childlike, snuggled down. With a tender smile she brushed his forehead with her lips. Then, moving silently, she crossed the room and gently closed the door.

Now the three of them were grouped beneath the colonel's bedroom window. From above, the snores were sawing through the night. A huge medicinal Scotch had sent the colonel off to sleep. It was getting light and soon the world would be astir.

'We'll have to get rid of that,' said Roberts gazing fondly at the bomb. It stood embedded in the ground. A gigantic lethal dart.

'Too bloody right,' said Fletcher. 'But first, Marie.'

Soon Marie was safely back in bed, awake, remembering the sweetly fumbling Johnny responding to her touch. How different from the predatory hands of Fletch, she thought. She heard the jeep move off and felt a deep enduring warmth. Curling up, she cupped her naked breasts and murmured; 'Johnee, love me. Love me, Johnee,' and contentedly she drifted off to sleep.

'I know just the place to dump it,' Roberts said. He turned off the track and bumped the jeep along. Soon they came to a timbered strongpoint that had been built there by the Japs. The Japs had hacked away the ground below to form a cliff. Dismounting, the two men peered across the edge.

'Just the job,' said Fletcher and he flung the bomb to earth. Each of them grabbed an end. Once again there was a cheerful, 'One — Two — *Three*,' and Pompous Perce's nightmare went sailing out of sight.

Laughing, they turned towards the jeep. BANG. The blast ripped up and sent them reeling, stunned and gasping, to the ground. Through ringing ears they heard the splinters whining through the air. A million birds criss-crossed madly in the sky. The village dogs went berserk. Reaching up, a smoke cloud hid the sun. Bits and pieces crashed and splattered all around. Voices ricocheted. An echo rumbled in the hills.

Gradually, everything returned to normal. The drifting smoke began to thin and wisp away. The world had got its breath back.

Fletcher sat up and checked for hurt. 'Rob, you all right?' he called.

'Yes, I'm fine. You?

A chuckle. 'Good as new.' Another chuckle. 'Just as well it didn't go off in Perce's bed.'

Roberts chuckled too. Then said: 'It's all our fault.'

'Our fault! Why?'

'We forgot to pee on it. Forgot to put it out.'

Then the two of them were laughing. Laughing till the tears ran down. Roberts found he couldn't stop, the laughter just went on. Then suddenly it stopped. Suddenly he was stonecold sober. For several hours something had been niggling at his mind. No more. The drunken haze had gone. He now knew exactly what it was. It was the photograph. The photograph of Brigadier Po Kyin. The photograph of Brigadier Po Kyin saluting General Slim. Po Kyin, the epitome of the dashing cavalier. Just one thing wrong. The forefinger of the saluting hand was just a stump.

PART THREE

RETRIBUTION

16

Driving hard and fast, they were back at Marie's in record time. This time there were no shenanigans at the wheel. The door was barred but Fletcher's shoulder saw to that. Roberts strode across the room, grabbed the photograph and held it to the light. Yes it was Po Kyin and yes his right forefinger ended in a stump. There was another photograph that he'd missed, a snapshot. This was of Po Kyin, in uniform, laughing and holding up his hands in mock surrender. This too clearly showed his mutilated hand.

Roberts' mind was whirling. Suddenly, everything had fallen into place. Stevens, poor hard-done-by Sergeant Stevens, had been proved right. Incredible though his story was it was now proven to be true. It was Po Kyin — resistance hero, a brigadier with DSO, MC and bar, who had been the liar. No wonder Stevens, a press-ganged hireling of the Japs, had been totally disbelieved. Even he, the defending officer, had fallen for it too. But then so had everyone else involved. Roberts thought of the way he had taken it out of Angie and his toes curled up in shame.

'Boys, boys! What's all this?' A bewildered Marie, rumpled, naked and clearly straight from bed had come into the room.

'That's what you are going to tell me,' said Roberts grimly.

But Fletcher intervened. 'Steady on, old son,' he said and, smiling, slapped Marie's bottom. 'Get some clothes on, Marie, you're too big a girl to be running about like this.' Another slap. 'And how about some coffee whilst you're at it?'

Coaxed by Fletcher, Marie told them what she knew about Po Kyin. It was quite a lot. First she produced another snap. This, clearly taken several years ago, was of three men in Burmese clothes: a rather young Po Kyin, another man of similar age, and a very much older man — paternal-looking, grossly fat, and wearing an upper-class Burmese head-scarf. 'Po Kyin, Aung San and a friend of theirs, U Saw.'

Roberts studied the snapshot closely. So this was Aung San, the two-timing commander of the BNA. He was young, slim, good-looking and not at all the ogre he'd expected. In fact he looked quite a decent sort. Well, be that as it might, so much for Po Kyin's evidence that before that fateful night he had never known or even met Aung San.

Fletcher took the snapshot. 'That elderly

bloke's U Saw all right,' he said. 'It's the man I told you about, the rabblerouser. The one whose name you used to put the breeze up Perce.' Fletcher pulled a face and reeled off what he knew. 'A politician. A pre-war premier. Interned by us for his pre-war flirting with the Japs. A self-seeking bastard who would shop his mother if the dividend was right. Now he's in Rangoon and doing everything he can to undercut Aung San.'

'He can't be all that bad then,' said Roberts drily.

'Not all that bad!' Again Fletcher pulled a face and then said sourly, 'Politicians like him? I've shit 'em.'

Roberts laughed. 'Very delicately phrased, as usual,' he said. Then he turned his attention back to Marie and gave her quite a grilling.

Yes, she'd known the three of them. This just before the war when she was at Rangoon University. No, she knew nothing about their politics. Or any other politics come to that. An earthy grin. 'I had other things in mind.' No, the only one she'd ever seen after that was Po Kyin and that was not until early 1945. Then she got to know him well. In fact very well indeed! Yes, during the war she had been friendly with the Japs. She had kept her nose clean, there had been no other way. 'A girl had to survive, Robbie.' No, the Japanese were not all bad, in fact some of them were very nice. They had helped to keep the wolf from the door when things were bad. Then Po Kyin turned up. He had taken her by surprise by arriving in the middle of the night. She gave another earthy grin. 'Just after a Japanese officer friend had left.' Without as much as a by your leave he had set up a radio in the loft, from which he had sent all sorts of messages back to India. Well yes, it had been quite a risk but (she gave a reminiscent smile), Po Kyin was worth it. 'No, the Japs had never suspected anything untoward. She said laughingly: 'I had many social visits and, like Caesar's wife, I was clear of all suspicion.' Yes, Po Kyin had helped her in many ways. Particularly with money. In what way with money? Well, by then many things were scarce and Japanese notes were useless. Only silver rupees had any worth. 'Oh yes, he gave me many of these to buy black market goods.' With another laugh she added: 'He told me he had a private silver mine in the Toungoo hills.' What did she know about Mutaguchi? Not much, it seemed. He had been a man to avoid. By then he'd left Toungoo. Had left just after Major Willis and his stores were captured. How did she know all this? It was in the papers. It was on the cinema screen as well. How long was Po Kyin there? Oh for several months, even when the Japanese had gone. He was in uniform then of course. That was when that snap was taken. No, she had never seen him since. He had gone away. Had said that he would pick his personal things up later on. No, he never did. She thought it was due to his being badly injured in a crash. Had that worried her? No not really. In fact she was rather glad. She could never have made love to a man with missing limbs. And in any case she was by then making love with Fletch.

They paused for another pot of coffee, then Roberts resumed his grilling.

'Did you know he was in Toungoo, giving evidence at a trial?'

'Yes, Fletch told me. Told me that you were involved as well.' She giggled. 'Fletch said it was just so that you could get Angie to drop her knickers.'

Fletch had the grace to look away.

'But you didn't contact him at all? Give him back his things?'

'No, that was up to him. In any case I knew that Po Kyin would not take kindly to sharing me with Fletch.'

Roberts gave a doubting smile. 'But Po Kyin was a brigadier. Fletch is just a captain.'

She tossed her head. 'Fletch has his arms

and legs.' She gave another giggle. 'Something else as well.'

'Can you tell me anything more about Po Kyin's pre-war life?'

'No, not really. But U Saw could. Po Kyin told me that he and U Saw had gone to Japan together. They must have known each other well.'

By now Roberts knew he had milked her dry. But would she be prepared to repeat it all in court. He asked her. The reply: A toss of the head. 'If Fletch wants me to, of course . . . '

Once more seated in the jeep, Roberts studied all three snapshots. Fletch was busy with his last farewells. For today Fletch was going home. For him it was a case of 'Rangoon here I come'. Well perhaps he could find the time to see what U Saw had to say. It would certainly be worth a try.

Now about the trial. He would have to see the colonel right away. Tell him what he'd learned, show him the snapshots and demand that Stevens be released. But with Po Kyin so involved it wouldn't end at that. Far from it. By all accounts the anti Aung San lobby wanted him put on trial. Not just for being a traitor but for an appalling murder too. The news that he and his lot were guilty of the Willis group betrayal could easily tip the scales and send a shock wave through the London negotiations. Perhaps even lead to a bloody civil war. Roberts whistled through his teeth. God, what a can of worms, he thought. He shrugged it off. It was now a matter for Pompous Perce, not him. His sole concern was setting Stevens free. And yes, if possible, put things right with Angie when she returned from Mandalay.

Suddenly impatient, he gave a toot. 'Come on Fletch,' he called. Almost immediately Fletcher ambled out and climbed into the jeep. He gave a chuckle. 'Quite a night,' he said. Then: 'I'm starving. Let's have breakfast at the club.'

'A good idea.' The jeep set off.

When they arrived Washington was having breakfast on his own. The little restaurant was full and his table had the only vacant seats. They joined him but he was not too pleased and he made that clear by saying sourly: 'Thought of any more fairy tales to get that bugger off?'

Fletcher clapped him on the back and said cheerfully: 'Now don't be like that. Some fairy tales do come true.'

'Sorry, Fletch, I was referring to Roberts here, not you.'

'Were you now,' said Roberts equably enough. 'And what fairy tales are they? Could you be referring to Po Kyin's evidence that he had never met Aung San? Or that he could not speak a word of Japanese?'

'Leave Po Kyin out of it,' said Washington. 'Without his evidence that bastard Stevens would have got away scot free. If you must know, I was referring, amongst other things, to that missing finger yarn and all that cock about the reflection in the fanlight.'

Roberts smiled. He was thoroughly enjoying this. 'Were you now,' he said again. 'Well, hang on to your hat, Washington. I've got something to show you that'll shake you rigid.'

'Oh,' said Washington, suspiciously.

'Recognize any of these three jokers?' Roberts laid a snapshot down as if he was playing cards. It was the snap of the three Burmese. 'With your Burma background you'll probably know all three of them.'

Washington studied the snapshots closely. Then, without looking up, he said: 'Po Kyin, taken several years ago and, I think, the former Premier U Saw. But I could be wrong. The third chap? No, his face means nothing.' He looked up. 'So?' Roberts nodded approvingly. 'Two out of three. Not bad. Now have another good look at number three.'

Washington studied the snap again. Then shook his head.

'No?' said Roberts. 'Well I think we're going to see a lot of him quite soon. That's the great Aung San, my friend. The man Po Kyin told us that he hadn't seen till forty-four. And yes, you're right about U Saw. That snap was taken when he and Po Kyin were swanning off to cherry-blossom land. Po Kyin stayed a year. So much for not knowing a word of Japanese.'

Washington was staring at the snaps. His jaw had dropped.

Roberts rubbed it in. 'Now about those other fairy tales.' He slapped two more snapshots down. The ace and king of trumps. 'Take a shufti at those, my friend,' he said.

Washington did. He shrugged. 'So what,' he said. 'Po Kyin getting a gong from Bill Slim. Po Kyin larking about.'

'Hold them up to the light.' Roberts gave a laugh. 'Better still, a fanlight.'

'I don't get you?' Washington frowned, puzzled.

Fletcher butted in. 'The hand man, the hand,' he rasped.

The penny dropped. Washington's breath hissed in. Suddenly the awful truth had him by the throat. He couldn't speak. Po Kyin, the man whom he, whom everyone would have trusted with their lives, was the man who had betrayed them to the Japs, the man who had

237

brought about his torture and had caused the death of Gordon Willis and so many of their men, including Po Kyin's signallers too!

A bearer was at the table, pad and pencil poised. 'Your pleasure, Sahibs?' he smiled.

'The works. For two,' said Fletcher. 'One with coffee, one with tea. Oh yes, and a brandy for Captain Washington here.'

Surprised. 'A brandy, Sahib?'

A nod. 'You heard. Better make it a double and make it quick.'

'Sahib.' The bearer scuttled off.

Washington looked and sounded crushed. Almost in a whisper, he asked: 'Where did you get these from, Roberts?'

'Friend of Fletch's. One time friend of Po Kyin too.'

Washington carefully jollied the snaps together and patted them into place. His face was white. 'So where do we go from here?' he asked.

'Good question. First of all I must tell Colonel Perceval. Show him the snaps. Get him to adjourn the trial. Free Stevens. Then someone, Fletch, I hope, will have to see U Saw. Get him to confirm what Marie Gomez said.'

'And Po Kyin?'

'All going well, he'll replace Stevens in the dock,' said Fletcher. 'A lot'll depend on whether U Saw gives evidence, of course. Someone will have to see him. Pretty quickly too. Before Po Kyin gets word of this and queers the pitch. U Saw's a politician. He'll need careful handling. And the sooner the better.' He cocked an eye at Washington. 'Like today for instance. And by you.'

'By me?'

'Why not? You've spent donkey's years in Burma. You know the people. You speak the lingo too. What's more you've got a personal axe to grind. So why not you? Who better?'

'But you said 'today'. U Saw's in Rangoon.'

'No problem. I'm off today.' He glanced at his watch. 'In exactly an hour from now. I'm going down by jeep. I was taking an MP driver to bring it back. But if you come down with me, you can bring it back. That'll suit everyone. Can you be ready in an hour?'

'I can, I can. I'll meet you here.' Washington grabbed the snap of Po Kyin holding up his hands and scrambled to his feet. In moments he was gone.

'Good. So that's settled,' said Fletcher, leaning back.

The bearer had arrived and was fussing with a tray. Fletcher eyed the breakfast with delight and rubbed his hands together. 'That looks good,' he said.

'Captain Washington's brandy, Sahib.'

'That looks good as well.' Fletcher knocked it back in one.

An hour later Roberts was talking to a very startled Pompous Perce. Fletcher and Washington were hurtling south towards Rangoon.

17

Washington, accompanied by the Rangoon
APM, pulled up at U Saw's house. Not with
Fletcher though. Fletcher had washed his
hands of the whole affair. 'Count me out, old
son,' he'd said. 'Get involved and I'll be kept
in this pox-ridden slum of a city till it's all
been sorted out.' He grinned. 'My regards to
Po Kyin though. All going well, he'll swing.'
Another grin. 'Couldn't happen to a better
chap. You can tell him that from me.'

However, he had persuaded a policeman
friend, the Rangoon APM, to lend a hand. He
was a very useful acquisition, for numbered
amongst his duties was keeping tabs on
prisoners on parole and U Saw was on his
list.

Like many more at GHQ the APM was
very much against Aung San. Like most
policemen he viewed everyone as black or
white: no greys. In his book Aung San was
black, jet-black. 'Anything that'll trip that
bugger up is fine by me,' he'd said. 'But a
word of warning. Aung San has friends at
court. Friends in very high places. Bill Slim
for one. The Supremo too, I'm told. I've also

heard that he is going down very well with Attlee.' A sniff. 'But then, what would you expect from a bloody red?' Then he'd brightened up. 'However, it's not all bad. The governor's agin him and so is the C in C. And, being a rival politician, U Saw hates his guts. But even so, Georgie, you'd better watch your step. U Saw's as devious as they come.'

U Saw met them at the gate. He looked every inch the Burman. A prosperous Burman too: gold toothed, squat and grossly fat, he was dressed in a scarlet *longyi* and a snow-white linen shirt. From underneath the *longyi* his sandalled feet peeped out. The toes were manicured and painted red. On his close-cropped skull he wore a pink Burmese headscarf that clashed violently with his nail varnish. Smoothly yellow, his face was like a moon. Gingery eyebrows bushed above the cold and calculating eyes that summed them up.

However, he made them welcome. A plump bejewelled hand waved them to a group of canvas chairs. Speaking in Burmese and smiling, he said: 'Gentlemen, please be seated.' The bejewelled fingers snapped and, like genies summoned from a lamp, two minions appeared with an extensive range of drinks. Washington was impressed. On parole the man might be but, on the face of it, U Saw lived in style.

Still speaking in Burmese, U Saw said softly and politely: 'Welcome to my humble home.'

'I'm afraid you'll have to speak in English,' said the APM, 'neither of us can speak Burmese.'

U Saw's lips tightened slightly. Then, as politely as before, still smiling and still speaking in Burmese, he said: 'How impertinent. You rule but you disdain to learn our tongue.'

Then, having made his point, he asked, in English: 'What would you gentlemen like to drink?'

It was gin for the APM. For Washington, a Scotch.

U Saw translated their wishes to his servants, saying: 'For the taller English pig, a gin and tonic. For the smaller pig, a Scotch.'

Placidly, Washington gazed around the garden and admired the view. He could be devious too!

'Now, gentlemen, to what do I owe this honour?' A click of the tongue. 'But I forget my manners.' U Saw raised his glass. 'Your health,' he said.

'Cheers,' replied the APM.

Washington opened fire. 'We've called

about a Brigadier Po Kyin,' he said. 'He was, perhaps still is, a friend of yours?'

U Saw's response was a dead-pan look. Behind it, Washington could sense the buttons being pressed, the tumblers turning, a balance being struck.

'Well, not necessarily a friend, Captain.' Pursed lips. 'These are troubled times. Shall I just say that Po Kyin and I have met.'

'Before the war?'

'Possibly before the war.'

'Perhaps I could jog your memory. I understand that just before the war you and Po Kyin paid a visit to Japan. Yes?'

Taking his time, U Saw mulled this over. Then: 'As Premier of Burma I visited many places, Japan amongst them. Just normal diplomatic courtesies, of course.'

'Of course. But, on your visit to Japan, you took Po Kyin with you, did you not?'

U Saw pondered. 'So many years ago. So many visits. So many people . . . '

A lengthy wait. Washington let silence do its work.

' . . . I may well have done. If I did it was perhaps a little tactless.' Then defensively, 'But we were not at war. There was nothing wrong in that.'

Washington waved a dismissive hand. 'U Saw,' he said curtly. 'Cards on the table. I'm not concerned with what you have or haven't done. All that will be on record. I need to know about Brigadier Po Kyin's pre-war background. I'm in a hurry. I need to know it now.'

'I trust the brigadier is not in any sort of trouble?'

Without replying, Washington drained his glass. His eyes bored in to U Saw's face.

Again the dead-pan look, the buttons being pressed, the tumblers turning. Then, seemingly deep in thought, U Saw poured another round of drinks and passed them to the visitors.

Then suddenly he relaxed. It had taken a little time but a balance had been struck. He said: 'Your hurry must be due to our recent return from London. So why should I not tell you all I know?' Leaning forward, he rested his arms on his knees and held his glass tightly in both hands. There was a look of candour on his face. 'I met Po Kyin, and others like him, at Rangoon University. They, like me, in fact like all patriotic Burmans, wanted, wanted desperately, an independent Burma. We still do. Only our methods differ.'

'And what are, what were, Po Kyin's methods?'

U Saw's smile did nothing to soften the calculating eyes. 'Po Kyin, and his very close friend Aung San, were two of the 'Thirty Comrades'. Young Burmans who had fire in their bellies. Young men who were convinced that the only hope of freeing Burma was with the backing of the Japanese. All, like me, were ardent supporters of the Nippon/Burma Friendship League. When invited to Japan, I was asked to bring one of the 'comrades' with me. This I did.'

'Po Kyin?'

'Yes, Po Kyin. For me it was a brief diplomatic meeting between two heads of state. Po Kyin however accepted an invitation to stay on for a year, in order to learn the language. To become a link between our countries.'

U Saw shrugged 'Why not? As a subject race we had to learn the language of our English lords and masters. So why not Japanese?'

'Why not indeed. But when Po Kyin came back — what then?'

'They were very difficult times, Captain. The Japanese had struck. Everywhere their armies were triumphant. It was clear that Burma would become involved as well. The 'comrades' looked upon this as a golden opportunity.'

'And?'

'With one exception the 'comrades' absconded

to Japan.' U Saw put on a mask of woe. 'Left the King Emperor in the lurch.'

'And that one exception was our friend Po Kyin?'

A nod. 'Yes. All the others were trained by the Japanese to form the nucleus of the Burma National Army. As you know, at first, they took up arms against the Raj then came back to the winning side.'

'And Po Kyin?'

'Most strange. Something must have happened in Japan. What it was I never knew.' U Saw pursed his lips. 'By that time I had been interned. I had been on my way back to Burma.' Sadly, U Saw shook his head. 'In doing this your Mr Churchill made a big mistake — '

Washington cut him short. 'But about Po Kyin?'

'Quite simple. Po Kyin sided with the British. He fought as an officer in the Burma Rifles. Got back to India in the forty-two retreat. Then, by all accounts, he covered himself in glory.' U Saw slapped his knees and straightened up. 'The rest you know.'

'And now?'

'And now he is Aung San's right-hand man. Now he is a man whose ambitions have played havoc with his brain. Believe me,

Captain, your Mr Attlee would not be wise to trust these men.'

'No?'

'No. Whatever they are saying now, they will take Burma from the Empire. Po Kyin knows this well. His aim is to be the commander of an independent Burma's forces. His ambitions do not stop at that. If anything happened to Aung San then Po Kyin would take his place. Become not only the commander of the forces but chief of state as well. Aung San would be wise to watch his back.'

As he said this, U Saw's fingers tightened on his glass. 'Or so he thinks. But he is wrong, so wrong. A far better ruler is waiting in the wings. A man with real experience. A man with brains. A man whom your government could trust.'

The APM, impressed, 'Like your good self, for instance?'

A nod.

'And if Mr Attlee turns him down? What then?'

Again the tumblers were falling into place in U Saw's head. This time it took almost a minute for a balance to be struck.

Then he said, ruefully: 'We are plagued with dishonest and over-ambitious men, gentlemen.'

'I am afraid you're right,' said the APM sadly.

'The Aung San-Po Kyin partnership is a case in point.'

'It is?'

'It is.'

'So?'

'I am loyal to the British crown.'

The APM gave a nod of professional integrity. 'Of that I have no doubt.'

'Yes. I too want an independent Burma. But as a dominion within the British Empire. I plan to reiterate this to your Lord Mountbatten, tell him other important things about the treacherous Aung San.'

'Such as?'

There was a calculating look from the hard, cold eyes. 'In confidence, of course.'

'Of course.' Unseen, the APM crossed his fingers.

Then came some startling information that made the APM sit up.

'The two of them are plotting an insurrection. If the London talks break down Aung San will take what he wants by force. To accomplish this, Po Kyin is building a private army for him. He is gathering the necessary stores. With all this he plans to oust the British.'

The APM snorted his derision. 'Poppy-cock,' he said.

'No not poppycock, Major. Thanks to the Japanese the peoples of the East have history on their side. Look around you, Major. Everywhere there is revolt. Indo-China, the Dutch East Indies, Malaya. Even India itself. Now in Burma. Take your blinkers off, Major. The white man's rule is drawing to a close.'

'With respect, U Saw, that's nonsense.' The APM showed a clenched fist. 'We are strong. We'll crush any such insurrection. Nip it in the bud.'

U Saw shook his head. 'With equal respect, Major, it is you who are speaking nonsense. Yes, at the moment you are strong. But not for long. England is bankrupt. Your armies are melting fast. You would have to use your English soldiers. Politically you dare not use your Indian troops to crush revolts. Your English troops are getting few in number. They are weary of the war. They have no stomach for a fight. They only wish to get back to their homes in England.' He gave a humourless smile. 'They say 'let the wogs fight it out amongst themselves'.' Again the mirthless smile. 'Wogs like Aung San and Brigadier Po Kyin. And yes, even a wog like me. You must face the realities, Major. Under your Mr Attlee the English are going to swap their greatness for free false teeth and spectacles. Lean back. Hand all their worries to the state.'

Angered, the APM showed his teeth. 'Don't write the British lion off just yet, U Saw. The Germans and the Japs made that mistake.' He flicked a hand. 'More to the point, tell me more about this insurrection.'

U Saw waved a podgy finger. 'I remind you that this is all in the strictest confidence.' The finger stopped and pointed. 'Except of course to my very good friend Lord Louis. Your Lord Louis is a very great man. He must be told at once how helpful I have been.'

The major showed two open hands and an equally open face. 'But of course,' he said, tongue in cheek.

U Saw was concentrating on his glass, turning it around as if searching for a fault. Then, without looking up, he said: 'The insurrection is being planned by Brigadier Po Kyin, from his estate in Golden Valley. The whole estate is packed with guns and warlike stores of every kind. Much of it has been handed over by the Japanese. Men are being trained in secret. The reconstructed BNA has been limited by the British. But it is being duplicated. It will then be duplicated again. It will then have four times the strength expected by the British. Similar arms dumps are being established up and down the country. You employ many civilians in your army installations. Most of these civilians are Po Kyin's spies. Those still loyal to the British are being bullied and threatened into line. Assassination squads are being trained. Many important people will be murdered when the moment comes.'

The APM took a long deep breath. If all this was true he was on to something big. Something for the C.-in-C. himself. Something that if stamped on quickly could finish off Aung San.

'Why are you telling us all this?' he asked.

U Saw's grip tightened on his glass. He sucked in a breath. 'Because Aung San and Po Kyin will bring disaster to my land. They are ruthless men. Men with a lust for wealth and power.' Then, bringing the words out one by one: 'They must be shot.'

As he said this, there came the crack of breaking glass. Glancing down, Washington could see that U Saw's glass had broken in his hands and that a trickle of blood was running down.

Ignoring this, U Saw said: 'Power must go to a truly patriotic man. A man with the best interests of his land at heart. An honest man who will work with and not against the British.'

It was said with so much fervour that, for just a moment, the two of them believed it.

U Saw was wrapping a handkerchief around the cut. 'Finish your drinks, gentlemen,' he said, 'I must attend to this.' He made his way across the lawn and went inside.

'Well, well,' said Washington. 'Do you think it's true?'

'Must be. U Saw knows that if it isn't his feet won't touch. It's true all right.'

The APM rubbed his hands together. 'Tomorrow we'll put the auditors in. Check the stocks.' He smacked a fist against a palm. 'Put an end to Po Kyin's little game.'

'And Po Kyin himself?'

'We'll pull him in. Give you the chance to nail him for that Major Willis business. As Fletch said earlier on, we'll see the bugger swing.'

Washington stood and banged his glass down on the table. He'd had a sudden griping in his gut. He groaned. Damn and blast it to bloody hell, his dysentery was back. 'I'll see you in a jiff,' he said and hurried to the house.

The door was open. As he entered he saw that his host was on the phone. With an apologetic smile he said: 'Sorry to bother you.' He patted his stomach. 'I've been taken short.'

U Saw put his hand across the phone and, in Burmese, told him where to go. As if uncomprehending, Washington shook his head.

'First door along,' the Burman said, this time in English.

'Thanks.' Washington acknowledged with a hand and disappeared inside. He was only just in time! Through the door he could hear U Saw speaking on the phone, saying in Burmese: 'Sorry about that, Po Kyin. I was telling a shit of an Englishman where to shit.' This was followed by a laugh. 'In his own nest! That's very good, Po Kyin, very good indeed.'

Po Kyin! Washington pricked his ears. 'You devious sod,' he muttered. Then, between the spasms of his gut, he listened in. U Saw was saying: 'A Captain Washington is enquiring after you. Yes, he's here right now. With the head of the army police. No, it's something to do with your pre-war life. Your twelve months in Japan. That's what I thought. Yes, something personal. That's why I am ringing to let you know. Think nothing of it. It's good to be of help — no don't ring off. There's something more. Someone has told them that you are planning a revolt. Well maybe it is a nonsense but they think they're on to something. In the main it is that you are gathering arms and men in Golden Valley. If you say so, but from what they said you are in for trouble. If what they say is right it could jeopardize the London talks. Be the end of Aung San's hopes. Yours too. Well, if it happens you know who your real friends are. Me too. Worth thinking about, Po Kyin. You and I could go a long way together. Oh yes, when the British are out of course. True, true. Just one more thing. If you have to lie low for a while, use my little place on the Inya lake. (A laugh) You can use Ma Kin as well. I'll warn her to expect you. Oh yes, she'll be very nice to you. I'll see to that. No, think nothing of it. What are comrades for?'

As Washington emerged U Saw put the receiver down and smiled. Washington smiled back and, patting his belt, he said ruefully: 'Our bodies always cut us down to size, U Saw.'

Still smiling like the cat that had got the cream, U Saw replied amiably, 'They do indeed.'

He ushered the two of them to their jeep and waved them off. His parting words were: 'I implore you to tell Lord Louis everything I've said.'

'We will indeed,' said Washington, speaking for them both.

Once on the road he told the major what

he'd heard. However, he did not mention U Saw's offer of the bungalow and the woman on the Inya lake. For reasons of his own he decided to keep that information to himself.

Po Kyin took the warning in his stride. He would have to move the arms, of course, before the military police arrived. But that would take . . . what? Two or three hours at most, for most of the arsenal was kept stored on the ten-ton 'Macs'. So there was no call for any panic. He had planned for an emergency such as this and had no doubts at all that he could clear it in the time. All he had to do was give the word. His men would do the rest. Come to that, there was no real need to hurry. After all, any such raid would need sanction from the very top. And it was Sunday and the 'very top' would be enjoying their weekend break. Yes, and a long weekend at that. It would be well into Monday or even the following day before the wheels began to turn. And even then, the way things were, they were bound to play it carefully, very carefully indeed. As the Americans would put it, Aung San was a 'very hot potato' and, before taking any action, those involved would try and pass the buck. Even as far as London if they could. And his eyes and ears at GHQ would keep him well informed. Yes, it was a nuisance but nothing more than that.

He had plenty of time to see that the cupboard was bare when the military police arrived.

However, even so, he was glad of U Saw's warning — and of his offer of Ma Kin too! Not that he had any illusions about U Saw. A man with ice-water in his veins. A man with a heart of stone — (if he had a heart at all, that was). If anyone needed watching it was him. There was an adding-machine behind everything he did. Always a balance to be drawn. Sooner or later, U Saw would present him with a bill. But then, that was to be expected. Burma was at a crossroads and the stakes were high. Everything now depended on how Aung San got on in London. If that went sour he would have to think again. It would be just as well to have U Saw on his side. Clearly U Saw thought so too.

But enough of that. Forewarned was forearmed. There was no point in wasting time or taking risks. So, Po Kyin gave the word. That way he could not lose. However, Po Kyin hadn't reckoned on a man like the APM.

★   ★   ★

When Washington told the APM what he'd overheard he let off steam, 'That double-dyed

257

devious sod,' he fumed. Then, simmering down; 'But at least it confirms that what he said was true.' Then the APM realized that, even as he spoke, Po Kyin would be shifting the arms and explosives and whatever else he had. Someone would have to get their skates on before he stripped the cupboard bare. The APM put his foot down and raced for GHQ.

But here he got a jolt. The duty officer listened but he didn't want to know. 'Sorry, old boy,' he said, 'the answer's no. A raid like that right now could start a civil war —'

'But that's what I'm trying to stop.'

'No, you've got it wrong. Not a war with Aung San's lot. I mean here at GHQ. He's got 'em all at daggers drawn. It's a problem for the big white chiefs, not an office boy like me.' A shrug. 'No way am I getting involved. My boat sails in two weeks' time. I intend to be on it. Our friend Po Kyin will have to wait.' Again he gave a shrug. 'Why not? Another day won't hurt. No way am I going to stick my neck out. It'll have to sweat till Monday.'

At this the APM blew his top. 'For Christ's sake, man what are you? A bloody clerk or what?'

He was answered with a grin. 'Well yes, if you put it like that. In fact, for the next two weeks I'm anything that'll see me on that boat.'

God, what a way to run an army! The APM overcame an urge to knock the grin off that smugly selfish face. It'd be satisfying but not worth the repercussions. 'You useless prick,' he snarled, 'I'll deal with it myself.'

The grin stayed put. 'Suit yourself, old man. It's your career, not mine.'

'Right,' the APM grabbed the phone. A crackle. The operator's voice. 'What unit please?'

'HQ, Military Police. And quick.'

And quick it was. Within seconds he was speaking to Captain 'Tiny' Moore, OC of the Rangoon Military Police.

'Tiny. APM. I'm at GHQ. I want every man you've got and I want 'em now. You too. This by . . . ' a glance at his watch ' . . . eighteen thirty hours. That'll give you almost twenty minutes. Arm your chaps with Stens. And you'd better bring your Brens as well.'

A whistle of surprise came down the line. 'Almost twenty minutes! You're not in any hurry then?' A chuckle. 'OK. Wilco. Out.' The phone banged down.

Back at GHQ the operator plugged in another outside call. Gave the crank a whirl. Again the crackle. Then from the other end:

'Brigadier Po Kyin . . . '

'Tiny' Moore flicked a switch. The alarm bells shrilled. Even as they rang the RSM came rushing in. Tiny met him with a grin. 'Christ, you were quick,' he said.

But the RSM was not alone in this. From everywhere around came the scurrying of movement, voices, engines starting up.

'APM's in a flap,' Moore told his RSM. 'Wants everyone at GHQ. Wants 'em now. Leave one bloke on the radio, another on the desk. Everyone else to go. Stens all round. Bring the Brens as well. Radio the mobiles they're to pick up the foot patrols and go direct. Everyone here to leave when ready. Make their own way there. OK?'

'OK.'

'And, Frank.'

'Sir?'

'Last man there's a cunt.'

A grin. 'I'll pass that on.' Then, barking out his orders, the RSM bustled off.

In even less than the twenty minutes the MP jeeps and trucks arrived at GHQ. Delayed by an urgent phone call, 'Tiny' Moore was last. His late arrival was greeted with a cheer. Tongue in cheek, the unit wag asked: 'Sergeant-Major, what is it we have to call the last man in?' A good natured laugh cracked out. 'Tiny' was liked and respected by his men.

The APM grunted his approval. Maybe, with the war now over, the army wasn't what it was. But at least 'Tiny' and his men were on the ball.

He himself had been on the ball as well. By now he had got the bit between his teeth, and to hell with the consequences if things went wrong. Scrounging a blackboard from the map room, he had sketched a plan of the roads approaching Po Kyin's house, and an outline of the house and garden. Chalked in were the red-capped men. 'Now, this is why you're here,' he said.

Washington had not been idle. He realized that a fugitive Po Kyin would go to earth. And that, in this case, he would almost certainly take up U Saw's offer of the hideaway by Inya lake. So he had searched out and tackled a pre-war friend in Civil Admin. Asked him if by any chance he knew where U Saw's mistress lived. It appeared that he did. 'Well, strictly *entre nous*, old boy, it's a posh little lakeside bungalow off Pagoda road. You can't miss it, it's opposite the Chinese temple.'

Then the friend had pursed his lips. 'Her name's Ma Kin. But watch your step, Georgie. She's quite a looker but underneath all that she's a real tough cookie. That applies to U Saw too.'

Washington was pleased. He knew the area well. He recalled it with affection. That part of the Inya lake had seen many a happy day. Many a happy night as well. So the Chinese temple had survived the war. That too was good.

By now the APM had briefed his force. His plan was simple, it had to be, for already it was dark and everything was happening in a rush. However, the moon would soon be up, the redcaps knew the ground and each man knew exactly what to do. Watches had been synchronized. Pistols, Stens and Brens all checked. The swivel scanning-lights tried out.

'Right, all aboard,' he said. The sea of redcoats eddied, moved apart. Voices. Bustle. Engines whined then roared. Vehicles rocked as the compound cleared in a haze of dust. Then, nose to tail, the raiding force set off.

Once clear of the Rangoon road, all lights were doused. Only the APM's lead jeep used its lights. (A cavalcade of approaching lights would never do.)

They had less than a mile to go. Then, one by one, the jeeps peeled off and came to a halt, facing in towards the house. The military police dismounted and spaced themselves between the gaps. The whole estate was being ringed by the silent red-capped men. Others, further back, set up 'hollow' roadblocks. These ensured that all vehicles, on whichever road they came, could be turned away or trapped where they were. Expertly, the Brens and scanning-lights were placed to cover all the entrances and exits. The ring had closed.

The APM and the searching party had dismounted by the gate. A great iron affair. Fortunately it was padlocked back against the wall and so presented no problem. A tarmac drive climbed into the night between an avenue of shrubs. For just a moment everything was dark, foreboding and as silent as the grave. It seemed that surprise was on the redcaps side. Then, from somewhere up ahead, there came a rumbling. A rumbling that grew louder all the time. Underfoot, the ground began to quake.

The APM raised a signal gun above his head. A click. A crack and a green-over-white signal climbed into the sky.

It was a signal to the jeeps. Instantly their headlights blazed, the scanning-lights came on, a brilliant ring of lights that danced the redcaps' shadows on the trees and lit up Po Kyin's house and grounds. Also lit up was a line of ten-ton Macs which were coasting down the drive. All nose to tail, all with their lights switched off.

Po Kyin's ears and eyes at GHQ had served him well but, thanks to the APM, not quite well enough.

Taken by surprise, the drivers of the Macs switched on. Their engines coughed and roared. Then, with there klaxons blaring, they made for the open gate.

'Christ!' Scattering, the APM and his men jumped clear. Just one of them stood firm — the RSM. Every inch the policeman, he was standing upright in the middle of the drive, his right hand raised at 'Stop'.

Instinctively, the driver of the leading Mac obeyed. Slamming on his brakes he locked his wheels and the gigantic truck came slithering down the drive, tyres smoking, rubbering two black streaks.

The RSM stood his ground. The truck came on. Then, barely inches from his boots, the Mac juddered to a halt. The RSM's hand came down.

Crash. The truck behind had rammed. Glass flew. There was a scream of riven steel. The engine bellowed as, still in gear, the wheels dug in. Short-circuited, the klaxon blared.

The RSM signalled with a thumb. Scared stiff, and with hands above their heads, the crew came tumbling out. After a a warning burst from the MP's Stens the others followed suit.

All but one, that was. The crew of the last in line rebelled. Wrenching at the wheel, the driver put on speed and veered across the drive.

Again the redcaps scattered as the truck came through. Then, with engine roaring, it went plunging, bounding, crushing through the grounds, mowing down trees and shrubs, shedding bits and pieces and flattening everything in its path. Once clear of the trees it made a beeline for a jeep, and smashed into it. A shower of sparks rose up. Redcaps started running for their lives. There came a scream of tortured metal as the jeep was crushed. *Whoof.* The jeep's petrol tank blew up in a searing sheet of flame, then another as its jerrican went up too. The redcaps' Stens rattled. Fences, trees and shrubs, even the grass, caught fire. The Mac was burning too. Undeterred, the driver aimed his vehicle at the road. There was a burst of tracer as the roadblock redcaps opened fire. Bullets spanged, punched holes, splintered woodwork, made a pattern of stars across the windscreen. Trailing a sparking red-black-yellow shroud, the Mac veered off in a crazy sweeping arc, bucking, crashing through everything in its way. The crew, bouncing about like marionettes, were aiming for the roadway further on. Tracer streaked from all four Brens. Bullets sparked and thudded but still the driver carried on. Only fifty yards to go. Then a flash paled out the moon. The Mac fragmented in an instant, smoke-rimmed ball of fire that seared and boiled and spread. A thunderclap split the night. The whole world shook. Then a choking tidal wave of black came billowing, blotting out all light. Debris, large and small, rained down. Bits of bodies too. Gasping and crouching beside their jeeps, the redcaps hugged the earth, the sound of the explosions ringing in their ears.

Then, very gradually, it grew quiet. A redcap's 'Jesus Christ!' came over the air. Then the rays of the rising moon began to probe. The blackness lightened, softened into cream, then went away. The rebel Mac had disappeared. From the crater came a thin white wisp that rose and thinned and gossamered away.

The signal gun cracked again. The ring of red-capped men closed in. Dazed and shaken, the crews of the Macs gave up and the searching and the questioning began.

The haul was greater than the APM expected. Grimly content, he said: 'Well that's one insurrection that won't take place.' There was a fly in the ointment though. But then, as the APM consoled himself, there always was. Po Kyin had got away. Had left just before the net closed in. Had left, according to his men, to mastermind arrangements at the other end. Where that 'other end' could be they either didn't know or, much more likely, didn't care to tell. He intended to tell Washington that his quarry had got away. But he discovered that he couldn't. Washington was missing too.

18

Standing by the gate, Po Kyin was feeling pleased. True, the telephone call from GHQ had been a shock. But, by then, the move was under way. The call had merely served to speed things up. The men had responded well. When he had left to come on here they had almost finished loading. They would now be on their way and here, at the alternative base, everything was ready to take the Macs. The whole affair had gone so smoothly with scarcely a ripple on the way. The APM and his merry men would draw a blank. It would then be a case of apologies all round and the APM would bite the dust. Po Kyin preened himself. No two ways about it, planning paid. Some would call it luck. Well, admittedly Lady Luck had smiled, smiled twice in fact. First with U Saw's warning and then with the call from GHQ. But luck, real luck, that was, usually required a push. A push that proved that the harder one worked, the luckier one became. What good would the warnings have been without the previous planning? No, good fortune did not depend on luck alone.

Expectantly, he peered along the road. The

moon was up and, although they would be travelling without their lights, the Macs should be in sight. But no, there was nothing, no sound or sight of movement. Suddenly, he felt a stirring of unease. Then, from a long way off, he caught the sound of small-arms fire. Or was it his imagination? He strained to hear. No, it was not his imagination. What was more, it was coming from the direction of the house. Ice-cold fingers clutched his gut. This was trouble! Hampered by his leg, he climbed on to the jeep. He sucked in a breath. It was trouble right enough. Away in the distance he could see a ring of tiny lights and they were surrounding his house. From them came little streaks of red and waving beams of light. At that distance and against the backdrop of the night, the scene was like a jewel, scintillating like a brilliant diamond brooch. Something really lovely. Angrily he pushed the fantasy from his mind. Even as he did, a flash lit up the sky. A fireball seethed and boiled and rose into the air. The sound of the explosion followed and a tremor shook the jeep.

Po Kyin knew a moment of despair. This spelt disaster utter and complete disaster. The APM had beaten him to the punch. He was puzzled. How could he have got there in the time?

What now? What now indeed! One thing was for sure. Aung San's enemies at GHQ would be triumphant. They would make a song and dance, milk it to the full. They would have him arrested, put on show. Use the discovery of the arms as a stick to beat Aung San. They would lose no time. Any moment now they would be working on his men. Sooner or later one of them would break, would betray him and betray the whereabouts of the second base. Right now they would expect to find him when they searched the house. They would expect to catch him with the arms, red-handed. Any moment now they would discover he was missing and cast a net across Rangoon. They would block all the roads, check his usual haunts and put pressure on his friends. There was no alternative, he would have to disappear, and quickly too. But disappear to where? Well, that was not a problem. It would have to be U Saw's love-nest by the lake. Ma Kin would be expecting him. And that was good. He knew Ma Kin of old. Had known her way back in her student days. He would be safe enough with her.

Po Kyin offered up a prayer: 'Thank God for Ma Kin and her haven by the lake. Thank God for U Saw too.'

Now, how best to get to Ma Kin's house?

He would have liked to have gone direct. But now, that would mean skirting Golden Valley and, almost certainly, tangling with the police. It would be better to take a long sweep round. True, that would keep him on the road for much longer, but it was the better of two evils. But either way, the sooner he was underneath her roof the better. He made up his mind. Minutes later he was on the main Prome road, driving very carefully so as not to attract the attention of the military police patrols. He had three or four miles to go. He kept a watchful eye as the road unwound.

Soon, over to the left, he could see the residence of Dorman-Smith, the Governor. It was floodlit, with men on guard. A lazy Union Flag hung from the mast. Now, approaching on the right, he could see the Pegu club. As usual it was ablaze with light but, significantly, there was no sign of the redcaps normally there on duty. Then came a row of largish houses, well spaced out. He passed all safely. Now GHQ came in sight — the lions' den! There were flags and signs of every hue and Gurkha sentries at the gates. Then, with GHQ now behind, the right fork was coming up. A flash of moonlit water through the trees indicated the Inya lake. Still there was no sign of any roadside checks or military police patrols, in fact, no MPs at all.

Then he turned right and right again on to the long straight Pagoda road and still not a thing was in sight. He had an urge to put on speed. But no, that would be tempting fate. Over to the left and picked out by the moon, was the Chinese temple. Good, he was almost there. Now there was just the narrow turning to the right. The jeep came round. Still nothing seemed untoward and there were just a hundred yards to go. The jeep coasted to a halt. Po Kyin whinnied with relief. He'd made it. Then his stomach lurched. Picked out in his lights stood a jeep. An empty jeep — an MP jeep at that — was parked beside the house. The driver had dismounted and, standing in the porch, was talking to Ma Kin. The driver turned. Again Po Kyin whinnied with relief. It was not a redcap, it was his old friend and comrade from the past, Captain Georgie Washington. The old friend and comrade who'd been enquiring from U Saw about his pre-war life. Alarm bells sounded in his head. What the hell had his pre-war life to do with Washington. Could be something quite innocuous of course. Something to do with the Toungoo trial? It would be nothing to do with the raid, of course, or the MPs would be here in force. But, in that case, why all this right now? And much more to the point, what was Washington doing here?

Could be that he and U Saw and Ma Kin were friends? That could well be. Washington had lived for many years in Burma. But no. Something told him it was something far more sinister than that. He switched off his lights, unbuttoned the holster on his belt and joined Ma Kin and Washington on the porch. Washington did not seem overjoyed to see him!

Smiling, Po Kyin slapped Washington on the back. 'Why Georgie, what a surprise,' he said. It certainly was! 'You must come in.' Closely followed by Ma Kin, he pressed Washington through the door.

Once inside, Ma Kin unbuckled Po Kyin's webbing belt and hung it, together with the holster, on a hook. With a smile she took Washington's belt and holster too. In perfect English, she said: 'Welcome to my humble home.' Then, with a gesture to a curtain made of beads, she led them through.

So much for a *humble* home, Washington was thinking. It was anything but that and that applied to Ma Kin too. As his friend at GHQ had warned, she was a good-looker and a real tough cookie too.

'Please make yourselves at home,' she said, 'I will get you both a drink.' She gave a hard professional smile. 'Two Scotch and sodas.' It was a statement, not a query. The beaded curtain swished and she was gone.

Po Kyin had seated himself, sideways, behind a desk, resting his gammy leg on a partly opened drawer. As invited, he had made himself at home. Washington too sat down, but upright on a high-backed chair.

A box of cigarettes was on the desk. Po Kyin flipped it open with his hook. A smile. 'Smoke?' he asked.

'No.'

A wary look came over Po Kyin's face. He shrugged. Again using his hook, Po Kyin helped himself. It was most expertly done. But then he had trouble with his matches. Fumbling several times, he looked across expectantly.

He was answered by a stony face. Washington made no attempt to help.

Po Kyin pursed his lips. He gave another shrug. Then, very neatly, he lit his cigarette, waved out the match and placed it carefully on a tray. Leaning back, he took a long deep pull, then let the smoke dribble from his mouth, all the time eyeing Washington through the smoke. The cigarette glowed again. Another trickle of smoke issued from his mouth. Still he stared steadily at Washington.

'Something's troubling you, Georgie.' Like Ma Kin a minute or two ago, it was a

274

statement, not a query.

'Several things are troubling me, Po Kyin,' answered Washington coldly.

'To do with the Toungoo trial?'

'Partly. But there's more to it than that.'

'Oh?'

Just then the curtains swished and Ma Kin came in with a tray. She placed it on the desk. On it was a bottle of Johnny Walker, a syphon, two crystal tumblers and a small white cardboard box.

Ma Kin poured two measures. Big ones. She gave one to Po Kyin, neat. She turned to Washington.

'Soda?'

A nod. 'A splash.'

'Say when.' The soda syphon fizzed.

'When.'

She handed him the glass. Again came the professional smile. Then, to Po Kyin: 'I'll leave you two alone. I'll leave the bottle too. If you want anything else, just call.' Once more the curtain swished.

Po Kyin raised his glass and, with a smile, said 'Down the hatch.'

Washington nursed his glass and said nothing.

Po Kyin's glass banged down. He sat up straight. When he spoke his voice was harsh. 'Right, Washington. Whatever's on your mind, let's have it.'

Washington opened fire. 'For starters, your evidence is crucifying Sergeant Stevens.'

Po Kyin nodded. 'So that's it.' Then, curtly: 'And so it should.'

A nod came back. 'On the surface, yes. But Roberts, the defending officer, has been digging. Digging deep.'

'Bully for Captain Roberts,' said Po Kyin drily.

'Yes, you could say that. Now let me tell you what he found.'

Po Kyin laughed. 'Why not, my friend?' But there was precious little humour in the laugh.

'In your evidence you said, amongst other things, that you'd never met Aung San till forty-four. You also said that you knew no Japanese.'

'So?'

'So. Roberts has found a witness who gives the lie to that. A witness with a snap of you hobnobbing with Aung San. This was just before the war. The witness maintains that before the war you went to Japan to learn the language. That you stayed there for a year.'

Po Kyin's head came up. 'Marie Gomez,' he said, almost in a whisper.

'Yes, Marie Gomez. What's more, she says that when you were hiding in Toungoo you were flush with money. Silver money. That you boasted that you had a silver mine in the Toungoo hills.'

'Of course I had. Funds dropped to me by Delhi.' Po Kyin looked amused.

'Oh, and what about not knowing your friend Aung San. What about not knowing any Japanese?'

'So, I gilded the lily,' answered Po Kyin, still amused. 'I shot a line, as the RAF would say. This was mainly to enhance my standing with the British. No harm in that. At least not as far as Sergeant Stevens is concerned.'

'But that's only the start. There's the story you told of seeing Stevens stealing the silver from the dump. That story doesn't fit. There are five witnesses who swear that Stevens wasn't there. That he couldn't possibly have been there.'

'Diehard Japanese officers,' Po Kyin said contemptuously. 'Burmese peasants on the make. Coming from them, what sort of evidence is that?'

'But it isn't only that. There is Stevens's evidence of seeing the man who betrayed us. Or at least, seeing his hand. The man who must also have taken the silver. A man who spoke good Japanese but with a Burmese accent. A man who, like Aung San, hated British rule — '

Po Kyin butted in, saying with a sneer: 'Oh

spare me the poppycock of that reflection in the fanlight. Believe that and you'll believe anything, anything at all.'

Washington ignored the interruption. ' . . . A man who had a forefinger missing from his hand. His right hand.'

'As I said, poppycock.' A pause. 'What exactly are you driving at?'

'I'll tell you what I'm driving at, Po Kyin. It's a description that fits you, fits you like a glove. Even to the mutilated hand.'

'Me!' Po Kyin's look was one of outrage. The look gave way to a rueful smile. Sadly, Po Kyin raised his hook. 'Stevens saw, or rather he said he saw, a missing finger, not a missing arm.' Then, more in sorrow than in anger, he went on: 'Georgie, do I have to defend myself against a charge like this?' He shook his head. 'Do you really think that I, I of all people betrayed you and the group to the Japanese?' He shook his head again, saying, 'Whatever gave you that idea?'

It was said with such a depth of feeling that Washington began to have doubts. But he pushed them aside. Extracting the snap of Po Kyin holding up his hands he flipped it across the desk.

'That,' he spat.

Po Kyin took the snap. He studied it closely, taking his time. 'Well, well,' he said.

'Caught with my trousers down.' He picked the snap up with his hook. 'Has the court seen this?' he asked.

'Not yet.'

'Good. What their eyes don't see their hearts won't grieve at.' With that, Po Kyin tore the snap across and put the pieces in his pocket.

'No point in that, Po Kyin. Marie Gomez had a snap of you saluting General Slim. It clearly shows your hand. By now Roberts will have shown it to the court.'

Po Kyin's voice was soft. 'So, the delectable Marie Gomez has dropped me in it. But then of course she didn't know. Why should she? Why should anyone have given it a second thought.' Again the lopsided grin. Sadly he shook his head. 'That bloody fanlight, that bloody, bloody fanlight.'

Washington felt detached. Not, for the moment, angry, just perplexed. His face was full of hurt. 'Why?' he asked almost in a whisper. 'Why?'

For what seemed an age, Po Kyin stared across the desk. Stared through Washington as if he wasn't there. The only sound was the ticking of a clock.

'Why?' Now that was quite a question. Remote, without seeing, without hearing, Po Kyin went back to the past. Events appeared like slides projected on a screen.

Click-clack: The last meeting with the Thirty Comrades. The bowl in the centre of the room. The oath. Each man slitting a finger and swearing allegiance in a mixture of their blood. The meeting breaking up and going their separate ways. The Comrades departing for Japan. He, on Aung San's orders, had gone off to join the Burma Rifles as an undercover man, a Burmese 'Trojan Horse'. He had sworn, no matter what, to undermine the British from within.

Click-clack: Click-clack: Click-clack. Slide after slide that were the memories of the past four years.

Click-clack: The war. Burma was being raked from end to end. Then came the long retreat, blood, sweat, appalling thirst, and tears. Refugees, in tens of thousands, were dying on the way. Dying from starvation and disease, from man's inhumanity to man. Then came the Division breaking up, crawling into India, racked with malaria, dressed in rags, but exultant that, with the humbling of the British, an independent Burma was in sight.

Click-clack: The British were fighting back. He had joined an infiltration group so that he could sabotage their work. There had been months of training, then months out of action with a badly damaged hand. That mine, that bloody, bloody mine. There had been no news but many disturbing rumours about Aung San's BNA.

Click-clack: Toungoo from the air, with the railway yards aflame. Parachuting. Landing in the hills. Meeting the legendary Major Willis and Washington, his right-hand man. He had felt an instant respect and liking for them both. Being taken to the dump. Knowing that, at long, long last, he could strike a devastating blow for Burma. He had had to stifle all his scruples to carry out his oath.

Click-clack: Returning to the dump. Secreting the silver somewhere else, as insurance against a future rainy day. Setting up the scene for his 'escaping', naked, from the Burmese woman's bed. Walking to Toungoo, arriving late at night, meeting Major Mutaguchi. Pointing out the three locations on the map; this with his mutilated hand. That bloody, bloody hand: Jeeping through the night with a Japanese lieutenant, arriving at BNA HQ.

Click Clack: The reunion with Aung San. Being briefed. The shock of learning that the BNA was changing sides. Being sick at heart at what he'd done. Aung San's 'Forget it. Charge it against the cause, my friend.'

Click-clack: Becoming Aung San's go-between.

Fighting as an officer of the BNA. Using the British as, previously, they had used the Japanese. He endeavouring to offset with bravery what he had done to Major Willis and his men. An MC. A bar to it, then a DSO. The DSO pinned on by General Slim himself. Being photographed saluting General Slim. (Again that hand, that bloody, bloody hand!)

Click-clack: The final mission against a diehard group of Japanese. The L5 ambushed as it was coming in to land. Tracer streaking past, then ripping through the plane. A squelching impact as a leg shattered. Blood along the perspex. An eyeball hanging down. The L5 on fire, careering through the trees, sounding like a thousand milk churns clattering. Turning over in the air. Agony from just below a knee. A bumping, drawn-out, crunching grind. Screams of pain and fear. A shattering crash. A flash of light. Then nothing.

Click-clack: Pain. Discomfort. Weeks in bed. Plaudits from both the comrades and the British. A visit from Mountbatten. A visit from Aung San.

Click-clack: His injuries mending fast. A hook. An artificial leg. A patch across an eye. More promotion and another gong.

Click-clack: Politics. Becoming Aung San's right-hand man. As a national hero, pushing

Aung San's case at GHQ. Covering up the Toungoo gaffe by fending off all whispers. Scotching the rumours by making a scapegoat of an Anglo-Burman sergeant. And why not? The Anglos, to a man, were against an independent Burma.

And now? And now, coping with disaster: the betrayal of the arms dump, the insurrection. The exposure of the ill-timed betrayal of Major Willis and his group.

★ ★ ★

All this, and more, was the answer to Washington's plaintive 'Why?' But would Washington understand? The answer to that was no. Only if England herself was subjugated and under foreign rule would Washington understand.

'Georgie, you ask me 'Why?'.' he said. 'It's a long story but the answer is very simple. Perhaps too simple. It's simply because we, like you, like all the English, cherish our freedom above all else.'

'And that justifies your betrayal of your British and Karenni friends and comrades?'

Po Kyin shook his head. 'The British and Karenni are our enemies, not our friends. We, the Thirty Comrades, took a solemn oath. Sealed it with our blood. We swore that come what may, we would put an end to British rule. To any foreign rule. Once we are free we will welcome you as friends. Until then, you will remain our enemies.'

For what seemed an age they were silent, eye to eye. Once more the only sound was the ticking of the clock.

Then Washington heaved himself to his feet. He pushed through the beads and retrieved his belt and holster from the hook outside. The curtain swished again. Washington had drawn his .38 and was aiming it across the desk.

Seemingly unconcerned, Po Kyin hadn't moved. Ignoring the menace of the gun, he poured himself a drink. Making a gesture with the bottle, he asked: 'And you?'

With a snort, Washington shook his head.

With a shrug, Po Kyin took a sip. 'Well, Georgie, where do we go from here?' he asked. Thoroughly relaxed, he could have been asking about the weather.

'I know where you're going,' said Washington harshly. 'I too took an oath.'

Po Kyin raised his eyebrows. 'Oh?'

The pistol was aimed at Po Kyin's face. 'After what happened in Toungoo, I swore to Sergeant Stevens that the three of you would swing,'

'The three of us?' Po Kyin looked puzzled.

Three flicks of the gun. 'Stevens, Mutagu-chi and Ekesta. But of course it wasn't that poor sod Stevens, it was you.'

Po Kyin's lips formed the makings of a smile. 'So you intend to turn me in?'

Washington's face was grim. 'No. Your friends at GHQ would probably get you off. Turn a blind eye like they did about the headman Aung San murdered.'

'So you don't propose to turn me in?' Amusement still played on Po Kyin's face.

'No. I intend to do the job myself. Even up the score for Gordon Willis and his men.'

'And for what the Japanese did to you, perhaps?'

Washington bared his teeth. 'Yes, that too.'

'All very melodramatic Georgie?' A grin. 'Like a second-feature film.'

'Is it? I don't think Willis would agree with you on that.' Washington cocked the pistol with a thumb. His hand was steady.

Po Kyin nodded towards the gun. 'That'll make you a murderer too,' he said.

'No. An executioner, not a murderer.'

Po Kyin's good hand flicked the air. 'That's what Aung San said about the headman.' Another flick. 'What is it, Georgie? One law for an Englishman but another for Aung San?'

It was the moment of truth. Washington's

285

finger tightened on the trigger. So it was justice at last. This was the man who had caused the death of Gordon Willis and his men. Had caused the agony, yes and the indignity, of his treatment by the Japs. And, on top of that, had engineered an innocent man being blamed. But even so, could he shoot him, like this, across a desk? Yes, he could. 'Die you sod,' he snarled and pulled the trigger.

A metallic click. He pulled again. Another click.

Po Kyin was smiling. He hadn't turned a hair. 'When I said 'all very melodramatic', Georgie, I meant just that.' Saying which, he tapped the little cardboard box that Ma Kin had brought in on the tray. Six bullets tumbled out. Po Kyin explained, 'Just a little precaution that Ma Kin took on my behalf.'

Behind him, Washington heard the curtain swish. Half-turning, he saw that Ma Kin was in the room. She had a pistol in her hands, presumably Po Kyin's. She looked most capable of using it too. However, she handed it across the desk.

Taking it, Po Kyin said: 'Pour Georgie here a drink. One for me as well. And, Georgie, put that useless gun of yours away. And sit, man, sit.' His gun hand was steady too.

Both Ma Kin and Washington complied.

Then once more the curtain swished.

For a while the two men sat in silence. Then in a wry but surprisingly friendly way, Po Kyin said: 'I suppose that your pulling the trigger like that gives me the right to do the same?'

Suddenly, Washington was tired. 'Killing' a man like that had drained him. His body sagged. Somehow he no longer cared what happened. 'Do what you like,' he said. 'I'm not that fussed.' Then, with an effort at a sneer: 'After all you've done, what's one more?' Then he rallied. 'But at least I've put an end to your insurrection. Killing me won't alter that.'

Po Kyin set his teeth. 'True, true,' he said.

Another lengthy silence ensued, with Washington on the verge of sleep and Po Kyin deep in thought.

Then Po Kyin sat up straight. 'Georgie,' he said, 'let's get down to cases.'

Washington forced up heavy lids. 'Well?'

'I've got to disappear. Till Aung San gets back, that is. Till all this fuss dies down. In forty-eight hours I could be safely tucked away. There's just one snag though.' He gave a quizzical look. 'And that, my friend, is you.'

Almost indifferently Washington murmured 'So?'

'You, given half a chance, could queer the pitch.'

Washington nodded.

Po Kyin raised his gun. 'The most sensible thing for me to do is to kill you here and now. As you yourself said, 'What's one more?',' A friendly grin. 'Rather tactless, I thought. But believe me, Georgie, that would go against the grain.'

'Oh? Developing a conscience, Po Kyin? Getting soft?'

'A bit unfair. But yes, you could say that.' A pause. 'There is another option. Something that would be entirely up to you.'

'And that is?'

'You stay on here for the next two days and nights.' Po Kyin glanced towards the curtain. 'Ma Kin would look after you,' he grinned, 'especially in the nights. In fact I'm proposing that you promise, hand on heart, officer and gent and all that, to give me the forty-eight hours I need. After the way you pulled that trigger, I think you owe me that.' Po Kyin gestured with the gun. 'How does that solution strike you?'

Washington came to life. 'Bollocks to that.' He spat.

'Georgie, you're certainly a glutton for punishment,' said Po Kyin sadly. He gave a long appraisal. Then: 'Well perhaps that's just as well. It would be a lot to ask. However, there is a third solution, a compromise. And why not?' He smiled, 'You British are very good at that.'

'And what sort of compromise is that?'

'Quite simple. In fact I should have thought of it before. It'll be a bit embarrassing for you I'm afraid but as I said, quite simple. Over there, in the corner, U Saw has a safe. By the look of it, it weighs a ton. I'm going to chain you to it for the next two days.' A pause for thought. 'No, I'll make that three days. The way things are I'd better, if you'll excuse the pun, play safe. Ma Kin will make you as comfortable as she can.'

Then the good-natured banter disappeared. Po Kyin's face and voice were grim. 'A warning Washington. Don't try any tricks. Ma Kin will have a gun. She knows how to use it, too. With things like that she's as tough as any man.' Even more grimly: 'She knows what'll happen to her if things go wrong. Do I make that clear?'

Washington nodded.

'Good.' The smile was back. 'One final thing, Georgie. A request. When Ma Kin lets you go remember you are an officer and a gent. Don't take it out on her in any way.

She's only doing what she's been told. OK?'
'OK.'
'Good.' Po Kyin drained his glass. 'Ma Kin,' he called.
The beaded curtain swished.

19

Very carefully, as if they would suddenly fly away, Colonel Perceval laid the snapshots on the desk. Then, exchanging glances with the JAG, he blew his cheeks.

Roberts was amused. The Walrus and the Carpenter to the life, he thought.

'These put a new complexion on the case,' the colonel said.

The JAG nodded his agreement. But he was thinking that 'a new complexion' must be the understatement of the year. These photographs were dynamite. If, or rather when, the news got out it would blow the Aung San controversy sky high. Reverberate across the world to London. But that wasn't all. It would affect the JAG's leave as well. God, he thought, what a time to choose. The trial, to use the current American jargon, was almost buttoned up. At the most it would have taken just a day to dot the i's and cross the t's. Then it would have been the joy of 'Kashmir, here I come'.

Not now, the JAG thought sourly, not with this particular cat amongst the pigeons. He would now be lucky if he got any leave at all.

Disaster. All was lost. Damn. Damn. Damn.

But just a moment. Perhaps all was not lost. Surely Stevens, a self-confessed renegade, was not worth all the trouble, let alone the inconvenience that this would bring? So why not let sleeping dogs lie? Why not rule that the snaps were inadmissible and then ensure that they were 'lost'? After all, it would be for the greater good of all concerned. Well, nearly all. There could be no doubts on that. What was more, a whisper in a certain very important ear would rebound to his advantage later on. And the accused? Well, as things were, he stood an even chance of getting off. A consummation now devoutly to be wished! This verdict would get everyone off the hook. And if he was proven guilty? Then he would advise the defence to throw themselves on the mercy of the court. Plead his youth and the extenuating circumstances. The accused could then possibly, yes, quite possibly, receive a lighter sentence. And if not? Well, it was all for the greater good. However, there was a fly in the ointment: Captain Roberts. The chance of his not using the photographs was slim. He had already shown what an awkward customer he could be. Mentally, the JAG crossed his fingers. He would meet that if and when he had to.

He picked up the snapshots, placed them

in a folder and put the folder in his case.

'It is my submission, Colonel, that, at this late stage, the photographs are not admissible in evidence and should not be placed before the court. I will need to get a ruling from my legal lords and masters. In the meantime I strongly advise that the trial be adjourned until further notice. That in the interim, the accused be held in custody. This until a ruling has been made.'

Again Colonel Perceval blew his cheeks. No fool, he could read between the lines. He too was well aware that the photographs spelled trouble. That a 'wrong' decision could jeopardize his future. But then he felt relief. Why should he himself make any such decision? This was strictly a legal matter. This was why the JAG was here. A sense of relief flooded into him. All he, Colonel Perceval, had to do was pass the buck. Drop the whole thing in the Judge Advocate General's lap.

'That sounds eminently reasonable to me,' he said. Then, with an ingratiating smile, he turned to Roberts. 'And I trust that, as defending officer, Roberts, you'll go along with this.'

The lawyer caught the glint in Roberts's eye. He held his breath and girded his loins for battle. Come what may, those photographs must not be put before the court.

But, to the JAG's surprise, Roberts 'went along'. Was all sweet reason.

'If a legality is involved, Colonel, who am I to quibble,' Roberts said. 'But why adjourn the trial? I am sure of a not guilty verdict, with or without the snaps.' Holding up his hands, he went on: 'So why adjourn? If we do, the case will just go on and on for months with Stevens still in goal. So why not carry on?'

The JAG could hardly believe his ears. What a difference from the man's attitude earlier on. Perhaps Roberts too had an axe to grind? Then the penny dropped. Of course, it had to do with his age and service group. If the case dragged on he could, in fact almost certainly would, be kept back beyond his time. Yes, that was it. It only went to show that, whatever his protestations, each man had his price.

Overjoyed, the JAG rubbed his hands. 'In that case, Colonel, there is no problem. If I may say so Captain Roberts has made a very wise decision. He is absolutely right. The sooner this unfortunate case is settled the better for all concerned.' He gave a knowing smile. 'Present company not excepted.' He gathered up his files and locked them in his case. Rising, he put his cap on very straight. 'Till Tuesday morning then,' he said.

Roberts lost no time in breaking the good news. Sitting in his jeep they were face to face. Stevens's hands were trembling. Suddenly, tears were trickling and the snaps began to blur. For quite some time he couldn't trust his voice and when at last he spoke, his voice was trembling too.

'These prove that everything I said was true.'

Roberts gave a nod. 'They do indeed,' he said.

'They prove that the brigadier's a liar.' Anger replaced the wonder. Now, Stevens's voice was shrill. 'The bastard tried to get me hanged for something he did himself!'

'He did indeed,' said Roberts.

Stevens shook his head in disbelief. Again the anger surfaced. Almost beside himself with rage, he began pacing to and fro. Words were spilling out. 'The shit. The shit. The dirty rotten shit . . . ' Every now and then he paused and spat. Then the diatribe went on: 'The shit. The despicable, dirty, lousy, one-eyed shit . . . ' He kicked a stone and it clanged against the jeep. Roberts, feigning alarm, cowered in his seat and raised his hands to guard his head. Stevens glared. Then, realizing that the other man was clowning, he gave a rueful grin and began to simmer down.

'What happens now?' he asked.

Roberts proffered him a smoke. 'By tiffin-time on Tuesday, you'll be free.' He smiled.

Stevens waved the cigarette case away. 'And Brigadier Po Kyin?'

Roberts told him of Washington's going to Rangoon, and went on to say: 'On Tuesday Po Kyin'll be well and truly up the creek. Under close arrest. If all goes well, that is.'

Stevens stiffened. 'All goes well? What do you mean by that?'

'He has friends in very high places. They'll do everything they can to cover up.'

'Not much joy for them in that, surely? Not after you've produced these snaps in court. Not when the court has compared them with the things he said?'

'I won't be producing the snaps in court.'

'You won't?' Stevens looked puzzled.

Roberts told him of the JAG's decision. Then, seeing the alarm on Stevens's face, he said: 'Not to worry. There is more than one way of skinning a cat. The JAG took it for granted that the snaps he's taken are the only ones. In fact I got a friend in Photo-Rec to run me off some copies. Those you've got there are two of them. What's more, he knows nothing about Washington's visit to Rangoon. Washington is going to stir things up.'

Roberts switched the engine into life. 'Right now I'm going to run you home. With a bit of luck Angie and your dad will be back from Mandalay.'

They set off in the jeep.

'And the copies. The other snaps?'

Roberts grinned. 'I'm going to deliver a set to each member of the court.' He slapped Stevens on the knee. 'Once they've had a dekko you've no need to worry about their verdict.'

'And the brigadier? That lying shit, Po Kyin?'

'We'll have to wait and see. Wait till Washington gets back here. But, in any case, not to worry. I've got a set for Sir Dorman Smith, the Governor, and another for the C.-in-C. They both hate Aung San's guts.' He laughed. 'Let Po Kyin wriggle out of that.' He laughed again. 'Poor old Perce'll wet his pants.'

By now they had arrived at Station Road. The Stevens's house turned out to be empty. From a neighbour they learned that Angie and her father would not be back till Tuesday.

Disappointed, Stevens pulled a face. 'That means a dreary Monday on my own,' he said.

'Me too.' Then Roberts had a thought. 'I

tell you what. Why don't we go along to Thandaung and get Thein Maung, the muleteer, to take us to the dump. See what Po Kyin said you'd robbed.' He laughed. 'Who knows. With a bit of luck we could find a bag of silver.'

Stevens's face lit up. 'Yes, why not.' He too gave a laugh. 'It'll be finders keepers. We'll go fifty-fifty on anything we find. Don't worry about bringing anything to eat. I'll lay on some Burmese grub. OK?'

'OK. See you tomorrow then. O nine-thirty on the dot.'

A wave and Roberts was on his way, the tyres screaming with the tightness of his turn.

Stevens watched him go. He thought of Po Kyin. The JAG. The colonel. Then he thought of Captain Roberts. Takes all sorts to make a world, he thought.

20

The APM took stock. Arms and ammunition by the ton but no Po Kyin.

What now? Every senior officer he had tried to reach was 'not at home'. Clearly, self-preservation was the order of the day. But not with the APM. He had the bit between his teeth. He was well aware that there would be trouble over this, big trouble. But someone had to act and fast at that. And if that someone had to be the APM, then so be it.

The APM had no time for Aung San or any of his mob. They were murderers and traitors to a man. If it were left to him, the sooner they were put against a wall the better. It was time that someone showed them who was boss.

So the APM cast a net and things began to hum. The BIC reported that a man answering Po Kyin's description had been sighted in the docks. Reinforced by the RAF and Navy police, the APM sealed them off. Now his men were searching the area block by block.

The BIC, both in uniform and civilian clothes, were helping too. Through their grapevine they had issued a description and made it known that there would be cash for information leading to the brigadier's arrest. The APM was confident he'd soon have him in the bag for, even in Rangoon, a man with injuries such as his was rare. Not only that: the city teemed with Indians and Chinese, people who had a virulent dislike of all Burmese and who, with or without cash reward, would be glad to turn him in.

Soon, every exit from Rangoon was sealed, with 'fallback' roadblocks further out. Every ship and railway train was being searched. everything on wheels that left Rangoon was checked and checked again.

Of course there was always the chance that he would try and slink away on foot. Well, let him try. BIC and military police patrols were everywhere and as someone pointed out, 'On foot', singular, was right!

So, in the biggest manhunt since the search for 'Colonel' Baker and his men, the night wore on.[1]

★   ★   ★

It was now an hour past dawn. Lieutenant Ne Win of the BIC drew up by the MP jeep. He

---

[1] See 'Colonel Baker's Dozen' — Robert Hale.

could see that a wheel had dropped into a drain. A wing was crushed, the nearside headlight had a squint and oil was pouring from the sump. Standing by was the gigantic MP captain, 'Tiny' Moore, and his red-capped MP driver.

'Morning, Tiny. Need any help?' called the lieutenant,

The captain turned and raised his eyes to heaven. 'Thanks,' he said. 'I'd appreciate a lift. How far are you going?'

'Toungoo.' The lieutenant gave a friendly smile. 'That far enough?'

'More than enough. I've got a roadblock at the Pegu fork. Can you drop me there?'

'I most certainly can. Jump in.'

Whilst 'Tiny' was giving instructions to his driver, Ne Win checked his jerricans and tightened the trailer cover. He had over 200 miles to go and the battle-scarred road was rough. Then, orders having been given, the captain jumped aboard and the jeep moved off.

'Tiny' jerked a thumb towards the trailer. 'So you're not on the search,' he said.

'No, I got away just in time. I'm off on leave. A fortnight in Toungoo. My family lives there.'

'Lucky old you.'

'Yes, you could say that. Long time no see.

But about the search — any news of Po Kyin yet?'

'No. But I guess he's hiding somewhere in Rangoon. Waiting for things to quieten down. For my money, he'll probably try and get away by ship.'

'Think so?' Ne Win shook his head. 'Not Po Kyin. My bet is that he'll make for Siam and get across the border. Get to Toungoo, then up the Mawchi road. Once he's across the Salween he'll be home and dry.' Then, reflectively: 'He could make for Mandalay, of course, and make his way to China.' He laughed. 'I hope it's Siam. I'll keep my eyes peeled. Might spot him going through Toungoo. There's a reward I hear. Come in very useful on my leave.'

By now Ne Win was weaving through the traffic and, knowing that he was safe from MP checks, he put on speed.

The road unwound with tracts of nothingness on either side. Then, over to the right, was Mingaladon airfield with Daks and L5s buzzing about like flies. Then they passed a rubber plantation, a dump of wrecked and rusting trucks and a group of burned-out tanks. Then came a few more miles of nothing. Then they came upon a line of military and civilian vehicles, nose to tail.

A redcap directed them to join the queue

but, recognizing his CO, the MP waved them on.

'Morning, Taff,' Ne Win gave a smiling greeting. He was answered with a 'Sir', and then they were sweeping along the line, covering the stationary vehicles with their dust. The line seemed endless. Then came a sudden bend, a barrier across the road and a rash of red-topped caps.

Ne Win coasted to a halt and 'Tiny' Moore got out. 'Thanks a lot,' he said. 'Anything I can do for you, just let me know.'

'A pleasure.' Ne Win glanced at the queue behind. 'You've done me a favour too.'

'Tiny' slapped the bonnet. 'OK.' He smiled. 'Have a good leave and remember to keep your eyes peeled. You never know. You might be right about Siam.'

Smiling, Ne Win eased the jeep and trailer through the gap. Once clear, he put his foot down and the jeep began gobbling up the miles.

He passed a reservoir with a pipeline four feet thick, then came a largish village, then another and yet another. Then, stretching way ahead, was just miles and miles of nothing. He took a few more miles at speed. Then Ne Win brought the jeep and trailer to a halt. He dismounted, unzipped his fly and, whilst scouring the landscape, he pissed against a wheel. There was nothing all around. And beyond that nothing, rose the blue-green Pegu range.

Zipping up, he took a last look round. Still there was no sign of life, no sound. He peeled the cover from the trailer. 'Brigadier, it's safe to come out now,' he said.

21

As promised, Roberts arrived at 09.30. on the dot. It was just another Burmese morning but today there was a magic in the air. By now the sun was riding high in a deep-blue, cloudless sky. His cap was on the seat and the morning breeze was ruffling through his hair. Cool and caressing, it rustled through the trees, picked up bursts of chatter, billowed soft green waves across the fields and teased the surface of the lake. Already, people were going about their everyday affairs. Children were scuffling at their play and, with flowers in their jet-black hair, girls were giving him the eye. Roberts stretched full length and a rich contentment welled up in him. At times like this, life could be very, very good.

Smiled at by the latest passer-by, he gave a toot.

Stevens bustled out. He too sensed the magic of the day. But then, why not? It had been wonderful to sleep at home after all those months in gaol. Wonderful to fear the trial no longer. Above all, it was wonderful to be free.

He jumped aboard and within minutes

they had crossed the Sittang bridge and left the town behind. They passed through an avenue of flame-in-the-forest trees, then the jeep was rocking along the worn-out Mawchi road. Thick bamboo grew on either side. Here and there stood a tank, now overgrown with green. Occasionally a bamboo shack appeared, a shrine and, every now and then, there was a rattling as they crossed a Bailey bridge. Once, a foam-capped cascade tumbled down. Overhead, trees were fending off the sun, leaking little bursts of light that dazzled briefly and were gone.

Roberts filled his lungs with the clean, cool air. It was a morning to remember. And what a contrast to those other mornings of a month or two ago: mornings with the rattle of machine-gun fire and the empty crack of shells, and the road swarming with troops and tanks and guns. But now there was hardly anything on the road. All in all it promised to be a perfect day. If he had been there on his own he would have broken into song. The jeep purred on . . .

Now, which way? They had come to a junction where four tracks met the road. However, not to worry, a road sign said 'Thandaung'. Roberts swung the jeep off and bumped it along a track.

Soon the village was in sight. He could see

that it was no different from any of the others he had come across in the past three years — there were no tracks as such, but a clutch of bamboo houses perched on stilts. Above them grew giant trees. Through them, wended dusty, palisaded paths. Here and there was a well. And there was the usual scattering of naked kids and sleeping dogs. Somewhere an arthritic axle creaked and groaned. And, as the jeep pulled up, a cockerel strutted past them with a bristling comb. The war was a million years ago.

'OK, Andy, see if you can find his nibs.'

It turned out that Stevens couldn't. The mules and the denigrated brother-in-law were there but it seemed that the muleteer would not be back for several days.

Both men felt a wave of disappointment. Like kids, they had set their hearts on having a dekko at the dump. Roberts shrugged it off. 'Perhaps some other day,' he said. As he spoke, he was gazing at the mules. What wonderful beasts they were, he thought. Without them we would have lost the war. His mind went back to the mule-trains on the march crossing the mountains, swimming rivers, splashing across the streams. Ah yes, and the screw-guns crashing into action — huge Indian gunners and gigantic, eager mules. Some had been nearly as big as that huge one over there. Now that really is a mule. A king of mules, no less.

As if conscious of his gaze, the animal swung its head and regarded him with intelligent big brown eyes. Why yes, this must be the mule that had guided Watanabe to the dump. He mentioned this to Stevens and the sergeant saved the day.

'Perhaps it could take us to the dump?' he said. 'It was quite a time ago but they say that an elephant never forgets and it could apply to mules as well.'

Roberts's spirits surged. Why not? The day was young and they had little else to do.

'Have a word with brother-in-law,' he said.

Brother-in-law proved anxious to oblige and in next to no time he, Roberts and the sergeant were striding behind the mule.

Roberts crossed his fingers. They had come to the fourtrack junction. Now, would the lead mule know the way? It did. In fact it took it, literally, in its stride. Without slackening speed it turned along the left-hand path.

The mule pressed on for several miles. Then, quite suddenly, it turned and left the track. Roberts gave a cheer. But it was followed by a groan. There was nothing here that could possibly have been the dump. To make things worse, the mule had turned around and was striding back towards Thandaung.

Disconsolate, the three men followed. Then again the mule turned off. It forced its way through a stretch of jungle scrub, then halted in a glade. All down one side was an open-sided cave with rotting canvas hanging down. All around were various odds and ends. Unconcerned, the mule began to graze.

'Well I'll be damned!' gasped Roberts.

It was the dump all right. Delighted, and to the amusement of the others, he gave the mule a kiss. Then they searched around. But, like Mother Hubbard's cupboard, the dump was bare.

'Not much chance of any silver here,' the sergeant said.

Roberts gave a rueful smile. 'No, I guess you're right.' He pondered for a while. Then: 'You know, if Po Kyin did hide the silver somewhere else he'd have been here on his own. The silver would have weighed a ton so he couldn't have carried it far.'

He checked his watch. 'I tell you what,' he said, 'We've managed to find it and we've got bags of time. So why don't we split and scout around? The track's the boundary. You take that side, I'll take this. Brother-in-law can stay here with the mule.'

'Why not?' Stevens grinned.

'Right. Be back here in two hours' time.'

Still Stevens grinned. 'With or without the cash.'

Roberts gave an outright laugh. 'Yes, but fifty/fifty on anything we find. OK?'

'OK.'

The two of them went their separate ways. Stevens was content. The chance of finding any silver was remote. But then, so what? After all that time locked up it was good to wander free. To go whichever way he chose. The nightmare of the past three years was coming to an end. Tomorrow the court would set him free. Free to pick up the pieces of his life. Well, he consoled himself, but for Captain Roberts it could have been a whole lot worse. The question now was what he and Dad and Angie were to do? They had the house, of course, but precious little else.

Lost in thought he wandered through the scrub. But something was niggling at his mind. Something was not quite right. What was it? It was like trying to recall a dream. Now what the devil was it? Think. Think. Think. It was something that had caught his eye. Yes, something red. Something small and red. Something that had glinted from the trees. Totally preoccupied, he had passed it by. Now whatever could it be?

Intrigued, he retraced his footsteps. He'd

gone just fifty yards or so and there it was — a little red spot that was glinting in the sun. He pulled the scrub aside and there, to his amazement, was an army jeep and trailer. A jeep with BURMA INTELLIGENCE CORPS stencilled on its front and six jerricans of petrol in the back. He now saw that the sun had caught the near-side red reflector.

Now what in heaven's name was a jeep and trailer doing here? There could only be one answer: someone from the BIC was treasure-hunting too.

Well, why not? True, the chances of success were almost nil. But then, who was he to talk?

With a bit of luck, he'd find whoever it was. Amused, he continued through the scrub. Every now and then he stopped to listen. But, each time, he heard nothing. Then suddenly the jungle opened up and there, right in front of him, was something most unreal. It was some kind of geological fault. Rising from the scrub it was like a gigantic carbuncle. Most of it was cleanly smooth and white but at the top it was pitted by a scattering of holes. Some big, some small. But, more to the point, at the side of the topmost pit was a pile of canvas bags. Lying on the bags was a bush-hat and a tunic shirt. The ends of a bamboo ladder were poking from the hole.

Stevens's 'I'll be blowed,' jerked out. The driver of the hidden jeep had found the cache! 'Lucky old BIC!' he thought. An envy welled.

Then Stevens got a shock. Even as he spoke, a head emerged. Its face had a patch across one eye. The head was followed by a shoulder on which sat a canvas bag. There was an arm around the bag, which ended in a hook. Po Kyin!

Stunned, Stevens sank behind a bush. It was the brigadier right enough. Stripped to the waist, his features drawn and dripping sweat, he clambered up the last few rungs. The canvas bag thumped down. Po Kyin flexed the elbow of his mutilated arm and adjusted the holster on his belt. He gave a quick look round then jerkily, he disappeared down the hole.

Swiftly and silently Stevens clambered up the 'carbuncle' to Po Kyin's pit. Peering down he saw that the pit was about ten feet deep and two or three feet wide. The sides were smooth. The ladder was roughly made of green bamboo. As far as he could see there was just the one bag left. This, Po Kyin was hefting on a shoulder.

Incongruously the words *Pull the ladder up, Jack* flashed across Stevens's mind. In a reflex action he did just that and threw the ladder down the 'carbuncle'. As he did a bellow came from down below.

Stevens's pulse raced. His hands were trembling. Blood was pounding in his head. He was in a state of shock and he'd need to simmer down. Sitting on the bags he made himself relax. Closing his eyes, he took in breath on breath. He ignored the shouts that were coming from the pit.

Gradually his heartbeats quietened down. Now what? Should he fetch the captain to the scene? Or should he handle this himself?

The bellowing had stopped. Gingerly, Stevens peered across the edge.

Gun in hand and standing in a crouch, Po Kyin was peering up. But the light was shining in his eyes and the face above was in darkness. 'Who is that?' he called.

Stevens had a sudden surge of hate. 'It's me,' he hissed.

'Me! And who the bloody hell is me?'

'It's me, you shit. Sergeant Stevens. The man you saw stealing all this silver.'

There was silence from down below. Then 'Well, well.' A further silence. Then a pseudo-jovial: 'Well stop playing silly buggers, Sergeant, and put that ladder back at once. Let me up. Let's talk this over. Man to man.'

'You'll stay where you are, you shit.'

Po Kyin's voice came up cajolingly: 'Oh

313

come on, Sergeant, it's bloody cold down here.' A laugh. 'I'll catch my death. I can't stay here for ever.'

'No? What makes you think that?' Stevens answered callously.

'Now cut that out, Sergeant. That'd amount to murder.'

'Yes, like having me hanged.'

There followed a lengthy spell of quiet. Then: 'That's all in the past, Sergeant. Water under the bridge. Think of the future, man. Let me up and we can sort things out. Share the silver.' Then, urgently, 'Come on, man. The ladder. Trust me.'

'As if anyone could trust a shit like you,' Stevens answered contemptuously. He surveyed the piled up bags. 'And in any case, who are you to bargain? The silver's all up here.'

A flash of humour from down below. 'Less one bag.'

'Keep it. Count it,' Stevens roared, enraged. 'It'll help to pass the time.'

Again there was a lengthy spell of quiet. Then: 'In that case I'll come up and get it.' There was no trace of humour now. 'Get you, too.'

Stevens assessed the depth of the pit and the smoothness of the rock. He considered Po Kyin's artificial limbs. He had a feeling of relief. There was no way Po Kyin could get out. He'd got the bastard trapped. Leaning in, he stabbed two fingers in a V. 'OK, come on up,' he jeered.

Crack. Stevens jerked away as a bullet whistled past. Then, from down below he heard Po Kyin calling: 'Right, you halfchat peasant, I'm coming up.'

From the pit came a sound of movement — a funny sort of scraping and, with it the sound of panting breath.

Stevens risked a peep across the edge. He gave a gasp. Po Kin had got his back against one side, his feet against the other and the gun was resting on his lap. Slowly but surely he was inching his way to the top.

Stevens panicked. Christ, what was he to do? A thought struck him: why not dislodge him with the ladder? No, he would grab it and then he'd be up here with the gun.

But the panting was getting nearer all the time.

Should he try and find the captain? No again. The captain wasn't armed. It would lead to both of them being shot.

The panting and the scraping sound were closer and louder still.

He risked another peep. Po Kyin was half way up. *Crack.* Another shot whizzed past. What to do? What? What? What?

And then the answer came. He should have thought of it before. He'd give Po Kyin the bags of silver.

'Brigadier,' he called, 'you can have the silver. Have the lot.'

The panting and the scraping stopped. 'Good. Now get my bloody ladder.'

'OK. But first your bloody silver.'

With this, Stevens grabbed a bag and raised it above his head. It was as much as he could do. Then, with a yell, he hurled it down the pit.

There came a yell, a crash, a groan, looking down, he saw that Po Kyin was trying to struggle to his feet. He felt another surge of hate. This was the man who had tried to get him hanged. Who would have wrecked both Dad's and Angie's lives. The man who had betrayed Major Willis to the Japs. The man who had planned to steal the silver for himself. All so that he could rule the roost, become a big shot with the other sod Aung San.

He grabbed another bag. 'That's two you've got,' he yelled, 'now here's the rest.'

The bag caught the brigadier fair and square and smashed him to the ground. Then the other bags rained down, burying and crushing him beneath their weight. As the last bag hurtled down, it split. There was a shower of silver coins. Now all were gone. The bush-hat and the tunic followed.

Gazing down the still and silent pit, Stevens hissed: 'All yours, Po Kyin. Don't spend it all at once. I'm coming back.'

Then suddenly he was tired, so tired. His body was trembling and he was very close to tears.

Taking his time, he made his way back to the jeep. He seated himself and lit one of the captain's cigarettes. He had nearly half an hour in hand. Time to have a think.

Again, he asked himself: What now?

Three years ago he would have given his very soul to have had this wealth. Now it was his, all his. And not only the silver but the jeep and trailer too. Yes and all that petrol. Enough to get him and his family out of Burma. Now the question was, where to? Siam? Or India perhaps? And if that did not work out, why not make their way to England. Fulfil Angie's dream. Yes, why not. But better any country than a Burma run by, and for, the Burmese and the Burmese only.

He stubbed his cigarette. He didn't have to make his mind up right away. Dad and Angie would be back tomorrow and he'd be free. Then the three of them could decide just where to go. Discuss all the things they could now afford to do.

Stevens was on cloud nine, but still on the edge of shock. His daydreams carried on. Mum would be so pleased about it too. There were so many things she'd gone without, so many things he'd give her. Then a pang shot through his heart. No, he wouldn't. Couldn't. Mum had been dead and gone these last three years! His eyelids pricked. The pain was as cruelly keen as it had been at the time. Unmanned, the tears were trickling down his face. Oh Mum, oh Mum. Why not you as well? Then he was sobbing as he never had before and never would again.

Then, fiercely, he dashed the tears away. As a family, they had been so close. Mum, wherever she was, would somehow know, and would be overjoyed for him and Dad and Angie. Wherever they went, whatever they did, they'd be sharing it with her. Dear, dear, all-loving, all-forgiving Mum.

Now it was time to get back to the dump.

Roberts was whispering endearments to the mule. Seeing Stevens emerge, he gave the mule a final pat. Then, turning to brother-in-law, he pointed to the track. It was time to be leaving, for they had quite a way to go. It had been a pleasant if an uneventful day. He had thoroughly enjoyed it. By the look of him, Stevens had enjoyed it too. Well, good for him.

Stevens joined him. 'Any luck,' he asked.

Roberts, smiling, shook his head. 'No, but then I didn't really look. I don't suppose that you did either. But at least it passed the afternoon.' He gave a shrug. 'I'm sure Po Kyin's got it snugly stashed away.'

Stevens had gone over to the mule and had taken its velvet muzzle in his hands. Gravely, he nodded his agreement. He gazed into the big brown eyes.

'Yes, you could be right,' he said.

22

So Sergeant Stevens was released. Shortly afterwards Captain Roberts sailed for home. The world wagged on.

Aung San realized his dream of an independent Burma. A victorious but exhausted Britain was in no mood to say him nay. So he returned in triumph and in next to no time Burma was freed from British rule.

The triumph soon turned sour. Thugs in U Saw's pay slaughtered Aung San and his ministers as they sat in state. For this, U Saw was put on trial and hanged. The ensuing turmoil led to civil war. Chaos reigned. Then an iron fist came down. The revolt was crushed and a military dictator ruled. Soon the country fell apart and the land, whose rice had fed the East, could scarcely feed itself. British companies read the writing on the wall. They packed their bags and left. The infrastructure crumbled as despotic rule prevailed. Inevitably, Burma regressed and slipped into the past. It had been said that, under British rule, the Burmese were a poor people in a prosperous country. There was truth in this. But now, with independence, they were far, far poorer in a bankrupt land. This continues to this day.

With the departure of the British most of the Anglo-Burmans left as well. Many of them brought their twilight world to Britain. For these, the pathetic dream of coming 'home' came true. It availed them little. Still they were neither fish nor fowl nor good red meat. A few managed to pass as white and flourished. These included Sergeant Stevens, his sister too. Not their father though. He was killed when dacoits attacked his train near Mandalay. Perhaps this was just as well, Stevens *père* would not have fitted in.

Stevens realized that in the post-war world the motor car would reign supreme. With the proceeds from the cache he bought an ailing garage on the outskirts of a sleepy country town, trading as 'Silver Lining Cars'. Fortune smiled, for the town expanded in the post-war boom and Stevens burgeoned with it.

Fortune was kind to Angie too. Against all the odds her *True Romances* dream came true. On the sea voyage 'home' she set her cap at a sex-starved REME Major. Surprisingly, it turned out well for all concerned. Stevens and the major hit it off and the major became an equal partner in 'Silver Lining vCars'. His technical know-how was the key to its success.

Robbie Roberts went from strength to strength. The local rag was far too small to hold him and a major provincial daily took him on. He quickly made his mark but, like all journalists worthy of their salt, he had set his sights on Fleet Street. His aim was good and he quickly achieved a byline as the chief crime reporter on a national. In achieving this he owed a lot to his old friend Fletcher of the Metropolitan Police. He too was doing well and as they climbed their respective ladders to success they scratched each other's backs.

Once, in a West End bar, they got to wondering what had happened to the post-war Pompous Perce. Being in their cups they made a bet on which of them could first find out: the long arm of the law against the ferrets of the press.

By one of those incredible coincidences that are an integral part of life it turned out to be a draw. For, two drinks later, Roberts suddenly stiffened and sat up straight. Grabbing Fletcher's arm he said: 'Talk of the devil, Fletch. Look who's just walked in.' He was gesturing to a prosperous looking couple who, arm-in-arm, had just arrived.

Fletcher looked. He gave a gasp. 'It's Pompous Perce himself.'

'Yes, but look who's with him.'

A moment of shocked surprise. Then, in strangled tones, Fletcher uttered: 'Well, I'll be buggered. It's Marie, Marie Gomez.'

Fletcher made to stand and go across but Roberts hissed: 'Sit,' and pulled him down. 'Don't spoil things for them, Fletch.'

Fletcher leaned back in his chair. Suddenly he felt good, so very, very good. A chuckle rumbled out. 'Good old Marie. Trust old Marie to make it too,' he said.

We do hope that you have enjoyed reading
this large print book.

Did you know that all of our titles
are available for purchase?

We publish a wide range of high quality
large print books including:
**Romances, Mysteries, Classics
General Fiction
Non Fiction and Westerns**

Special interest titles available in
large print are:
**The Little Oxford Dictionary
Music Book
Song Book
Hymn Book
Service Book**

Also available from us courtesy of
Oxford University Press:
**Young Readers' Dictionary
(large print edition)
Young Readers' Thesaurus
(large print edition)**

For further information or a free
brochure, please contact us at:
**Ulverscroft Large Print Books Ltd.,
The Green, Bradgate Road, Anstey,
Leicester, LE7 7FU, England.
Tel:** (00 44) 0116 236 4325
Fax: (00 44) 0116 234 0205

Other titles published by
The House of Ulverscroft:

THE MOONRAKER MUTINY

Antony Trew

A tired old freighter, the *Moonraker*, is bound from Fremantle to Mauritius. Haunted by his past, Captain Stone seeks solace in the gin bottle in his cabin. His niece, Susie, flirts with Australian passage worker Hank Casey, and Italian mate Carlo Frascatti grumbles at the motley crew. Then the radio operator receives a warning of a suspected cyclone ahead . . . The panic-stricken crew turn on their captain and abandon ship. Those left behind desperately struggle to keep the battered hulk afloat, whilst nearby, a coaster and an ocean salvage tug are each determined to profit from the *Moonraker*'s disaster . . .

THE PERPETRATOR

David Millett

When seven old men, survivors of a Lancaster bomber crew from World War II, book into a hotel for their annual reunion, someone has decided that they will suffer for the activities of their youth. They are to remain physically unharmed, but anguish and despair will ruin their final years. Unknown to them, their loved ones are no longer safe — the Perpetrator is making sure of that. The old men will never know the origin of the attacks. The Perpetrator does not seek overt dominance. The secret knowledge of what he has done will be satisfaction enough.

OUT OF ORDER

Charles Benoit

Jason Talley lives in Corning, New York. His friends are Sriram Sundaram and his wife, Vidya. But after Sriram confides he's planning to return to India, the next evening the couple are dead — the cops call it murder-suicide. Jason decides to fulfil Sriram's quest and books himself a trip to India. Travelling, he meets Rachel, and together, they embark on a journey into danger . . . Sriram was a computer genius who had sold out his colleagues, and Jason has sent details of his trip to Sriram's e-mail list, hoping to meet up with Sriram's past. But when he does . . .

DARTMOUTH CONSPIRACY

James Stevenson

September 1942: Luftwaffe pilot Karl Deichman must bomb the Royal Naval College in Dartmouth, despite knowing his cousin and childhood friend is resident there. Yet his orders give him no choice — the attack must proceed . . . After the war, Karl returns to England, haunted by the thought: *Did I kill Andrew?* His quest leads him to a former secret agent, a wartime spy, and an ex-RAF Spitfire pilot; but as he uncovers the secret of the Dartmouth Conspiracy, he is drawn into a lethal trap. And it will be more than sixty years before the final jigsaw-piece falls into place . . .

TO KINGDOM COME

Will Thomas

When the Irish Republican Brotherhood bombs Scotland Yard in May 1884, private enquiry agent Cyrus Barker and his apprentice, Thomas Llewelyn, set out to infiltrate the faction responsible. Working for the Home Office, the duo impersonate a reclusive bomb maker and his assistant, who are willing to help in the plot to blow up London buildings and destroy the monarchy. Accepted by the faction, Barker investigates the identity of the Brotherhood's leader, as Llewelyn becomes involved with an Irish lass with ties to the group. Now the detectives must risk everything to save London from being blown to kingdom come.

THE BLOOD PARTNERSHIP

Seth Garner

Ben Spencer is the ambitious young owner of The Blood Partnership, an online property marketing company. Over the past few months he has become heavily involved with every member of the wealthy property-developing Westlake family — including becoming engaged to beautiful young Caitlin Westlake — and now he's beginning to regret it. Things go from bad to worse when Ben's own family are targeted by the Westlakes. Now he must choose a side, and it seems the only way out is death — but whose will it be?